D1429360

The Cryptographer

The Cryptographer

Tobias Hill

W F HOWES LTD

This large print edition published in 2004 by
W F Howes Ltd
Units 6/7, Victoria Mills, Fowke Street
Rothley, Leicester LE7 7PJ

1 3 5 7 9 10 8 6 4 2

First published in 2003 by Faber and Faber
Limited

A CIP catalogue record for this book is available
from the British Library

ISBN 1 84505 630 2

Typeset by Palimpsest Book Production Limited,
Polmont, Stirlingshire
Printed and bound in Great Britain
by Antony Rowe Ltd, Chippenham, Wilts.

For my sister

He broke a twig
From a low branch of oak. The leaves
Turned to heavy gold as he stared at them
And his mouth went dry
He felt his brain move strangely, like a muscle.

Ted Hughes, *Tales from Ovid*

I

WINTER

She is late and he is alone at his table. Before he looks up, in that space, she sees him as clearly as if he were a stranger. He is an old man, there are spots on his hands and neck the colour of old meat, but his eyes are still beautiful. They make him uncomfortable: he would prefer to be less handsome, and so less conspicuous. And this is his favourite table, at his favourite bar, a stranger might notice it in the way he sits. His own place, where the waitresses cajole him to eat, *come on Lawrence, have something with that*, and the taxis give him a discount home.

'Anna,' he says, and she kisses him. Not as she always has, but as she would family.

'How are you?'

'Better for seeing you.' There are two glasses lined up ready. Cold dry white. He doesn't touch his until she has sat down, taken off her coat. He looks cold himself, though the room is warm. 'You're late.'

'I'm sorry, I tried to call. I left work when I could,' Anna says, smiling for him, but already he is waving her away, decorously, irritably, as if her

3

excuses are as faint and distasteful as smoke from an adjoining table.

'Work. And how is work, these days?'

'You know, it never changes.' She settles back in the leathered booth. 'You know how it is.'

'Awful. My poor protegée,' says Lawrence. 'Did I tell you I still have nightmares about it?'

'Don't,' she says, as if he is joking, and looks up to find that he is not. That he is only embarrassed, after all.

'Not the work. I mean of course the work, but the place. Her Majesty's Central Inland Revenue. *They say there was once a labyrinth where the way weaved between blind walls and lost itself in a thousand treacherous paths.*'

'Come on. It's not that bad.'

'Only because it has you at the end of it. But you're here now. Now you're here we both have something to celebrate. To drink to. I should thank you.'

'What for?'

'For your remarkable new client . . . Mister John Law. What else?' He beams with pride. 'Did you think I wouldn't find out? Are you surprised or impressed?'

'Definitely impressed.'

'Liar. Well may you smile. To your client, your career, and John Law, the Cryptographer.'

'The Cryptographer.'

They touch glasses. She isn't surprised; not as he means it. The acquisition of fact has been

4

Lawrence's life, after all, or its working constituent – his practised answer to the question *What do you do?* being a euphemistic *I work in Information* – so that his knowledge is not quite unexpected. She is only surprised by his happiness. He has been waiting to tell her all day. She can see it in his face.

She watches him drink, carefully, no more than a taste. Twenty-first century Chablis. He is measuring the day and night in wine, a glass an hour from noon until midnight. Hour-glasses.

'Alright, I give up. How did you know?'

'I still have my sources. What do you make of him?'

'Nothing, yet.'

'Oh, now.'

'The investigation hasn't begun. I haven't even met him.'

'But you know everything about him, you have the information at your fingertips, don't you? Of course you do.'

'You taught me that.'

'So I did.' He sits back. 'I might be able to help . . . well, I know when I'm not wanted. If you need advice, you know where to find me. I'm a little jealous, you see.'

'I'll keep you in mind,' she says, and drinks.

Her hair is still wet from the street, she can feel its coldness, the wine in her throat, the heat of her skin as the room warms it. It is to do with being watched, this self-consciousness. Watched

5

and wanted, though she has known Lawrence too long to be surprised by either the sensation or the desire.

'Not your everyday client, Mister Law. The extremely rich are not like the rest of us, or so we say. The rest of us, that is. Does he know yet?'

'I don't think so.'

'Then I feel sorry for him.'

'Do you? You make it sound cruel,' she says. Then, as she feels it, 'You almost make me sound like that.'

There is laughter at a nearby booth. Anna looks beyond its crowded source. The bar has sixty floors of view. Outside the rain has eased. The air is clear over the twin cities of Westminster and London, their silver-greys and golds.

'You know,' Lawrence says, bringing her back, 'in my own time I came to the conclusion that there were only two kinds of tax inspector. The failed police officer and the failed stockbroker. Both have reasons to be cruel.'

'Which kind am I?' she says, because he wants her to. And Lawrence smiles, gratefully, because he knows it, and also fondly, because he is drunk, and he is remembering the times they have been more or less than friends.

'You?' he says, his eyes quite bright. 'My dear Anna. Sometimes you hardly seem like an inspector at all.'

He walks to his cab one step at a time, waves as

6

if he has just won gold, and is gone. Anna drives home with the taste of good wine in her mouth. The intoxication is subtle, she is barely conscious of it; a tremor in the bloodstream. But it is always like this. It is like a memento of him, of what it is to be him. Which is one reason she does it to herself, after all.

It is past midnight. The streets are cleaned out with rain. The crowds are tiring but unsatisfied, congregating under neon. At night it is hard not to fall for London, Anna thinks, when the best of it is lit, and the worst is glamorised by darkness. The Capital of Money, people call it these days, as if it is not fully inhabited by those people at all, but by other things. Synthetics, metals, futures.

Only as she reaches the suburbs does she pick up speed, edging the limit. She is wakeful in a way she knows can lapse too easily into sleep. She turns on the radio. The signal keeps her going, moving through waves and intermittent stations.

She wishes she could have told Lawrence more, tonight. There was a time when she would have gone to him for advice gladly, when it would have been the first thing she would have done. Now she suspects, with an inspector's instinct, that he is not a man to trust with secrets.

Mister Law is full of secrets. The Cryptographer, people call him, or the Codemaker, and other things, expressions of distrust and ill-concealed admiration. It is the new millennium, after all, and no longer acceptable to admire the rich. But Law is

7

both distrusted and admired more than most, more than Anna entirely understands, and that will have to change. She will need to understand her client. Rule number one: information is the inspector's greatest weapon.

Now she is almost home. Two blocks east, five north. She turns into her road. The trees and street lights form a procession of shadow and illumination. The car is warm and dark as a head.

Her own job is simple in its way. Anna measures the worth of people. It is something they hide, often, and most often from themselves. It is not pleasant to be reduced to the margins of profit and loss, to see one's life scored. More than once, over the years, Anna has interviewed clients so frightened or angry they have forgotten the facts of their lives: age or birthplace, the name of a husband, a child. She has waited while they sit staring back at her, dumbstruck at their own stupidity. It isn't the potential for loss which does it, Anna thinks, so much as the imminence of measurement. The relentless picking-through of days.

There are clients who appear guilty even when they have nothing to hide. They watch Anna as if they expect her to hold up their accounts, as a doctor will hold X-rays to the light, and find them wanting. Those are the ones who equate worth with worth, money with success, and believe they have failed. It is not what Anna believes of them herself. She has seen too much of money for that. It is not what she hopes for; she doesn't dream of money in itself. But then, as Lawrence says, sometimes she hardly seems like an inspector at all.

It is eleven years since she joined the Revenue. Inevitably there have been more clients than she remembers. The names tend to escape her first, followed by the faces. The lives stay with her longer. But when she works well she comes to know them all for a while: even the most difficult clients, the richest and the most impoverished. She knows who they think of, when they think of money. To understand the rich, Anna believes, you should know who they are rich for.

Sometimes it is only themselves. More often it is the children they mean to have, or meant to. Anna has investigated clients who talk of nothing but the people who wouldn't believe in them, the ones who said they would fail. For them wealth collects in sweet, cold drops.

Then again it can be a stranger they imagine. A woman seen once, on a bright street, in a bright dress, smiling. Someone they want to have or to be. And it can also be the dead. The dead can be a reason. But Anna has found there is always someone.

She undresses in the dark of her room. Her clothes smell of the sour damp of the city. There is a little light from the lamps in the street. In the mirror she catches glimpses of herself. The curve of her hips, flesh, the shadow of her hair.

Her name is Anna Moore. She is thirty-six

9

years old, born in the last millennium. She is an Inspector A2 Grade. Which means she is good at what she does, one of the best, or so people say, so they tell her.

People like to think that money and love are opposites. Anna has come to be less sure. After all, both love and money tend towards others. And money arises out of greed and generosity. And greed and generosity are evidence of love.

This is the night's secret. Not only what she knows, but what she would like to know. Because even the Cryptographer must dream of someone. Anna would like to know who John Law thinks of, when he thinks of money.

It is the end of October, the last days of autumn. In the morning she opens the door and her car has turned white with frost. Doggedly she guns the engine. She has never much liked machines. She talks to them like stubborn children, pleads with them like small, recalcitrant gods. The radio comes to life and dies in a single galvanic burst of music.

The overground is ten minutes walk through the gloom. Anna finds a seat in the third carriage she tries. She takes a tablet computer from her briefcase and works with it resting on her knees, mailing the Revenue autopool, the Revenue-authorised garage, leaving her name and numbers and an imprecise list of mechanical symptoms. The screen illuminates her palms and face.

People always say she looks proud. She doesn't feel that way. It is only skin-deep. Not everyone has the face they deserve. Often, what people take to be pride is only her reticence. Her shyness, which is a form of gentleness.

Her hair is long, black, with the density of mercury. Her mother has always claimed oriental blood. In another time and place she might have sold it, Anna thinks, and this is an image of herself she likes, it is something she imagines of herself, a private fiction. Her clothes are handsome, more expensive than she can afford. She would say she is no longer young. She would also say that she is no longer beautiful, though people can be wrong about themselves, they can be their own worst judges, even those who calculate the taxes of the Inland Revenue.

Just before dawn the train stops between stations. The engine winds down in the twilight. Carriage by carriage the lights go out, like pearls spilled from a curved rope.

There is a murmur of disquiet, but at this hour no one really complains. Given the choice of silence or the office, they are content with silence. Across from Anna, a man with the face of a lawyer sleeps beside a woman with the arms of a dancer.

The engine thrums, accumulating power. Anna leans her face against the window. The glass is cold against her cheek. Outside is a landscape defined by trees. Each minute is lighter than the last.

Few people use their mobiles. Those that do

11

talk softly, as if they are afraid to wake someone. A pale black man asks for Miriam. The girl with dancer's arms talks to John. Anna listens to them with her eyes open. She is always listening to others. Overhearing: she thinks it is an inspector's habit. The man and woman say the same thing, everything and nothing. *We're on the train. Just waiting. We'll see you soon. We love you, love you. Love you.*

Her colleagues have arrived before her. Carl and Janet and Mister Hermanubis, all on one park bench in Limeburner Square, like three birds on a wire, like the jury of three monkeys, two out of three watching the crowd with mistrust.

Along with good clothes (that are nevertheless a little austere, a little old-fashioned, like the suits of undertakers) mistrust is something they have in common. They are Her Majesty's Inspectors, after all. They are in possession of the facts. They have seen the most unexpected clients lie, so that they have come to expect the worst of people, even of one another; and this not always without reason, since they know about wealth without possessing it, and know a few things about deception. They are not inclined to trust.

There are two kinds of tax inspector, Lawrence says, though depending on what he is drinking Anna has heard him say there are three kinds, or four. If there are three, it is those who find counting the wealth of others a torture, a temptation, or a

12

trial. If there is a fourth, it is those who take pleasure in their investigations. Anna likes to think her colleagues are all the fourth kind. It's only that the pleasures they take are different. One vindictive, one perverse, one vicarious.

They make room for her. She has a coffee from the station and it wakes her fast, like their chat. Mister Hermanubis gets up and mutters goodbyes like bad news. The crowd goes on past the Old Bailey, dealers and brokers in their own drab, mineral colours. They look camouflaged, Anna thinks absently. As if they could step back into the shadows of limestone around them, and disappear.

'Look at them,' Carl says. 'Suit boys.'

'And women too.' Janet Sullivan, her voice milder with lack of interest.

'Not from where I'm sitting.' Carl puts his tea down on the bench between them. Hefts his brief-case, clicks it open, takes out four immaculately wrapped sandwiches. 'From where I'm sitting they're all just offshore bank accounts.'

He offers the sandwiches around. They eat gratefully, clumsily, in more or less easy silence. Sullivan is a tall woman with small eyes, a quick temper, and – entirely unconcealed by these things – a mind like a steel trap. Carl has close-curled hair, like astrakhan, and a face that keeps tight to its bones. To Anna his features seem Semitic, Arabic or Jewish, though she has never asked. They are too close, professionally, to be close friends.

13

Their relationship lacks the trust for that, and also the promise. She knows that by the time they are inside the Revenue both inspectors will see her as the competition. Carl has said as much, more than once. Until then, this and every morning, they are each other's company.

The workers pass close by them. They are young, for the most part: their seniors, the successful ones, will arrive later, by car, in subterranean bays. And they look as if they are thinking of nothing, which is to say they are thinking of money. Anna recognises it in them. The way it fills their vacancies. The addictive mix of it. Two parts anxiety, one part joy.

They are thinking of security and independence, pleasure and power. They are thinking of the smell of new cars and the fame of personalised parking spaces. The feel of skin, footprints in sand, the gardens in emeralds, a passage of music, rain on glass, the taste of a mouth, the taste of wine. They are thinking of someone. Their faces as set as the stone of the banks and courts around them.

'The drive for five,' says Sullivan, 'the yen for ten, the gleam for fifteen.'

'What's that?' asks Anna, and beside her Carl readies the phlegm in his throat, a rattling laughter.

'The dealers say it. Five million buys you your basic wish fulfilment. Two houses, clean children and walk-in wardrobes. It's all worked out. It's what they aim for.' Sullivan smooths her skirt critically. 'You should know that by now.'

'What happens when they reach ten?'

'They get a free hula skirt and a week in Hawaii. How would I know? Right, I'm off. Places to go, people to scare. Fear and loathing to inspire.'

'Early bird, eh?' Carl squints up at her.

'That's right. I'm manoeuvring to shit on you from a great height, Carl. I'll see you then.'

'Not if I see you first.' They watch her cross towards the Revenue steps. Anna finishes her coffee. The morning is turning out fair. From the trees a drift of small red leaves has collected at the feet of the bench, like confetti. An airship passes overhead, rolling in the breeze off the river, its slogans high as houses.

GURU RICE – THE WISE CHOICE.

SOFTMARK: THE NEW MILLENNIUM IS NOW AVAILABLE.

'So,' says Carl, and Anna glances back at him. Now they are alone there is a change in his voice. He is trying to sound solicitous. She knows him well enough to know when he wants something.

'So what?'

'So, just so. Just making conversation.' He has the decency to look pained. Anna waits for him to go on. He is not a patient man, it doesn't take long. 'So, people are saying you've landed a big client. You must be pleased. Nice bit of luck, a

15

client like that. Lots of potential. A good person to know. When do you see him?'

She downs the last bite of immaculate sandwich. Unaccountably she thinks of Lawrence, although as far as she knows he and Carl never got on, have not been in touch since the older man's redundancy. Nor is there any great shortage of people at the Revenue willing to discuss business behind backs.

She should be resigned to it by now. Instead a faint, fine anger unfurls in her. The first of the day. 'Soon. I'd like it to be soon.'

'And the Revenue gets what the Revenue wants. I hope you're prepared, though. He won't be easy.'

'You've met him?'

'Not as such. No one's *met* him. What I mean is, when you're as rich as he is, you don't have to be nice. You don't need to make things easy for anyone.'

'Jealous?'

'Course I am,' he says equably, leaning back, getting the sun on his face. 'That's not the point. Don't worry about me, worry about him. Otherwise you'll find yourself out of your depth before you even know you're in deep water.'

'Sounds dangerous.'

'You can laugh now.'

'I'll pack a wetsuit, shall I?'

'A bikini might be better. I'll help you choose, if you like.'

'I'll manage, thanks for the offer. Look, it's a

random investigation. There are no inconsistencies in the accounts,' she lies. 'I'll be done inside four months.'

'If you say so. Quite a chance, his number coming up.'

'The same as anyone else. What are you thinking?'

'Nothing.' He watches her, calculating. 'You might need help, all the same.'

'Whose help?'

'Well, two heads are better than one, especially if one of them's mine.'

She laughs despite herself. Carl scowling over his cup. 'What?'

'I don't think so.'

'Alright. Why not?'

'I don't think we'd work well together,' she says. Which is, she thinks, already the guaranteed understatement of the day. 'And my clients are my own business.'

'Of course they are, of course. I don't mean to pry.'

'Of course you don't, Carl. Why don't you ask the Board?'

Reluctantly, hopefully, he smiles. 'You know why.' And immediately she does.

'Because you asked them already. You're unbelievable. And what did they say?'

'They told me to ask you.'

'Good. And I'm telling you I don't need your help. But thanks. Really. Thanks for the offer.'

She watches him swear and look away. The tension that has condensed in her begins to dissipate. In profile he is more attractive. His ancestry comes through more strongly. Something Phoenician, she imagines, by way of south London.

'You think you've got it all fixed up.' A muscle works in his jaw. Although he looks older, acts older, he is barely twenty. Little more than half her age.

'Carl,' Anna says, 'you don't need to be jealous of me. I'm not like you.'

'No, you're not.' He leans in on her. 'But everyone's driving for something, aren't they? The drive for five. You can't spend all day working with money and not want it. You know how the Revenue works, and how it doesn't. You wouldn't be the first to put that to better use, would you? Tell me you don't want more.'

'I don't want more.'

He nods. For a moment she thinks he understands. That she is not like him. That her desires are less utilitarian than ambition or wealth. Then he nods again. 'So you can give me a piece of Law.'

'Not for a hundred hula skirts,' she says, and he sits back and smiles balefully.

'You're a cunt, Anna. But I do mean that in a nice way.' He closes the briefcase on his lap, locks it, stands up. 'Eat up, you'll be late. What are you doing after?'

'Whatever you like.'

18

She watches him across Limeburner Square, his grey figure disappearing into the crowd. These are the people who dream of John Law, she thinks. She thinks of the drive, the yen, the gleam. The words like three steps down, a diminishing progression of desire.

Upriver at Westminster, Big Ben begins to strike, the first tolls hazy with distance, unchanged for a hundred and sixty years. In Anna's mind, childrens' rhymes. All the churches of the twin city, talking of money.

When will you pay me? Say the bells of Old Bailey.

When I grow rich, say the bells of Shoreditch.

When will that be? Say the bells of Stepney.

She will know everything about him. She will have the facts at her fingertips. Of course she will.

People say many things about John Law. Not all of them are true, of course. But Anna is an inspector of the Inland Revenue, a collector of taxes, not a member of a jury. And of course she can't help but know, when people say so many things.

They say he is Scottish by birth. This at least she half believes. She has not spoken to him herself, not yet, but she has heard him speak, naturally, and there is a certain inflection, a softness and edge, something which might once have been an accent. Now it is almost nothing, just as there are people who say he is nothing. Although Anna suspects this

19

is untrue. She is beginning to think there will be more to him than meets the eye. In the flesh.

They say that by the age of ten, John Law could program machine code as if it were his first language. They say that he was orphaned into a lifetime inheritance: also that he is the son of a single mother, a factory worker from the island of Coll, who appeared for a time on screens everywhere. No one has fifteen minutes of fame any more; instead they get an hour that nobody watches. As far as Anna recalls, the woman was dour and unremarkable except for her eyes, which were much like his. Kennedy eyes. The factory processed krill. This is old news. Anna heard of no gene test done then, and no one would care now if there was.

They say he is addicted, but no one can agree to what. In any week of coverage Law will overdose on crystal stim, be found drunk in an alleyway, downloading banned pornography, eating prohibited foods. On Sundays he will be recorded phoning for cheap prostitutes from glossy hotel penthouses.

No one says he is addicted to money. That is expected of him.

They call him the first quadrillionaire. They say that measured by the ounce, his body is 91,000 times more valuable than gold. They say he married his first love: they buy the social photographs. They say the marriage has gone bad. They say he has been cloned three times. His brain has been

20

regrown and he has taught it everything he knows. He keeps it for its company, like a bird that talks. They say his sperm has been refined. His wife will give birth to himself. So they say.

They say he can break the code. Of course they do. That more than anything: that most of all.

John Law is the man who made the first great electric currency. He did it alone, they say, in room nine of the London Savoy. He invented a perfect code, and from the code he made a money that would come to be used by billions of people. He called it Soft Gold. When Anna tries to imagine its ones and fives and tens, they are nothing but the fur of static on a screen, the hum of a wire in the rain. There is nothing to the new money except the code, and the code can't be broken.

In God We Trust, she thinks, as she works through the rhythms and formulas of the office. It was what they used to print on the American dollar bills. She remembers how you could smell the ink of the words and feel the paper in your wallet, the sweat in its seams. You could tell that other people had done the same. You could sense hot countries, cigar boxes, bank tellers' fingers. Greed and generosity. People believed in the paper, even if they didn't believe in the god.

It is only two years since they cancelled the dollar, the last exchangeable hard currency. Already Anna has trouble thinking of money that way. Of currency as touchable. The sour smell of alloy, the arcane traces of urine and cocaine on old notes. It seems to her that money was always meant to be this way. Invisible.

There is no sweat on Soft Gold. It carries no residue of human places. But people trust it because of the code, which can never be broken. In Code We Trust.

You have to trust, of course, she thinks. Because you need money. You need it even if you hate it. And in money, trust is everything.

These are the things that everyone knows, the bar-room apocrypha. But then Anna is not everyone. She is professionally knowledgeable. She is in possession of the facts.

People say that he is the richest man in the world. Anna knows enough to believe they may not be wrong. She knows, for example, that Law was rich even before Soft Gold. At the age of thirteen he designed and released a computer virus, Pandora, which in eight days was said to have done financial damage running into multiple millions. During the resultant periods of community service, Law put his talents to better use, inventing Asphodel Nine, a revolutionary system for embedding encrypted information in the genetic code of plants and flowers. The text of a secret in the stem of an iris. At seventeen he sold the patents to the US government for seven and a half million dollars.

According to the last Revenue report – four and a half years old – he owns property in cities on five continents. He is the only individual to possess land in Antarctica, an estate of lodges and ice caves. He has a yacht with thirty-seven rooms. Some of them will play any music you ask them for: anything, you just have to ask. The ages are measured in possessions, Anna thinks, stone, iron and silicon. And Law has everything. He might almost be living in a different century.

She has never seen him in person, but she knows what he is capable of. By chance, she has already been to the place that holds his code, the hall where his money is constantly being made and sent out into the world. She remembers it now, at night, as she cooks for herself. Rehearsing the facts of the case. Alone with a glass of drink beside her, the radio on low, old music, the windows clad with condensation against the dark.

The office is near Hatton Garden, London. Anna recalls that it has no discernable name. It is designed in a late-twentieth-century style, reconstituted Gothic, rough granite and fluted windows. It is larger than the buildings around it, although this is not immediately apparent. It hides behind road trees, itinerant late-lunch crowds, flower stalls. If a passer-by noticed it at all he would take it for a city block, not one building. And it is not noticeable. The passers-by pass on by, as they are intended to do.

The office effaces itself. Its mass is broken up by alleyways, service gates, inaccessible courtyards. The power is hidden in ordinary office architecture.

It is just an ordinary office. But there is only one door, with no name on it.

Years ago the building housed De Beers, the monopolists of diamonds, bankrupted by unnatural jewels. They were replaced by other companies with similar needs in security and unobtrusiveness. At one time there were two corporations and eight subsidiaries in the building. Now there is only one. It is called SoftMark. A company with a name like that could do anything, and so it does. Instead of diamonds it sells silicon. As well as making money, it makes money out of nothing.

Otherwise the office has changed little. Anna found she could still imagine the gem cutters inside, the stones raw as coal. None of this was as long ago as it seems, she knows. History gets closer as the times get faster. And they do change fast now. Today even tomorrow feels like yesterday.

She chops green fans of dill into a bowl of Arctic river prawns. The music plays. Water simmers on the hob. She scrubs black mineral earth from the silver skins of new potatoes.

The office has seven floors and six basements. Twelve storeys are comprised of SoftMark's business facilities – computer hardware and software – but the floor of the sixth basement is paved with silicon. There is nothing there except the pavement, black and vitreous. The basement is very large, an area of hectares or acres. Armed guards echo through the empty halls.

She has been there only once. It is not an easy

place to be, in any sense. She was admitted on Revenue business, one of nine. There was a moment when her colleagues were talking, all of them together, and she was alone.

She bent down to feel the pavement. It was cool to the touch and dark but also clear, like a window at night from the inside. The sensation she felt was not unlike vertigo. She saw – under her own reflected face – the silicon chips. Hundreds and thousands of them, small as the tesserae in a mosaic.

For as long as she could she stayed like that, looking. Once she saw a read-out illuminate deep below the surface, like a coin falling into a well. Then her superior was calling her name, and she had to go.

Don't worry about me, worry about him. Otherwise you'll find yourself out of your depth before you even know you're in deep water.

Anna believes that. It is something she can joke about, but not something she needs to be told. She has always taken care. A child dressed up for rain in her sister's favourite photograph; a girl watching river skaters, the skaters her parents, vague in the foggy distance; a woman smiling at the camera, but always carefully, a careful woman, always.

She wonders if John Law is the same. In her experience – which is to say her experience of others, her vicarious working life – it is almost impossible to be rich and careless, at least for long. But in the exaggerated stories people tell Law is more than careless. He is wild with the excess of his own wealth, mad as a Midas. There are famously few pictures of him, but in those Anna has seen he is often impatient, rarely at ease. She is not sure he looks cautious. It isn't carelessness, necessarily, but there is something, a recurrent expression. Restlessness, a contained volatility. He looks like a man who might take comfort in taking risks.

So Anna thinks. But then again, Anna is in possession of the facts. The fact is that the Revenue's interest in John Law is anything but random. If he were a careful man, he would never have become Anna's client in the first place.

For days her mind ticks over with him, so loud it is as if she hears it. She still has her regular portfolio, there are other clients to see, some of them wealthy, many well connected, and all of them difficult, because it is to her that the difficult clients will talk, if at all; it is a reputation she has, a talent for the unobtrusive retrieval of information. But her heart is not in it, now, and her thoughts are elsewhere. She wishes there was someone to talk to about Law, though there is only her sister Martha, who she sees the first Friday of each month at most, or her parents, old and divorced, divorced from their grown children, grown into new lives – or Lawrence. There is always Lawrence.

Those who know her a little would say she is too proud to doubt herself. Those who know her better would tell her she is taking her work too much to heart. So they would tell her, if they could see her now. Tonight she waits a long time for sleep. When it comes it is bad with dreams.

She is cleaning new potatoes again. This is a ridiculous thing to dream of, she thinks, even as it is happening, and she laughs at the pale things in her hands.

The water simmers. The old music plays. She is dancing a little, to herself, moving only fractionally; a dance of fractions. There is someone behind her in the kitchen. She doesn't remember him arriving. He is telling her about new potatoes. Somewhere in the world, he says, there are always new potatoes.

How many do you want? Anna says, and the man behind her says:

None for me. How many for you?

She laughs again. I don't want any either, she says. I don't know why I'm doing this.

What do you want, then? the man behind her says.

She says, I want to stop keeping watch. Let someone else do it. I'm tired of watching.

She doesn't say, *I would like to be watched.* Nor does the man answer. Anna doesn't look at him. Some part of her knows there are rules to this dream, old laws, and that if she turns round the man will die. She wants to tell him, to warn him of the danger, but the dream won't let her. Instead of speaking she goes on with what she is doing. She cleans the potato in her hands.

It is small and cool against her fingers. There is a scar on one side. When she peels at it the mark remains, under the skin. The flesh is like congealed ink. Anna takes a knife and cuts deeper. The water beside her begins to seethe.

Now the substance is exposed, glistening. The white flesh is stained through with fine dark lines. The pattern is not natural. It lacks that symmetry. Anna leans closer and goes still. She almost believes she can read them, these bright black capillaries. And then she can. She sees that the flesh is full of numbers.

What is it, Anna? says the voice behind her. It is soft, with only the trace of an accent. *Anna, what does it say?*

The next day she tries Lawrence, once at ten and again before noon. He picks up just as the machine kicks in. 'It's me,' she says.

'So I hear.' His voice is still rough with sleep. In the background a smoother version is asking her to leave a message. It stops abruptly. 'What's wrong?'

'Nothing.' She releases her breath, as if it could leave her lighter. She has caught him before the first drink, before he has lost his edge. In this state he still has something of his old keenness. It is what she needs of him, now she has made up her mind to need him. 'How are you feeling?'

'Why?'

'You're under investigation.'

'Liar.'

'How did you know?'

'Because I have nothing to investigate.' She hears him turn away to cough. 'My pension would hardly interest them, it hardly interests me. Because for an inspector, you're so terribly trustworthy, Anna, and such a terribly bad liar. Your sense of humour leaves much to be desired, by the way. Why don't you try to keep it for the evenings, when good people are past noticing?'

'You'll miss it.'

'Like hell I will.'

'Actually, I wanted to talk to you about something.' A siren goes past down in Limeburner Square or Pilgrim Street. '. . . Confidentially.'

'You can trust me,' he says. And Anna hesitates.

'I know. There was something else too. Do you remember Carl?'

'Who?'

'Carl Caunt. Young. Ambitious. He was still a trainee, when you —'

'I remember. The loud one. What about him?'

'Yesterday we talked about the Cryptographer. He'd already heard.'

At the other end of the line there is a sound that might be laughter. 'He is an inspector, after all. It's his job to hear things. You don't think I told him, do you? Do you?'

'No.'

'Christ, I can't have seen him in years. I imagine

29

that everyone at the Revenue knows by now. Don't they? It's hardly top-secret information anyway. Anyone who doesn't should be sacked for lack of enterprise.'

She almost flinches. This is also what he is like: sharper than she will ever be. It is two years since his own enforced retirement. His voice is less forgiving when he is sober. She knows he still blames the Revenue, but there are occasionally times when Anna wonders if he blames her too. If he knows that he should.

'So Carl Caunt knew. Good for him. And what did you say?'

She adjusts the phone against her shoulder. 'I told him that it was a random investigation, and that there were no inconsistencies. I said I didn't want any help.'

'And how many lies did this entail?'

'Three,' she says, 'I think.'

'That's rather a lot, Anna. For such a little amount of telling.'

She takes a deep breath. 'Can I talk to you about it?'

'You know you can. But not like this.' Anna is not sure whether he is talking about the telephone line or himself.

'When?'

'Tonight.'

'Where?' she says, and Lawrence says:

'Here.'

★   ★   ★

His apartment is old, dark, gentlemanly. An extension of himself, or something he would like to be. There is a shaving mirror by the window overlooking Little Venice. In the kitchen, florentines in a paper box. On the desk, a mechanical clock with a steel face. By the bed, a small vase of violets. She knows all these things as he opens the door, smiling, and that nothing will have changed. Somewhere a singer is practising to the sound of a piano. It sounds almost real.

'You look tired. They work you too hard.'

'It's not them,' she says, and Lawrence nods.

'What can I get you?'

'Coffee.' She follows him into the kitchen. The smell an alchemical admixture of tobacco and old cooking. 'You always make it better than me.'

'Of course. It takes years of practice.'

'I have years.'

'Hah. Not enough. I also bought some cakes. You must be hungry . . . will you stay for supper?'

'I have to get back.'

'You do work too hard,' he says, disappointed. 'I hope they appreciate it.'

'They seem to.'

'They haven't still got you buried away under Complaints?'

'No, I have an office on the thirteenth floor.'

'The thirteenth.' Lawrence briefly affects a pose of respectful disbelief.

'With a window.'

'A window! Well, we are going up in the world.'

She leans in the doorway and eats with her hands. Catching the honeyed crumbs, watching him work. His movements are economical with experience. It is how she remembers him. Not here but at the Revenue. Not doing these small things, but what he cared for most. Keeping watch. Setting the record straight.

She remembers the way he worked. A kind, instinctual, and relentless man. When he was like that, lost in the investigation, he was the perfect inspector. People said so, and Anna still believes it. The very best.

Later he became other things. When his drinking became more extreme Lawrence could be cruel. His exactitude became unforgiving, little by little, and most of all to the illiterate or innumerate, the unrepresented, those clients least able to ask questions back. But it was Anna who was the first to notice it. It was Anna who was closest, after all. Everyone knew that, in the place where everyone knew everything. It was Anna they came to first, when the complaints began.

She can remember herself, too. A decade younger. Not the youngest prospect, nor the brightest, but talented, in an unassuming kind of way, and set to shadow her more talented senior. Close to him as a shadow. Learning what came to him by instinct. Letting herself be taught. Loving him, of course. It seemed inevitable that she should love him. She thinks this was something else he tried to teach her.

Love. Of course. It takes practice.

'There!' he says, pouring the coffee into small cups. For Anna he adds hot milk. As he turns she smiles, so that her face will show nothing else. 'Alright?'

'Perfect.' She does not drink.

'Why don't we go into the study,' he says, and they do. The desk lamp is on under its green glass hood. Outside the night is coming on.

'Now tell me again,' Lawrence says, settling back, 'about your John Law,' and Anna says nothing. Now it comes to it she isn't sure she wants to talk about him, after all. She is still thinking about how strange it feels to be back here, in Lawrence's place. There were times when she almost lived here. She is thinking of the sex. Of Lawrence's skill as a lover, at once shocking and unsurprising. The passion of an old man. The appalling nights of failure, and the lovemaking when it came always fiercer, more desperate. The slack, warm musculature of his limbs.

It is a quiet room, this one, a natural study. She has always liked it, envied it, even. There are only the small or distant sounds of the mechanical clock. The singer floors away, singing piano scales.

'Anna?' says Lawrence, and she looks up.

'Yes. There is an inconsistency.'

'I see,' he says, surprised. It is not what he expected to hear, though he recovers well. Anna finds both things reassuring. She has been thinking it is a mistake to have come, though she needed this, needed talk. And it is too late now.

She drinks the coffee. Her mouth fills with its fine bitterness.

'So. What form does this inconsistency take?'

'A deposit box.'

'Containing what?'

'Nothing really, the usual hardware. Gold, a number of platinum ingots. But they aren't in his name, and they aren't declared among his assets.'

'Then among whose assets are they? The wife's or the son's?'

'The son. Nathan Law.'

'So. A vault into which funds are diverted, under the son's name, with a suitably uncooperative financial institution,' says Lawrence; and none of it is a question. Anna doesn't ask him how he knows. It is because he does, because he has the talent to feel his way through money, that she is talking to him at all.

'The Depository of the Gulf of Tartary,' she says. On the desk, the clock ticks softly behind its steel face.

'Perfect. And the Board chose you? Why not someone in corporate tax?'

'I don't know,' she says, although she thinks she does. Absently Lawrence taps his cup, as if there is something he is trying to put his finger on.

'Clients have a tendency to talk to you, don't they? You always had a talent for opening them up. Do you think that could be it?'

'Maybe. Maybe it's just because the discrepancies are in Law's personal accounts. There's no need to involve corporate inspectors.'

'Nor to rock SoftMark's boat any more than necessary. And how are they hidden, these discrepancies?'

Again she doesn't answer. Now she has the chance to explain, she finds herself reluctant to do so. She leans forward, quizzical. It is no longer an issue of trust. It is more to do with a kind of possession. Of having Law to herself.

'Anna?' Lawrence peers down at her, his concern exaggerated, amused.

'They're hidden between numbers.'

'What can you mean?'

'I mean that Revenue figures are rounded up or down to the nearest cent. To consistently round the figures the wrong way is fraud. Most people wouldn't have enough money to make it worth their while. It doesn't make much difference to us either, and if it does – if a few figures are rounded the wrong way – the amount written off is more than balanced out by the time we save in processing. But Law cares. The greater the transaction, the more accurately it is likely to be calculated, to the tenth or hundredth of a cent. And Law lives in a daily world of huge transactions. His fractions are worth millions. Last year his wealth was estimated to be greater than that of the billion poorest people on earth. Did you hear that?'

'I try my best not to notice these things.'

'If Law stakes ten billion on an overnight fall of a hundredth of a percentage point in the electric livre, he becomes a millionaire all over again – that's why he cares. And his annual accounts contain millions of expenses, disbursements, percentile profits, fractional commissions. Now it turns out there are also millions more than there need to be. His accounts are designed to generate as many divisions as possible. Finally every loss is rounded up, every profit rounded down. Because the fractions in the calculations are so small, no one has ever noticed. The figures have always been below the threshold where searches were designed to pick up errors. Two months ago, a new computer program was installed which examines individual entries down to one thousandth of a soft –'

'Please.' Lawrence puts out a hand. 'Stop. I'd almost forgotten how inane money can be. How long has this been going on?'

'Thirteen years. The Revenue has been deciding what to do for weeks.'

'And lo, they decided on you. The Board smiles on you, mortal.' He gets up, looks at her sharply, goes to the window. 'How much?'

'Hardware to the value of four million. The compound tax is three times that.'

'I see,' he says again. And then nothing else. He stands with his back to Anna, looking out at the Grand Union canal. She sees that it has begun to rain steadily outside, fine as net curtains. Upstairs the singer has stopped singing.

'You're surprised,' she says.

'Not that he would want more.' He shrugs. 'But yes, I am.'

'Why?'

'For one thing, that it should be such a small amount.' He turns back to her. 'Not to you or me. But I find it curious that he should take a chance with his life for that. Because his life must be very precious to him, don't you think?'

'Yes.'

'The rich tend to value their lives very highly. Have you found any other undeclared vaults and accounts, stashed away?'

'Not yet.'

'I rather imagine you will. Four million in Soft Gold?'

'Yes.'

'Six million dollars. You know I still think in paper, it's how I know I'm getting old. Four million must be nothing to him. How long will it take him to make that?'

'Thirty-four hours,' says Anna. She thinks: and seven minutes. Because she has already thought of this peculiarity. She has accrued the salient facts. To make legitimately what he has secreted away will take John Law less than two days. Awake or asleep; in terms of money it makes no discernible difference. 'Is there anything else?'

'Certainly,' says Lawrence. 'There is the fact

that the Revenue should have discovered this at all. With all due respect to you and Her Venerable Majesty's highly trained servants. But this is John Law, the inventor of perfect money.'

He is gesturing, now, as he talks. It makes him younger, Anna thinks. Just for an evening, he is doing what he loves. She thinks: I have given him that. She thinks: I am thinking of the wrong man. She watches him sit down, the desk lamp firing his face with light, hardly able to contain himself.

'If he wanted to avoid his dues, why would he not use cryptography? The immovable inspectors meet the unbreakable code. But no. Instead he attempts to hide this shabby business with false accounting. It's such a primitive way to go about things. It's almost pathetic. What else did the Board tell you?'

'Nothing.'

'Nothing? Well, they have always relied rather heavily on the dignity of silence. Anna, do take care, won't you?' says Lawrence. And sixteen miles across London, John Law looks up from his night's work at nothing, distracted by it only for a second, before he goes back to the blank white page.

For two more days she studies him. She suspects that she is as ready as she will ever be, that by the law of diminishing returns, if nothing else, she must be learning less with each hour she spends. All the same, she studies.

There is no end to it. She moves through

accounts in old money and Soft Gold, and online – there is no off-line, anymore – through sites and search engines, realms and domains. It is a world where she feels submerged. Half deafened, half blind, her hands pale and slow in a world of uncompromising quickness. It is as if she is waiting for something.

On the last day of the month she writes to him. It is still early, her office is barely halved with light. The electronic mail is bright as stained glass. She addresses the Cryptographer in the language of the Revenue, which is old, stilted, and relentlessly precise. She asks Mister Jonathan Keir Law to contact her. She asks for his primary business receipts over the last three years, his full-time and part-time staff lists and share dealings, and a meeting at his earliest convenience. She tells him that he is under investigation. Nothing else. After all, she is under no obligation to reveal the strengths of her position, or its weaknesses.

The reply comes within hours. Not from the Cryptographer, but from his personal accountants, a firm based in Philadelphia and Brussels. A Margaret Mutevelian informs Anna that Mister Law is in the United Kingdom. That he will be glad to submit his records immediately, if it is convenient. That he can meet her in five days, if she wishes, at his place of business. And as Anna reads this, the monitor bent towards her, her own bent head reflected in the glass, she realises that she is not ready, after all. That perhaps someone who feels as ordinary as her will never be ready for someone like him.

'Anna Moore,' Anna says to the door with no name. 'To see Mister Law.'

'Law,' the voice on the line repeats. Politely but neutrally, as if it has never heard this one syllable.

'John Law.'

'Yes,' says the voice. 'I'm sorry, but I don't have any record of another external appointment today.'

'Can you check again? Three o'clock. I'm here to see him at three.'

There is a faint sound, the crustacean scuttle of computer keys. 'What company do you represent, madam?'

'The Inland Revenue.'

'The Revenue,' says the voice, lightening. 'Oh yes. One moment, please.'

She looks away. Lunchtime traffic crawls towards Farringdon. She sees that a cyclo has overturned up by Hatton Garden, spilling bright-green plastic crates. It is an old-fashioned winter for the day, at least. The light seems preternaturally clear and sharp. The cold has put colour in Anna's cheeks. It makes her seem younger, although this she does not see.

There is enough time for a germ of anxiety to unfurl itself inside her. The old fear that what she does is more than what she is. *The Revenue. Oh yes.* Then the door opens behind her, and she turns to see a room full of flowers and a small man with large pores, a surprising moustache and an apologetically sweet smile.

'He's downstairs,' he says. 'I'll take you. I'm Terence. Sorry about the flowers.'

It is like walking into a wedding or a funeral. The reception desk is buried under a slew of lilies, maidenhair ferns and delivery forms. The scent of bouquets fills the long room. 'Your card,' Terence asks, and Anna hands it to him, a sliver of black lacquer embossed with her golden fingerprint. He uncovers a SoftMark laptop among the lilies, inserts the card into a slot. 'Thumb?' he says, and she presses it against the screen, feeling the invisible resistance of static.

'Is something happening?' she asks, and Terence shrugs.

'Nothing special.' He hands the card back to her. 'Nothing in particular. You know,' he says, and beams up at her, as if she does. 'This way, please.'

There are windows at the far end of the room, a deep courtyard, fountains. They reach them before Anna can think of anything she needs to say.

'Has Mister Law's accountant arrived?'

'Mister Law's accountants have been here for some time.' Terence motions her into a waiting elevator. 'There are a number of visitors here today. Have you been here before, Inspector?'

'Anna.' They start to descend as she says it. Her voice jumps with the velocity. 'Just Anna.'

41

'Of course. You're not the police, are you, after all?'

The floors pass slowly. Basement Three, Basement Four. The odour of lilies follows them down. Anna thinks of Asphodel Nine. The dream of cleaning potatoes. The text of a secret.

'I have been here once.'

'I knew it,' says Terence. The cubicle walls are lacquered to a finish. He winks at their reflections. 'It's the computers, you see. SoftMark computers never forget a face. Have you met Mister Law? Do you know him?'

'Not really,' she says. And then, 'No.'

'Everybody says that.' Terence is perpetually smiling. 'They say it just like that. Here we are now. Basement Six.'

The doors slide open. Beyond them is a great hall, a space of acres or hectares that Anna has seen only once but dreamed of many times, her mind embellishing it with a resonance and substance it does not quite possess. There is an echoing sound – a hubbub – that she associates with stadia and termini. The money hall is full of people and laughter, the clash of their voices. The crowd is so large and the scene so unexpected – Anna has readied herself for something so different – that her stomach lurches with a phobic sensation of panic. She is suddenly acutely aware of her work clothes, plain and handsome, and the briefcase at her side. The floor is black as far as she can see.

'What's happening?'

'Happening?' Terence looks surprised, as if he has only just noticed they are not alone. 'Oh. These will be new investors.'

'But what are they doing?'

He looks around, as if to check. 'Just as you see. They come to see how the company ticks. Or they come to get drunk and tell their friends about it later. But everyone needs investors, even Mister Law. No man is an island, even one who owns islands. I'll find him for you, if you'll just wait here. Anna? Inspector?'

'I'm fine,' she says. And then, because this is not what he has asked her, 'Thank you.'

'I'll find him,' says Terence, watching her. 'You wait here, will you?'

'Thank you,' she says again, but the receptionist is already apologising his way through the press of bodies, out over the smooth floor of money.

The fear drains from her as she waits. In its wake comes a fainter sensation of anxiety and a quickening of other feelings, harder, more manageable and familiar. Suspicion. An inspector's mistrust. Anna holds on to them as if they might save her from drowning. She wonders who these people are, with their soft, tanned features, the unformed faces of those to whom life has come too easily. She remembers the last time she was here, the first time she saw how Soft Gold worked. The flash of light beneath her outstretched hand. Miraculous, like a fish turning in deep water.

Somewhere a glass breaks against the vitreous

floor. Terence is out of sight. Anna keeps watch for him. Listens for his voice, over the babble of the crowd.

'Of course we're still cashflow-negative, but all things come –'

'Anyone that rich is a hypocrite – because only the hypocrites get rich –'

'That's your problem, my friend. You don't see that a billionaire in an aeroplane is the closest thing to God . . .'

'—must be ten years since the Diamond Jubilee. I hear the next will be her Silicon –'

'There he is! Do you see? There's the Cryptographer.'

Anna looks. *The Cryptographer*, someone hisses again, a woman with hair bright as wine. Whispers or hisses. There is a sharpness to it which means money or scandal. Anna follows the woman's eyes, and finds him. There he is. In the flesh.

Money lends him weight. Anna can't think of any other words for it, although it is the kind of construction her colleagues might use, might actually have used once, talking about clients and superiors. But then Anna is thinking of the word differently from Carl or Sullivan, who would mean by it social standing or a kind of mature power. Weight as compensation for lost looks.

This is physical. Not charisma and not fat or muscle, but something more essential. A density. Her own life feels suddenly light with lack of possessions. She realises she has been expecting John

Law to let her down, to be missable-in-a-crowd, an ordinary disappointment. And he is not these things at all. There is something extraordinary about him. It is as if the wealth he has created is present, all of it, under the pores of his skin.

The hall is underlit, guards and guests moving through pockets of spotlight. Where Law stands the illumination is dim, casting shadows under his cheeks and eyes. His features are not clear. He is smiling at something said. If there is an expression it is one of hunger. Anna feels a hankering to see him up close, under stronger light.

She moves nearer. Now she can hear his voice. She recognises the quietness. The quality that might once have been an accent. He is talking to a shorter man. To three men. And their voices are listened to, are carried into and over other conversations.

She finds herself trying to imagine his wealth. In real terms, magnums of champagne or cartons of late-night takeaway, a fortune measured in seafood and lemongrass. But the figures are incomprehensible, ghostly, like Soft Gold itself. They slip away from her. For a moment she feels – imagines she feels – the motion of so much money. It must be accumulating as Law stands here. He only looks so still, she thinks, because his money is not.

'There you are,' says Terence. 'I couldn't find you. But I see you've found him.' He has a glass in one hand. Clear liquid. 'I brought you a drink. It's just water. Sparkling, I hope that's alright.'

'I'm fine,' she says, and she is, now she has seen what she has come for. The receptionist withdraws the glass.

'I'll introduce you, then, and leave you to it.' Anna notices that for the first time he has stopped smiling. 'I should wish you luck, I suppose. Should I wish you luck, Inspector?'

'It's Anna.'

Terence nods, watching her. 'I trust him,' he says, abruptly, roughly, as if he would like to say more. Instead he gestures towards the Cryptographer, and Anna follows him.

He is near the centre of the hall, where the sound and sense of people is most intense. A woman older than Anna and with more apparent seniority waits beside him, apart from the encompassing crowd, humourless as a bodyguard. Two men are speaking to the Cryptographer together, excited, bullish with it, their voices falling over one another in the effort to communicate something already lost. A third is busy in the extraction of a business card. All the same he is the first of the group to notice Anna. His eyes appraise her, openly, as if she could present a threat to be respected.

'Mister Law?' Terence leans beside his employer, speaking in a quick undertone. And then they are all turning to observe her, the men necessarily quiet, Law himself smiling, holding out his hand.

'You must be Anna,' he says. 'I'm John.'

'Hello. I think we have an appointment to keep,' she says, although in fact it is not what she thinks at all. No you're not, is what she thinks. You're the Cryptographer, or the Codemaker, or John Law: John-Law, the words running together, double-barrelled, trademarked, impersonal as a surname. You're not John, she thinks. But it is not what she says.

His hand feels soft, surprising; vulnerable, like that of a child. Breakable. He is still holding her own fingers and the heel of her palm. She remembers the impression of density, of something subcutaneous, and pulls away.

'Of course,' he says. 'We have work to do. Do you enjoy your work, Anna?'

'Yes, I do.'

'So do I,' he says, and nothing else. He is still smiling, although it seems to Anna he is also frowning.

'Excuse me?' It is one of the other men, the observant one, leaning towards her. Another hand being offered. 'Tunde Finch, MRE. Anna Moore, is it? A pleasure. I missed who you were with –'

'Gentlemen,' says Terence, and he moves between them. 'I'm afraid Mister Law has business. Anna, this is Margaret Mutevelian—' The woman nods tersely. 'Mister Law will join you both as soon as he is done. Gentlemen?'

He ushers the men away from Law. Tunde Finch, MRE the last of them, the card still in his fallen hand, an empty expression on his face which seems as clear to Anna the inspector as spoken words – *this was my chance, my one moment, and I have lost it* – and then the Cryptographer is behind her, Terence murmuring at his side, and Margaret Mutevelian is walking with her to the elevators, leading her out of the company of strangers and up and away through the dim and luxurious corridors of the SoftMark Corporation.

The quiet envelops her. After the babble and hubbub of the hall it is almost tangibly calming, as if relief could be breathed in on air. The corridors are soft and stainless underfoot.

Along the walls are alcoves, lit plinths, vases of celadon and illustrated porcelain. It comes to Anna that there must be people working here somewhere. If so she doesn't hear them. Perhaps everything is mechanised, she thinks. She tries to remember what floor they have come out on. She feels a long way from daylight.

'Anna,' says the figure beside her. Margaret Mutevelian's voice is gentle, the English faintly Americanised. 'May I call you Anna?'

'Of course.' She smiles at the older woman. The accountant's face is handsome, her precise age indeterminate, the skin perfect with muscular or hormonal alteration.

'Well then. Such a nice name. And please call me Margaret.'

'Margaret.'

'Mister Law will be joining us soon, but I was hoping to ask you some questions first. Before we begin.'

It is an old relationship, that of inspector and accountant. A matter of diplomacy, since each is employed to consider the other with what amounts to a delicately veiled suspicion. There is a need for decorum, when the success of one may come to depend on the failure of the other. The tradition is as familiar to Anna as the language of the Revenue, and she feels herself relax into it.

The corridor forks. Mutevelian leads them to the right. Sure of her way, as if she has been here many times before. 'Would you mind?'

'Not at all, if you think it will help,' Anna says, but automatically; her mind is not in it. She is thinking of the Cryptographer in his hall of glass. His stillness, and the crowd around him.

'It will certainly help me. Thank you. So, how long do you think your investigation will last?'

'Six months. Perhaps less.'

'Six months?' The light of alcoves across her face. When Mutevelian looks away it is like observing the profile on a coin. 'I see. Then you believe you have found something? A discrepancy?'

'Six months isn't long. I wouldn't draw any conclusions from it.' And in her mind she goes over, not the dry minutiae of the investigation, but an entirely different order of facts. The Cryptographer's hands. His voice with the smile and the frown behind it. *Do you enjoy your work, Anna?* It is a strange question, she thinks. Strange for her. It is not something a client has ever asked her before.

They ascend a flight of stairs. There are narrow

windows here, bars of bezelled glass. Glimpses of courtyards, stone lanterns, a segment of bright November sky.

'Six months. But six months of Revenue time is not six months. It can be a lifetime,' says Mutevelian, and smiles. 'At least for the victims.'

'We prefer the term clients,' Anna says, and a part of her, the hard part, flexes like muscle. Be careful, she thinks. Take care. This is the accountant of a man with false accounts. This is not the time or place to let your mind wander.

'Of course.' Mutevelian is still smiling. Her teeth are crooked, an odd inconsistency in an otherwise perfected face. 'I don't recognise you, Anna. I know the British Revenue well, I've worked with them many times. The kind of people people have nightmares about – I mean that as a compliment, you understand. But I don't know you. I take it you are a Full Inspector? Ordinary or Senior?'

'We don't use those terms any more.' In the natural light Anna sees Mutevelian's mouth twitch. A moue of irritation.

'And what terms do you use?'

'I'm an Inspector, A2 grade.'

Along one wall is a sculpture of articulated steel, abstract, serpentine, draconian. At the corridor's end is a single door. Mutevelian stops in front of it. 'Well. They should have sent A1,' she says, mildly, as if she has said nothing at all, and Anna feels a rare slick of anger run through her, fluid as

50

plasma. 'Here we are,' the accountant adds, and opens the door.

The room is not large, and sparely furnished, but in its own way it is as much an expression of power as the hall of glass. There is a table fifteen feet long, a slab of some extinct dark wood, at which two men sit. There are two paintings, sparely lit, each of which Anna has seen countless times before, in countless reproductions, so that she knows them now as if they were her own possessions.

A window spans the entirety of the east wall. Outside there are trees, cedars and silver birch, yews and acer, the light falling through their branches and foliage; and nothing else. The trees are so old and dense, or the courtyard so vast, that there is no sense of the walls beyond them, or London beyond that. It is like looking at a motion picture, or through some impossible lens. Out of one place, into another.

'Mark Fugger, Marcus Cree,' says Mutevelian. 'This is Anna Moore.'

She looks away from the spectacle of trees to find the men rising from their places. They are inconspicuous in a way that Anna associates with all accountancy, and at this moment, inattentive with unexpected anger, she can distinguish them only by age. 'Inspector Moore,' says the older of the two, Midwestern American, and is transparently disconcerted when she does not take his outstretched hand.

51

She walks past him to the table. She can feel adrenalin still circulating through her, bright as mercury. It is not the strength it feels itself to be, she knows. She has never been insulted by an accountant – not professionally, as Mutevelian has done – but it is something she recalls Janet Sullivan describing. If the outcome of an interview seems inevitable, and undesirable enough, an accountant may try to obstruct it with careful offence. There is no law to say they must be subservient, and their first debt is always to their clients. But the Revenue has a long memory, and inspectors do not take kindly to obstruction. It is a risk few accountants are willing to take.

Or perhaps she is only telling the truth. Perhaps Anna is a surprise to her. There are other inspectors who could have been sent, after all, older and more experienced workers. They could have sent A1, couldn't they? Why, Anna thinks, did they send me?

She takes off her coat, lays her briefcase on the table, clicks it open. Willing herself to be calm. I am good, she thinks, as if saying it into a mirror. She lifts the tablet computer from its leather cavity. Aware of the time and the place and of the men behind her, unsure of themselves, waiting for their cues.

'Mark and Marcus will be assisting me in this case,' says Mutevelian, somewhere out of sight.

'Really,' Anna says, as evenly as she can. 'Well, you'll need all the assistance you can get.' And as she turns to them a door opens in the wall of glass, and John Law comes in.

'Margaret,' he says. 'I'm late again, aren't I?'

'No, sir, not at all,' Mutevelian replies, all decorous warmth. There is something on the shoulder of Law's suit, a minute fragment of leaf or seed from the trees outside, and around him the cold, bright air.

'Good. Well, it's a bad habit. I'm sorry to have kept you waiting.'

His gaze moves from Anna to the accountants. She is sure he is about to say more. Instead he glances back at her, and his expression changes. He is already turning away, closing the glass door, before Anna recognises amusement in his expression, and she feels another kind of anger, less certain of itself, touched with shame, at the fact that he has understood what he has missed.

'So then, sit down,' he says to them. 'Please.' The men find places beside him. Anna puts the table's length between herself and the triumvirate of accountants. When there is quiet she looks up. His eyes are there, waiting for hers.

'Would you like a drink?'

'No.'

'An antioxidant?' He takes a pastille case from his pocket. In the natural light of the room she can see he is not quite clean-shaven, perhaps a day's growth. It softens the pallor of his skin.

'No, thank you.'

'No.' He puts one green pill in his mouth, tucks

the silver case away, and sucks, gravely. 'Here we are, then. How can I help you?'

'This is only a preliminary meeting, you understand.' She switches on the tablet computer, its soft radiance on her fingers.

'I think I do.'

'The investigation is likely to comprise several interviews, given the nature of your finances.'

'I see. Then we'll have time to get to know each other.'

She ignores the irony which might not be irony, which might be what he means. He says it as if he means it. 'Today we'll talk about what you do in general terms. For example, how would you describe your work? Your business?'

A standard first question, unthreatening and unobtrusive, designed to put a client at ease as much as to elicit information. *Remember*, Lawrence once told her, *the first question should never be the one that matters*. 'My work is different from my business,' Law says, sucking like a child with a sweetie, and he is still watching her. His eyes haven't moved from her face.

'Your business then. How would you describe it?'

'My business is money.'

'You are the owner of the SoftMark Corporation?'

'I am.'

She looks down at the tablet screen. 'I understand that you own over eighty per cent of the corporation, and that the primary business of the corporation is computerware.'

'It is.'

'Mister Law,' she says, at ease with practice, 'I need you to be as transparent as possible in your dealings with me.'

He cracks the last of the pill between his teeth. 'Then I'll try not to disappoint you. The business of SoftMark is computers. The profile of SoftMark is raised by Soft Gold. When I created Soft Gold, the code required a place it could be housed. It needed dedicated power, and a financial institution behind it that people could trust. SoftMark was in a position to provide these things. Three years after the new money was set up, I was paid a previously agreed quantity of SoftMark shares. The quantity was dependent on the success of the new money. The new money was somewhat more successful than SoftMark had anticipated. Eventually I came to hold a controlling stake in the corporation. But I did so because Soft Gold is here. My code is here. My fortune is largely theoretical. I think of myself as a scientist, not a businessman.'

She types, *Nature of Business: Money*. The words look ludicrous even as she completes them, and she is angry again. 'Thank you.'

'You're welcome,' he says, and without looking she knows he is smiling.

'And what did they get?'

'I'm sorry?'

55

'I can see what you got from this. I can't see what they gained from you.'

'I see, yes. Alright.' For the first time since they have sat down he looks away from her. She is aware of it at the upper edge of her vision, and of the relief of it. 'When I came to them, SoftMark was already one of the most successful companies in the world. Now there is no need to qualify the term. I take full responsibility for that. I offered the corporation the most forceful advertising tool money could buy – their own money. I told them it would take their name into the pockets and minds of billions of people. I advised them to think of electric money as the ultimate product placement. As the junk mail no one would ever throw away.'

It is easier to watch him, now he is no longer watching her. He has begun to rock gently in his seat, as if with some suppressed excitement or anxiety. 'I also explained that, by offering preferential deals to Soft Gold users, they could gain unprecedented control of their own market sales. SoftMark now has a degree of pricing flexibility that other companies can only dream of.'

'You make it sound like a monopoly.'

'No.' He glances sharply back at her. Stops rocking. 'I didn't say that.'

'Excuse me. I didn't mean –'

'No problem.' He is watching her again now. Gauging her, she thinks, as if he has had her wrong. 'I also told them my money would make them indispensable.'

'Indispensable?'

Margaret Mutevelian leans towards him, murmuring blandly. In a voice like that, Anna thinks, one could say anything and still sound like a diplomat. Law hears her out, shakes his head, *no*, and turns back.

'I told them that if they could establish themselves as suppliers of a leading international currency, it would be extremely difficult for any domestic government to limit their growth. They would feel concerned, as they will when corporations expand to a certain point. But they would be reluctant to take any of the usual actions if Soft Gold were indispensable. They wouldn't want to rock our boat. The financial markets are volatile enough as it is.'

'The usual actions,' she says. There is a quality to her repetition which suggests incomprehension, she can hear it herself too clearly. The youngest of the men is smiling down at his laptop screen. Whether he is laughing at her or is only trying to understand what has been said, Anna cannot be sure.

'Anti-trust measures. Monopoly commissions, as you say. I needed them, and I needed them to believe me, and I believe they did.' Law pauses again, as if he is about to say something more; and again he does not.

'And were you right?'

'As a matter of fact,' he says, 'I was.'

She looks up at him. Not because she wants to,

but because it is time she did. Already she can feel the interview slipping away from her, the weight of it veering out of control. She wonders where it will take them. The accountants are writing hard in their little black electric books. Law is watching her as he did in the hall of glass: half frowning, half smiling. As if he has come across something he doesn't quite understand, whether in himself or in the woman who faces him.

'You didn't tell me what your work was.'

'You didn't ask.'

'What is your work?'

'Cryptography.' He leans forward. His eyes on hers. Kennedy grey. 'My work is the study of hidden things. You're here about the account. The one in the name of my son.'

The men look up one after the other, mute as court stenographers. In the time it takes Anna to make up her mind about what to say Margaret is already talking. 'Mister Law, I strongly suggest that this is not a constructive –'

'Margaret,' John Law says, but his voice is quiet.

'—avenue of discussion. It is not the place of the Revenue to –'

'Greta,' the Cryptographer says, and she turns. 'You can go now.'

She looks at him. The older of the accountants smiles, tentatively, as if someone has told a joke he is afraid not to understand. 'Sir?'

'You can go. Thank you, Greta. I'll be alright here.'

She says nothing, but stands, not entirely steadily though with a certain dignity. Without guilt, Anna sees that she is much older than she first appeared.

'I'll be fine,' Law says again.

'As you wish.' Mutevelian's cheeks have flushed, white at the bones, red at the cheeks. As if she has been slapped. She doesn't look at Anna as she passes, but her eyes are resigned. As if, Anna thinks, she has tried to prevent the inevitable.

The older man is the last to leave. He bows slightly as he closes the door behind him. The silence he leaves behind extends and intensifies itself in the room with the wall of glass and the two seated figures. Like heat in a greenhouse.

'I'm sorry.' Law's voice is still soft, there is no edge to it. 'Greta has been with me for many years. Sometimes she may defend me more enthusiastically than is strictly necessary. I'd like to apologise on her behalf.'

'She wouldn't want you to.'

'I'm sure she wouldn't.'

'I'd say she was trying to protect you from something.'

He stretches. 'Well, that's her job, isn't it? To protect me from you?'

No, she thinks. Her job is only to represent you. It would take something special, Anna thinks, to make Margaret Mutevelian go so close to the bounds of duty. But she says nothing, and again the air begins to fill with a jarring silence. A trembling begins, deep in the muscles of her arms, and she wills it away.

'You're not what I expected,' Law says abruptly. Anna tries to smile.

'And what was that?'

'I'm not sure. Someone less approachable. As it happens I rarely have the pleasure of meeting the Revenue at such close quarters. I thought you might be more chilling.'

'I can be extremely chilling.'

'Oh, I don't think so.'

'You'd be surprised.'

'Perhaps I would, then.' He stops, backs up. 'We're not so different.'

'What makes you say that?'

'We're both disliked.'

'Speak for yourself.'

'Professionally. I meant professionally. We both work with money.'

'You said your work was cryptography,' she says, smiling, quick-fire.

'Cryptography then.' Grinning. 'Cryptography and money are not unalike.'

'How so?'

'They both lay their numbers over the world. Grids of numbers, following the contours of hills and towers. And not only those inanimate things but lives, too, bodies and faces. You must see that in your work, as I do in mine.' He slows. 'A code can express anything, after all. Just as everything has its price.'

'Does it?'

'Sometimes I think it does,' he says. 'Don't you?'

When she doesn't answer he looks out at the courtyard. The light is lengthening, already it is beginning to go. A stooped figure in green celluloid boots moves between the grandeval roots of cedars.

'Do you like gardening?' John Law asks, the unforeseen question catching her by surprise. She shrugs automatically.

'I like gardens.'

He laughs, perhaps at her expense, but not as if the joke is unkind. Later she will regret not having laughed with him. 'Not quite the same thing.'

'Definitely not. You always have, haven't you?'

'How did you know?'

'Asphodel Nine.'

'Nice thinking there. I'm afraid they've wasted you on me.'

'I'll be sure to tell them.'

'You do that, Inspector.'

'Just Anna,' she says, but what she means is, *Wait*. They are talking so fast now, too fast, it seems to Anna, the rapidity of the words veering almost to the point of argument and back towards laughter. It is both more and less than an interview; more than she has hoped for, less than she can allow. He is only a client in the end, after all, and one with false accounts. But it is as if he is constantly just ahead of her, looking back. As if he knows where the conversation is leading them.

Wait for me.

She scrolls through her notes, lost in his millions, trying to remember what it is she is supposed to want to know. 'You were telling me about Asphodel Nine.'

'Was I?'

'Do you still receive income from it?'

'I doubt it. Greta would know. That was all a long time ago. I read that nine tenths of genetic code serves no function. I invented a way of writing one code into another. Vegetable storage space. I had—' he shifts uncomfortably again – 'I wanted to make my mark. Now can I ask you something, Anna?'

It is softer than she imagines it herself, the way he says it; an easy sound. A name like a smile. 'If you want.'

He nods at the courtyard. 'Do you like my garden?'

She looks, as if to check. 'Yes.'

'I'm glad. It's one of my favourites. I mean of my own. The trees here are transplantations, every one. I purchased them and brought them in full-grown. It takes a bit of work, but I think it's worth it. Some of these are already extinct in their natural habitats. There are sequoias as high as twenty-storey buildings. Taller than that and we'd need planning permission. One of the yews is sixteen hundred years old. They tell me it was alive in the region of York during the last days of the Western Roman Empire. There are natural bonsai from the Japanese Alps. The wind makes them. How do you put a price on things like that?'

'But you did.'

'I did. These are all priceless things, but I purchased them all in the end. They all had their price.'

He stops, as if waiting for something. 'Tell me about the account,' Anna says, and when he smiles again she feels her heart lurch and right itself.

'You haven't answered my question.'

What question? she begins to ask. The words are on her lips as she stops herself. She shakes her head. 'I'm afraid I'm not here for that.'

'Of course.' He sits up. His face falling into shadow as he does so. 'Of course. I am sorry. What was it, exactly, that you wanted to know?'

I want to know who you think of, when you think of money.

So she thinks, but it is not what she says. Anna's thoughts and words are so often distinct. In her it is a kind of professionalism, so she believes. She can feel herself beginning to blush, the blood rising in her skin like heat in air, she knows how it must look, and for a moment she wishes herself gone. But the client is waiting, his face as grave as when he first entered the room.

'The account,' she says again.

'Oh, you must know all about it, to be here.

Don't you? You must know almost everything about me.'

'If I knew everything, I wouldn't need to meet you.'

'Well,' he says, and smiles. 'And that would be a shame.' But he looks tired. A little of the brightness has gone out of him, as if the last of the courtyard's cold air has dissipated from around him.

'Will you tell me about it?'

'No,' he says slowly, 'I don't think I will. I'm sorry I did it, and I can pay. I can certainly pay. Will that be enough, do you think?'

'Enough for what?'

'For the investigation to end.'

She goes still. 'Well. You're not required to explain to me why you have acted as you have. You're not being charged with a criminal offence – we prefer our clients to be earning, as long as they can reasonably be allowed to do so. But if you're admitting a fraud, there's still reason for an investigation,' she says, wondering as she does so whether it is true, why she wants it to be true, what it means to want it. 'The Revenue is not in the habit of concluding matters at this point.'

'I see,' he says, but slowly, as if he has considered something else and decided against it. 'Do you happen to know what I owe?'

She types lightly, almost soundlessly, her eyes following the text as it surfaces on the screen. 'Eleven million, nine hundred and seventy-five thousand, four hundred and twelve soft,' she says, and adds, almost apologetically, 'and fourteen cents. Compound penalty interest over such a long time –'

'You'll have it by next week.'

She saves and shuts down, the tablet screen fading to the dullness of slate. The light in the courtyard has almost gone now. Anna looks for the gardener under the trees, but he or she is out of sight.

'Are we done?'

At the sound of Law's voice she turns back. The room's illumination has not yet come on automatically. In the gloom the Cryptographer's face looks surprised. 'Done. For now.'

He bows his head. 'Of course,' he says, and stands. 'Well. It's been a pleasure, Anna.'

'I rather doubt that. But thank you.'

'But it has,' he says. 'An unexpected pleasure, truly,' and she sees that he is smiling again, and is glad of it. 'Can I walk you out?'

'I'd like that,' she says. And he does. Out through the endless corridors, the porcelain and celadon, the rooms of glass and charged silicon, to where London waits under a clear sky for the emergence of night.

It is only later, when she is alone, that she realises she trusts him. It comes to her as something matter-of-fact, as if the issue has already been decided and she has known it for some time: as if her conscious mind is the last of her to know.

Despite his smoothness, his graceful assurance, his edge of arrogance, and all the evidence she has of his deception, she is like Terence in his room of flowers. She trusts him. It makes her laugh at herself in the dark.

For hours she turns the belief over in her mind, testing it. So it is later still, the small hours, when she remembers the question she never answered. The one John Law never quite asked. *Does everything have its price?*

'Now I remember why I felt sorry for him.'

'Why?'

'You could close the case. It wouldn't be hard, now the Revenue has its grubby hands on his grubby money. That's all they ever want.'

'Money isn't grubby anymore.'

'Money will always be grubby. You could talk to the Board. Those who smile on you so benignly.'

'I don't want to.'

'Why not?'

'Because it wouldn't be right.'

'Wouldn't it?'

'Because I want to understand him.'

'You had a specific job to do, and you've done it, and with commendable speed. What are you going to do with him now?'

They are below St Paul's, side by side on the grass, eating greasy street food from a Brazilian vendor. Anna can feel Lawrence leaning gently against her. It is only partly his age. The weather has turned milder, as it often does; a last manifestation of warmth before the true onset of winter. In the golden light they eat and talk on the greenness of old cemetery ground.

'You don't see.'

'What is there to see, Anna? Tell me. Enlighten me.'

'I want to understand why he did it.'

'It isn't your job to understand.'

'Oh, please.'

'I see.'

'No, you're being obtuse. You said yourself that what he did makes no sense. Aren't you curious?'

'Not in the slightest.'

'You are. You lie as badly as I do. Why have you changed your mind about him? He might do it again. He might use the code next time – then what? You know paying is just his way of getting rid of me.'

'And why shouldn't he?' He rearranges himself uncomfortably. 'He's done all the Revenue asks of him, after all. They aren't considering criminal charges. Are they?'

'No, of course not.'

'Then what would be the fault in letting him pay and be done? Twelve million soft is no small thing. Mister Law has paid the price of crossing the Revenue, and the country can make good use of a sum like that.'

'Paying is his way of removing any obligation to

explain his motives. He's tricked me. He's buying me out.'

'Of course he is.'

'Well, I want to know why, Lawrence. That's why. What?'

'Your friend was right.'

'Who?'

'Your accountant.'

'She's not my bloody friend. Why?'

'Because you are playing a dangerous game.'

'She never said that. What does that mean?' Anna says. 'I don't know what you mean.' But Lawrence only shakes his head and goes back to his food, mouthing palm oil from his hands, the light pale in his white hair, delicately licking the last remains from the tips of his fingers.

She goes back only once. She is on her way to somewhere else – an on-site interview with a software consultant in Bridge Street – and finds herself there before she knows it, outside the unassuming doorway.

It is afternoon, and the sky is all cloud lit through from above, tawny and lucid with incipient rain. Over the storeys of SoftMark Anna can see the tops of trees, the heights of the sequoias in John Law's hidden gardens.

There is a café across the narrow street. For a while she sits, watching the entrance. No one goes in, though one or two go out, salary-men dressed to kill. She is not sure what she is looking for, anyway.

She is going to be late. There are flies on the café walls, dull with the onset of winter. Dark and slow, as if they are waiting for someone to finish them.

It is the seventh of November, the first Friday of the month. Anna sits alone in a room on Cloak Lane, at a butcher's-block table lit by church candles. It is Martha's choice, this, a restaurant within brisk walking distance of two of London's criminal courts as well as Westminster's Temples of Law, with deceptively modest decor and remarkably immodest prices, so that while Anna waits she at least has time to scour the menu for the least exorbitant options.

She is early, and her sister is late. More often than not this is how it turns out between them. Although they tend to meet at Martha's insistence – as if between the scant pair of them they can hold their family together – it is Anna, on the whole, who waits, her life apparently less full than her sister's, her patience wearing thin. Just as, on other days, it is Lawrence who waits for her.

'Sorry,' Martha says as she descends. 'Sorry, sorry, I ended up with one fucking fraud all day, money is so boring, I don't know how you do it, I was going out of my mind in there. Anyway, here I am. Did you wait long? Am I a bitch?'

'No,' Anna lies. 'And yes, you are,' she adds, so that Martha, stooping to kiss her, mocks a scowl.

'When I'm a judge,' she murmurs, 'you'll make sure to call me Honourable Bitch,' and having kissed Anna she dumps herself into a chair. Beyond her Anna can see people turning, frowning at Martha's presence, or attentive, as if this is someone they almost recognise, or think they should. It is a quality Anna's sister has inherited from their mother. Anna has only their father's watchfulness.

'What was it?' she asks, but Martha is already hunched over the menu, rapt. Anna has to speak again before she notices her. 'The case, was it important?'

'Oh, probably. But not really, no. Some criminally greedy share dealing, no blood spilled. Allegedly.' Her cheeks are flushed with the heat of the room, the cold of the street. Anna looks back into her own shrewd eyes. 'The kind of thing Andrew likes to talk about, as if he weren't all talk. What are you having?'

'The risotto.'

'Don't be stupid.'

'Why? I want it.'

'I didn't bring you here to eat risotto.'

'You didn't bring me here.'

'Alright, please yourself,' she says, frowning, and then smiles with affectionate malice, like a sibling. They could be eighteen and ten again, twelve and four, for all the difference it has made between them. Nothing in their lives has changed them so much that they are no longer themselves. 'You can taste mine. White or red? Say red.'

They drink red. Anna watches her eat, voraciously, as she always has, not pausing until her hunger has been blunted on medallions of truffled hare, black cabbage, white asparagus. When she leans back it is with a sigh almost of relief.

'You look well,' Anna says, and when her sister sighs again, 'You do.'

'I believed you more the first time. You look tired.'

'Thanks.'

'It's only the truth. The whole truth.'

'If it is then you shouldn't bring your work home with you.'

'Funny.' She smiles again, with less conviction. 'Andrew says that too.'

'How is he?'

'He seems to be well.' The candles are guttering. She dips her thumb into the wax. Lifts out the small boat of her print. 'I don't see him as much as I'd like. The markets are hard this year. He's been busy, and so have I. What about you?'

'I've had a difficult client.'

'Violent?'

'No.' She has to laugh. 'No, nothing like that.'

'Then what?' Their voices have fallen. The restaurant is emptying out into the streets above, the background noise thinning down to the fundamental clatter of the kitchens. Anna and her sister speak with their heads bent over the remnants of their meal, small talk between siblings.

'His name's John Law.'

'Well, well.' The wax has hardened to the consistency of dead skin. Martha sets it down upright

71

by her glass, a pale coracle of lines and whorls. 'John Law, the root of all evil. You are doing well, aren't you? All Revenue eyes must be on you.'

'I suppose so.'

'You know, I never liked the look of him. He must be impossibly arrogant.'

'Not impossibly. Proud,' she says. 'Just proud.'

'Like you?'

'Oh ha ha. No, not like me. He deserves to be.'

'Do you like him, then? I never thought you were one for hero worship.'

'I didn't say he was my hero.'

'No, you didn't,' Martha says, the last of the candlelight dancing in her eyes. 'Does he like you?'

'Don't be silly.'

'I'm not. I bet he does. But you've finished with him now?'

'No,' Anna says, more or less to herself. 'I don't think I have.'

'Well,' Martha says, straightening. 'Anyway, I'm glad you came tonight. I've missed you. Are you glad you came too?'

'Of course,' Anna says, surprised, and she looks up at her sister, catching her by the eyes. There is something there still unspoken, Anna thinks, but before she can be sure of it her sister is already glancing away, raising her hand for the bill. Anna leans forward while her back is turned, picks up the wax imprint of her skin, presses it smooth and warm between her fingers.

★   ★   ★

72

In certain ways she has always been unlucky. It isn't the way Anna would describe herself – though she has always had a sneaking belief in fate – because in the time and place in which she lives everyone is potentially witness to every misery. A figure in the next tube seat, on the next webcam, the next news bulletin, under the next overpass. *It could be worse*, is what people always say, and it is always true, so unquestionably so as to be a particular kind of lie. A deception arising from meaninglessness.

A Revenue salary will never make Anna rich, but neither is she poor. She has never had to see someone die, or lost a loved one ahead of time, at least not to death. She has been in love and has been loved more than once (though she knows a great deal about secrets and lies; more, on the whole, than her lovers would like). She is not unlucky in death or love. It is something subtler than that.

She is unlucky in time. Too early. Too late. The younger sibling in a family not built to last, watching its decline and fall as long as she has had the faculties to do so. Always watching, and her parents always falling, or always about to fall, like woeful children themselves, or mismatched skaters on old ice. She is the younger sister of a brighter star, a louder, more talented, more beautiful sibling – so it has always been said – so that Anna has become to a degree the opposite of these things: slight, doubtful, wry. It is as if her character has grown to occupy her sister's vacancies. She was the youngest in her educational year, endlessly smaller, never quite catching up, wanting to ask the question, never asking. She has never been in the right place at the right time. She was the most mature Revenue trainee, abruptly old, passed over for the fast-track. She was the student in love with her mentor.

Too early, too late. But she doesn't think of herself as unlucky. Now least of all.

When she thinks of him – which is often – it is with a light heart. It is not the expectation of anything possible. It is only a sense of incipient lightness. It is the luck of it, the pairing of his name with hers, out of so many. Sheer serendipity. It is her heart lifting with something temporary, with desire, the hope of desire.

Something of Law has brushed off on her, like scent or gold dust. It isn't long before she notices. Almost overnight she has changed in the eyes of others. This is what it is like to be known, she thinks, to be thought of, not the watcher but the watched, and she feels a quickening of exhilaration.

Mister Hermanubis, stalking through the internal corridors of the Revenue like some Inspectorial demon, straightens up attentively as he passes her. *You can call me Sukhdev*, he says to her one morning, *Sukhdev*, and she tries but never quite manages to do so. Over sweetmeats from Oulu and coffee from Tunis Janet Sullivan confides in her that she

74

sees her children twice a month, entrusting worn photographs. (Three teenagers, all girls. Tall in the pictures, big in the bones.) The oldest waitress at Lawrence's bar meets Anna's eyes and inclines her head, as if she knows (and how can she know? Anna thinks. But there is her nod, just the same).

She sees Carl more often, and whatever has brought them closer has made them closer. A stranger might even mistake them for friends. Once, after dark, he makes a pass at her, which she gently evades. She is too old for him, she thinks. Or (and she is slower to acknowledge this, kinder to others than she is to herself) he is too young, his talk too incessant, his ambitions repetitive as hungers. There is a look he occasionally gets which Anna dislikes; an expression of amusement, and behind that, and feeding it, a warm human callousness. But on the whole she enjoys his company. Part of her is flattered. Part of her likes his difference.

He is talking now, as she drives. Soon they will be in a public place, a club Carl likes in Lower Marsh that extends under the Thames, bright vats of aquarium fish worlds away from the tonnage of river mud overhead, the crowd all backs and arms and body language. When Carl drinks too much he licks his lips, like a man busy licking his wounds. Until then she is still driving, and he is still talking.

'She works in systems. She said, I analyse systems, I'm a systems analyst. I thought fuck it. She tells you what she does and you don't know

75

anything about her. What does it mean? It's not like what we do. What we do is different. Hello, I'm a tax inspector. It's not hiding anything, is it? It's not exactly hiding your skeletons in the cupboards. You know where you are, with a tax inspector.'

The car is a confessional, Anna thinks. It is a professional observation, something to be remembered for later use. Partly it is the sense of closeness without facing. Partly it is the sense of being in transit, where nothing counts. In cars people will talk for the sake of it. Not that Carl needs any encouragement.

'Anyway. You don't want to hear all this, do you? And I want to hear about you. How's your code man?'

'He's very well. Thanks for asking.' Her eyes already narrowing with an edge of humour.

'Well, because I didn't expect to see you any more, that's all. I thought you'd be long gone by now. Vice-President of Morse. Deputy Dot Dot Dot. That's what I would have done. They're saying you closed the case.'

She shakes her head again. For a while neither of them says anything. It is Sunday, and the traffic eases them along almost of its own accord. They reach Waterloo Bridge and there are seagulls over the grey-green river, dozens of them. In the air they are elegant, balanced on nothing in the afternoon sky.

'Vermin,' says Carl. 'Someone should get rid

76

of them. There are viruses for that. It's tax-deductable.'

'I like them,' Anna says. Two of the gulls fly up from the bridge, quarrelling in mid-air. Lithe and muscular as dancers.

'Why?'

'They used to mean rain.'

'And that's good, is it? So what's he like?'

'Who?' She glances at Carl in the mirror. He is watching her, his dark eyes always on the move, as if he is trying to see through her. 'I don't know.'

'Come on.'

'I don't.'

'Come on, I'm not asking for the colour of his knickers, just tell me what he's like.'

She looks away from him, searching for directions. 'I expect he's your dream come true, Carl. He's powerful. It's as if there's some residue of money on him all the time. He stands out in a crowd and I don't think he minds it.'

'Do you like him?' He waits impatiently while she parks and sits back.

'I don't think he's a bad man. He's not immoral. I don't know if he's amoral. When I started at the Revenue I used to think that amorality was a necessary talent of the rich. Lawrence used to say that. I don't believe that now. Do you remember Lawrence Hinde?'

'Everyone remembers him. Stop avoiding the question, will you? It makes me feel like I'm with a client. Do you like him?'

She gets out and locks the doors behind them. 'Yes,' she says, over the roof of the car, 'I do.' She expects him to leer, to crack a joke, but instead he just looks away, down Coral Street towards the Waterloo Road.

'Why?'

Because I know he's lying, she thinks, and it doesn't make him less desirable. She thinks, because I trust him. 'Because he interests me,' she says. 'He's like something from the past or future. A Roman emperor in the twenty-second century. A science-fiction merchant prince. Something like that. Is that what you wanted?' And she looks up to find that Carl is no longer listening.

He is watching a figure in an adjacent doorway. There are two people there, in fact, both squatting on the pavement, but only one is holding out its hands. Begging, Anna thinks. It is not something she has seen for a while. Soft Gold means there is less to beg for or to give, now, only the old concretes of food, alcohol, cigarettes. In America, she remembers being told, there are beggars with card machines, but this was said to her with a slow smile and heavy eyes, as if the burden of these things is never gone.

It is a moment before she notices the hands themselves. The thumbs have been cut off. One has been severed at the base, the other near the knuckle. The amputations are healed but not yet smooth.

'Look at that, will you.'

'What—' Anna begins, quietly, although the figure makes no sign of hearing and it is not clear to her whether it is a man at all. She can't make out its features properly, its face is in the shadow of the doorway. Only the eyes are visible. They are watching her, unafraid.

'He's been fingered. That's what happens now, that's what they do. It started a few years ago. When they steal your card they take the print that goes with it. Sometimes they take both thumbs, to be sure. Fingering. Didn't you know?'

She does, of course. She has heard of it, seen it virtually, but never literally, like this, herself. 'I'm sorry.'

'What for?' Carl says, his voice unsteady. 'You haven't cut his thumbs off, have you?'

'For him, then,' she says, and she is, but she is sorry for Carl too. For the anger and fear milling in him. She is sorry for herself.

'Don't be.' Carl starts to walk. 'He wouldn't want you to.'

She follows him without a word. They turn out of the confines of Coral Street, up the main street. The sky is clearing to a fine blue, lighter than at midday, an Indian noon.

'I heard something,' he says eventually. 'About your merchant prince.'

'What?'

'It's not exactly moral.'

'Carl.'

'I don't know if you'll like it.'

'You won't know unless you tell me,' she says, trying too hard to be playful, to bring out the playfulness she likes in him. He smiles as if by rote.

'It's about the flower code. The one he hid in flowers.'

'Asphodel Nine?'

'Whatever. I heard there was another one, something he came up with later. They say he sold it in thirty countries. It was along the same lines.'

'What lines?' she repeats; but already she almost knows. She is too familiar with the way people think, the uneasy stories they tell. The grotesque and gothic shadows cast by the rich and famous.

'This one you don't hide in flowers. You hide it in people.' He stops, hawks into the gutter with practised precision, begins to walk again. 'You could have bank numbers in your fingernails. I could have chemical formulas in my liver. Anything. You'd never know. Useful. I might not even know myself.'

She laughs without conviction. 'Carl, if you believe that —'

'I didn't say I believed it,' he says, dogged now, 'I'm saying it's what people are saying.'

'People say anything.'

'And sometimes they're right. Worse things happen. There's more, too.'

'Oh, spare me —'

'No, listen,' he says, fervent, pleading, almost, and she does, because everyone does; everyone wants to hear. Because after all, it might be true.

It might be good. 'This code, whatever he calls it. Twenty years on, and the people who carried it are all dying. Dropping like flies, all over the world. They get some kind of cancer.'

'What kind?'

'The rare kind, I don't know. Cancer of the fingernails. I didn't say it was true, I'm just saying. Personally it makes my skin crawl.'

'It must be getting thin.'

'What's your problem? It's not like they'll lock him up, anyway. He'll just pay compensation until one day everyone's forgotten what he's paying for.'

Future tense. She blinks surprise. 'He's actually being charged?'

'Not yet. I heard there's a civil case being put together in Japan. Four deaths. The government lawyers have been on it for a couple of years. They're keeping it quiet.'

They reach the bar and stop outside. 'What would happen,' she says, 'if it was true?'

'Nothing, if he can live with it.' Carl sneers admiringly. 'Nothing, he's got too much money to lose. He couldn't go under if he tried, and they wouldn't let him anyway, there's too many people with their money on him. Of course, if the Japanese get in there there'll be others wanting the same. All the lawyers on the planet must be sharpening their knives. He might have to sell a couple of islands. I thought it might help you to know, anyway, just in case. Just in the interests of your interests.'

81

'I don't know what to say,' she says. 'You're disgusting. Thank you.'

'And that's supposed to be a compliment, is it?' He leers at last. 'I need you, Anna. You're my pacemaker. Always one step ahead of me, that's how I like you, where I can see you. Your seagulls are wrong, by the way,' he calls back from the club entrance. 'You should listen to your uncle Carl.'

She looks up, the late sun catching her eyes. The sky bright as magnesium. The gulls high, turning slow orbits, as if they have found the secret of perpetual motion.

By nightfall it has already begun to rain, not hard but with a kind of steady patience, ominously English, that suggests it has settled in for days. Anna stands in the warmth of her own place, her four thoroughly mortgaged walls, the house she bought with the hope that it would be home for more than herself, letting her coat drop, taking off her damp clothes, her shoes, smoothing the moisture from her hair.

She is thinking of her father as she stands there, her hands aloft. His nightwatchman's uniform dark after rain. The sound of him coming home, ordinary and mysterious. In the mornings the girls surreptitious as mice, ingeniously quiet, hopelessly bumping into things, their whisperings.

She remembers him as a loving but solitary man, always waking to his family with a faint look of surprise, and, Anna understands now, disappointment. His tiredness on long summer days, like a nocturnal animal in the zoo. His cheap books in English and Yiddish. The music he would try to explain, his voice already old when Anna was young. *A woman's grace is in her hair*, he said, the time she turned fourteen and cut off its shoulder-length. She cried for three days.

She wears it long again, now. Graceful, she likes to think, hopes, though it seems to her too that she has chosen a life largely without grace.

In the end it was Anna's mother who left, but it is her father who has gone out of her life. She doesn't know where he is in the world, or what he is, alive or dead. She imagines him as a nightwatchman still, out in the November dark.

Rain corrugates the windows. On the study desk a vase of Siberian iris, two days past their best. Shelves of books. Anna is known for them. *You and your bloody treeware*, Carl says. Her office is the same. Other inspectors put their clients at ease in other ways. Or not, depending on their inclinations.

Her eyes dilate in the familiar darkness. Now, she thinks. Now then, John Law.

Her briefcase is in the hall, beside her shoes. She brings it into the study and sits. She takes the tablet computer from the case, opens its prop and turns it on. The names of components begin to appear, hardware and software. The machine rediscovers itself, extremity by extremity, like a man who has been sleeping too long and wakes in an unfamiliar place. Then the screen lightens and fills with words.

PLEASE IDENTIFY YOURSELF. ENTER YOUR CARD IN THE SLOT PROVIDED. PLACE YOUR REGISTERED SKINPRINT AGAINST THE DESIGNATED AREA OF THE SCREEN.

THIS COMPUTER CARRIES A TRACER DEVICE. IF YOU DO NOT ENTER A MATCHING CARD AND SKINPRINT WITHIN 120 SECONDS, THE REVENUE WILL BE ALERTED TO YOUR CURRENT AND FUTURE LOCATIONS.

'Good evening to you too,' Anna murmurs, but her heart gives its usual start. There is always the thought that her card might be lost, and that the computer will find her out in that ordinary weakness. Or something worse: that the machine will discover some deception she has forgotten herself. As if she is not who she believes herself to be.

She has the card, there. Of course she does. She hasn't misplaced her hands. She obeys the

procedure and the warning words fade and van-
ish.

WELCOME, INSPECTOR
ANNA MOORE.

She hits a key and this text, too, dissolves.
Beyond is a vista of manila folders floating in a
gas-blue sky, like Magritte men in bowler hats.
Each folder bears the name of a client. Anna moves
through the archives until she reaches Law. Beside
her the rain taps and taps, like something waiting
to be let in.

She double-clicks. The life of the Cryptographer
fills the glass, twenty-one working years of profit
and loss. Each file is larger than the last: their
total would fill half a paper library. As large in
numbers as in life, she thinks, and at random she
opens a year. It is an early one, the figures still
in hard currencies, archaic as Imperial measures.
Law's invention still waiting to be conceived.

04/03/02–12/04/02 . . . Deutsch Bank
24 . . . Security architecture . . .
€22,512.54.
01/07/02–20/07/02 . . . Chaum
Associates . . . Watermark encryption . . .
$32,500.15.
03/10/02–07/10/02 . . . University of
Chicago . . . Merkle hash trees . . .
$7,312.09.

12/11/02–30/11/02 . . . Lyugun KK . . .
Cryptography . . . ¥3,608,000.07.

She smiles, because there is nothing as quaint as old prices; and also because she knows these figures well, has imagined the life they represent. The young freelancer, handsome, mercantile. A desirable human commodity. The expanses of leisure between contracts. Rooms at the Savoy, when the time comes for him to be more inventive. It is a different life from that fainter, earlier one – of the boy and the virus and community service – and from the existence Anna has glimpsed herself.

The three images could almost belong to different people, or at least to one person much changed. But people do not change so much, Anna thinks. Not under the skin: not at heart. They alter less than they think, sometimes less than they would like. It is as if the heart were lined, like the imprints of fingers. She sees it in herself and those she loves, but also in those she is paid to watch. In the records of the Revenue it is the details that differ – the profits and loss, the employments and entitlements. The clients remain themselves. Ambitious or miserly, generous or at ease, they are constant through the years of numbers.

These are parts of John Law, Anna thinks. Out of nothing she thinks of his hands, their childlike softness. Perhaps all I have to do to understand his actions is place his elements in order. The merchant prince, the cryptographer, the delinquent. Or is that the wrong way round?

There is a sound from the kitchen, a clatter of plastic. 'Burma,' Anna chides, without taking her eyes from the screen, and the cat comes through the dark to purr and coil guiltily against her feet. With one hand she roughs his damp ears. With the other she touches a key, and the document folds back into itself. Another touch and the Internet appears.

Her hand hovers. There are Carl's grotesque stories to be explored and denied, though the net is no place for reliable proof – it is a whispering gallery of the most gothic rumour, and rumour Anna has in abundance. But there is also the need and wish to understand what Law is doing, or what he has done. Some instance or circumstance, anything that will shed light on why a man with more money than he will ever live to spend would hoard it away, secretly, shabbily, like a bankrupt.

She types his name. The search engine blinks only once.

Results 1–10 of about 2,880,000.
Search took 0.11 seconds.

1. Homes of the Rich & Famous
You can be your own tour guide inside **John Law**'s fabulous estate of Erith Reach. Part One – the Arboretum to the Master

Bedroom. Just click on the place you wish to be and it will be so . . .

2. Why John Law Is Richer Than You

How to Become Rich As **John Law!!!** This is wonderful free site showing you TEN EASY STEPS to the best in dreamy lifestyles . . .

3. Masters of Reverse Engineering

. . . while **John Law**, the most dangerous and powerful industrialist in the world, continues to ignore the advances made by Schrodinger's Caterpillars, the Cult of the Undead Cow, the Three Blind Anonymice and many others . . .

4. Neon Geisha Palace

. . . linked with the names of movers and shakers around the world from Rory James Gates and **John Law** to the stars of webcast and the golden screen . . .

5. Save a Cow – Eat The Rich

. . . is Anneli Law (wife of Virus Code inventor, crypto-fascistologist **John Law**) who on 24 June 2012 carried out what is arguably the most appalling single act of shopping in capitalist history. Her purchases included 300 Louis XIV gilt chairs, 16,000 tons of Italian marble, the island of Miyako,

Japan, and 400 Victorian lampposts . . .

6. Welcome to Soft Gold
Soft Gold was created by **John Law** of the
SoftMark Corporation . . .

Her eyes come to rest. The entry is the first in
scores, Anna suspects, that will be ostensibly sane.
And it is familiar, she has been here before, years
ago now. It is part of the Cryptographer, and part of
the merchant prince. Two out of three, she thinks,
and clicks.

The destination window opens and is immediately submerged under a snowdrift of advertising
banners. They impose themselves, layer after layer,
their plaques gaudy as neon. Anna closes them
away. Beneath them all is a single site.

SoftMark
The New Millennium is Now Available.
Welcome to Soft Gold, the world's favourite
money. You are minutes away from joining
a global community of more than three bil-
lion users. Would you like to know more?
Just touch Read Me.
ReadMe

It is a decade, at least, since Anna registered to

use electric money herself. Nor is it the kind of site one visits twice. But it is part of John Law, the part of him people know and love. Which is to say this is where the money is.

She touches the screen. The writing gives way to writing. She thinks of palimpsests. The motion of script reflected in her eyes.

Q. What is Soft Gold?
A. Soft Gold is the world-famous currency from the SoftMark Corporation. Soft Gold is made of electricity.

Q. Where does Soft Gold come from?
A. Soft Gold was created by John Law of the SoftMark Corporation, the world's number one provider of computerware. It has no national base or boundaries. It is used by more people, in more countries, than any other currency in history.

Q. What happens when I install Soft Gold?
A. The first thing you will notice will be the SoftMark icon in the top left-hand corner of your screen whenever you work online. This is the visible confirmation that Soft Gold is used at your site. Visitors to your site will recognise it as a symbol of quality and security – so will anyone you email. Don't worry if you don't like the icon: it comes in a fully adjustable range of over 10,000

font and colour combinations. When you install Soft Gold, all online activity on your computer is protected by the Soft Gold Code. This is a free security measure for every site that uses Soft Gold, and is guaranteed 100% secure. When you trade in Soft Gold, you can be sure that every user has the same 100% site security as yourself, wherever they are in the world.

Q. How much do I have to pay?
A. Nothing at all. Soft Gold is a freeware product issued by the SoftMark Corporation for the benefit of others. At SoftMark we believe you shouldn't have to pay money to use money.

She laughs under her breath. There is something warming about the predictability of the corporation. At least, she thinks, they keep their cynicism pleasant. And then she remembers that it is not They but Him, that it all comes down to someone she believes she trusts, though she has reason not to. The cat jumps up, wanting attention, kneading her into shape, and she tidies him down with her hands.

Q. How does Soft Gold work?
A. You can think of your package of the Soft Gold Code as a wall and a gate. The wall keeps out undesirable material. The gate can

recognise units of the Soft Gold currency. Every gate has a unique and coded ID number, and your gate will accept Soft Gold only from other gate systems with a genuine ID. Because all users of Soft Gold have this freeware package installed, and because the Soft Gold Code cannot be broken, the Soft Gold currency can never be forged.

You will find that you cannot see the workings of your gate. This is so that all transactions in Soft Gold remain essentially anonymous – just like those made in the old money you grew up with.

Q. What makes the Soft Gold Code so special?

A. The Soft Gold Code is universally recognised as the first totally secure encryption system. The code is unbreakable because its rules change every two weeks. This is not long enough to break the code: in fact, it is estimated that the most advanced quantum computer would never be able to break one static sample of Soft Gold!

Your wall and gate system will receive the two-second logarithm change, as it happens, every fortnight, direct from the SoftMark Corporation. You are left free to work in the knowledge that your money is secure, now and in the future.

Q. Why do some people call Soft Gold the 'Virus Code'?

A. Don't worry – this doesn't mean that using Soft Gold will make you unpopular in the office! Some people use the term 'Virus Code' because of the way Soft Gold can change its structure, just as viruses do. In fact, Soft Gold is a kind of 'tame' virus. It is this flexibility that makes Soft Gold unbreakable.

Q. Who controls Soft Gold?

A. No one does. The Soft Gold Code creates its own currency without human interface, and monitors supply and demand for this as part of an internal programme. Each unit of money it creates is a fragment of the code that represents a single fixed denomination. Each time the money passes through a gate system, its code signature is updated according to the latest logarithms. Units of Soft Gold are electronically shrink-wrapped and tamper-proof.

Q. Who owns Soft Gold?

A. The Soft Gold currency is owned by anyone who wishes to use it.

If you have no more questions,
then welcome to SOFT
GOLD, the world's favourite way to pay!

To Join Now, Touch Here

By using this product, you agree to the following rules and regulations:

1. The Soft Gold Code is owned by the SoftMark Corporation™. The perimeter wall and gate system of your site are incidences of the Soft Gold Code and are owned by SoftMark. Any attempt to tamper with the wall or its gate system is strictly prohibited. Tampering will render your computer static and will act as notification to the relevant authorities. In the case of tampering your right to anonymity will be foregone and your personal details will be recorded.

2. Tampering with Soft Gold currency will render it unacceptable as legal tender and is a criminal offence under the 2002 International Electronic Information and Goods Act. It is not possible to modify, reproduce, redesign, redistribute or republish the Soft Gold currency or code. Attempts to perform any of these acts will send notification to the relevant authorities. All criminals will

be prosecuted to the full extent of national and international law.

3. For the avoidance of doubt, SoftMark is not responsible in any way for the content of sites or mail using this product. SoftMark does not represent or warrant that the information contained in any such material is legal or accurate.

4. Guarantee limited to fund replacement. This product is installed at the user's risk. To the fullest extent permitted by law, SoftMark will not be liable for incidental damages arising out of or in connection with the use of this product. This is a comprehensive limitation of liability that applies to all damages of any kind, including loss of data, income or profit, loss of currency due to theft, fire, flood or crash, loss or damage to property, personal injury, or death.

5. All rights reserved.

The telephone jolts her back in her chair. The cat is off her before she can lift him away. She gets to her feet and hunts around, trying to see in the dark, to place the mobile by sound or memory or anything, echo-location, so that by the time she finds it the phone has rung too many times, and she is wondering if something has happened, if something has gone bad, out in the world.

'Anna?' the telephone finally says in the voice of her mother, mildly bored and curious and everlastingly amused. 'Are you alright? What's wrong?'

'It's you. Nothing, I thought it was some kind of an emergency.'

'Can't I have emergencies too?' her mother says, as if she is asking for another slice of pie, a fuller glass of wine.

'Of course you can. Are you?'

'No,' she drawls. 'You know I never do.'

'You poor thing, that must be terrible. Would you like me to get you one?'

'Yes please. What emergencies do you have?'

'Oh, all kinds,' Anna says, and then the line fills up with long-distance static, hush-hush. She walks to the window, steadying her breath, waiting for the interference to pass. Each year her mother sounds more American, less like herself. Which is to say less like the mother Anna remembers. It surprises her every time.

Her eyes still ache from small print. She closes them and sees numbers. The life of Law in negative. As she opens them the line clears. 'I'm still here,' she says.

'Oh good. You were selling me an emergency.'

'Well, we have half-price deals on death by work-load, and I believe we still have some inadvisable relationships. Or did you have something special in mind?'

'Don't you have anything with naked men in it?'

'Naked men, hmm, not really, no.'

'Well, could you please have one ready for me next time?'

'We'll try our best, madam,' and she stops speaking to find she has been smiling without knowing it, knowing only that her mother is smiling the same crooked smile, the Atlantic rising and falling between them.

'So. How is the good old U of K?'

'The same. Ageing disgracefully. How are you?'

'The same. Ageing disgracefully. Single again?'

'You know I am,' Anna says, more uncomfortably, because her mother is not, doesn't need to be asked. Her life, like her, theatrical, limelit, always lived in the presence of others.

'I don't. You don't call. Your sister does.'

'I've been busy.' Biting back the easy anger. She glances past the computer towards the shelves. High up on their narrow purchase there is a picture, Martha's favourite photograph. Anna dressed for rain. Her sister stands behind her in a sunlit room. Unlike Anna she is out of focus; only the amusement is visible in her face. She is trying not to laugh. She is loving Anna so much she can hardly keep her hands off her.

'We're all busy,' her mother is saying. 'This is the twenty-first century, the world only keeps turning because it's chasing its tail. Sometimes I've been too busy for you too, I know, but I'd like to know you're alive. I think I deserve that. At least I always tell you what I think. And I happen to think you work too much. I think you should be out chasing that other kind of tail.'

'Actually, I don't think men constitute tail.'

'You haven't been out in a while, have you?'

'I have. I do.'

'Well, do it more, because I want to be a grandmother before you hit forty. Don't forget. What happened to your nice older man?'

'He died.'

'Don't tease. I liked him.'

'Only because he made you feel young,' Anna says, too fast, immediately regretting it, and her mother tuts.

'Don't let's fight. I just called because I'm coming over with a new friend next month. I thought we might spend Christmas together. Just the day. One day, that's all. We can have it at Martha and Andrew's, if you like. It'll be the five of us. Sweetheart?'

She walks back into the light radius of the computer. On the screen fractals are forming like ice on glass, an endless succession of whorls and filigree and branches. Anna touches the keyboard and the saver disappears. Beyond it the computer is still online. The new money still waiting to be chosen.

To Join Now, Touch Here

'Sweetheart? Anna?'

'I'm still here. What did Martha say?'

'Martha says yes, of course. Which just leaves you.'

'Christmas sounds fine.'

'Really? Well, that's wonderful. You can tell me all about your emergencies then. I'll email you. Okay? I love you. Bye for now. Bye.'

She puts down the phone. Beyond the periphery of the screen's illumination there is a mewl of complaint, and Anna gets up and goes through to the kitchen, abruptly conscious of her own hunger. Opening the fridge, the freezer, knowing the animal will be there behind her when she looks, like the man in her dream. She is making food for them both when the telephone rings again, and she walks back through with her hands full, the cat trailing her like an accomplice, its bowl, her plate and glass carefully deposited before she answers.

'No more advice today, thanks—' she begins, but as she does so she realises the line is wrong, too clear for long-distance, the caller closer than her mother will ever be.

'It's me.'

'Lawrence . . . it's late.'

'I couldn't sleep.'

'What time is it?'

'I don't know. It's late.'

'It's the drink.'

'I know. I know that. Anna,' he says, and stops.

'What?'

'Will you talk to me? Just for a while. Until I can sleep again.'

'You know I will,' she says. And she knows that he does. That he always will, and he doesn't even know why.

'Oh, thanks. Oh good. You're very kind. Well. Were you asleep? Did I wake you?'

'No, I'm still up.'

'What were you doing?'

'Talking to my mother.' She begins to pace. More wakeful now, clear-headed. Nocturnal.

'Eve is here?'

'No, thank God.'

'Oh yes. I tried you. You know, I always liked her.'

'Funny, she was just saying the same about you.'

'Was she? How very kind of her. So. And what are you doing now?'

'Raiding the fridge.'

'So late.'

'For Burma.'

'Lucky Burma.'

'Actually, I still have work to do.' She leans back against the window, tentatively relaxing. The cold against her shoulders. Sometimes, at nights – most times – Lawrence can be himself. Sometimes not. The rain taps, taps against the glass.

'You work too hard.'

'So everyone tells me.'

'And you know what else people say.'

'What?'

'All work and no play.'

'I do play, as a matter of fact.'

'Oh, I know. On what are you working, Anna?'

'Nothing much.'

'On him?'

She can hear his voice beginning to alter. It always creeps up on her, the way his natural warmth intensifies beyond the threshold of comfort. It has happened before, this, more times than Anna cares to remember. And it would be easy to hang up, the easiest thing, to leave him to himself. But here she is. Still listening.

Lawrence thinks it is because she still loves him. He has never said it but she knows. And she has never told him that whatever it is she feels – a kind of love, certainly, and at times more than one – is outweighed by guilt. There has never been a time to explain.

It is years since the complaints against Lawrence, and his forced retirement. Anna remembers being called before the Board. The relief on finding she had not been found wanting herself. She tried to explain the drinking, the mood swings, and they knew it all already. She told them she felt Lawrence was losing respect for himself, and they nodded and looked up from their screens, as if they knew that too.

And it was all true. Within the Revenue it was almost public knowledge. What Anna can't recall is why she didn't lie. It wouldn't have been so hard. Instead there is only a recollection of her own certainty, a belief that she was doing the right thing. For Lawrence's dignity and for the clients. For the Revenue and for herself. She was practising what Lawrence taught. Setting the record straight.

Cowardice, she thinks. It was cowardice not to lie.

'On him?' he says again. 'Are you working on your John Law?'

'I am, yes.'

'You know, I could almost be jealous.'

'Don't be.'

'Ah. You'll tell me when I should, won't you?' His voice thickening, whimsical. 'You know, I never trusted him.'

'You seemed to like him enough the other day. You told me to let him go.'

'You should. That was why I was ringing, in fact. Anna, I do think you are being rather insistent with this. It would obviously be better if you let him –'

'It isn't obvious to me.'

'Really, you could allow him the benefit of the doubt.'

'What is there to doubt? And since when are you his guardian angel?'

'Look, what I mean is. What I'm saying. People treat him like a god. A handsome, pecuniary little household god. They believe in his invisible money. And who am I to judge? He may be the best god they'll ever have. But he isn't a saint.'

'What does that mean?'

'Oh, come on. He's a money man, Anna, you've seen enough of them to know. John Law's had his years of big-swinging-dickery. He's the same as all the rest of them, he's just acquired the taste to hide it.'

'He doesn't see himself as a money man. He calls himself a scientist,' she says, anticipating Lawrence's snort of derision before it comes. And in the back of her mind is Carl's appalling rumour. The story of human code. The dream of new potatoes, the figure waiting behind her, the pale flesh full of numbers.

'Anyway,' she says into the radio silence, 'it's a free world. He can be what he likes, I don't have to like him.'

'But there's no such thing as a free world, is there? You should know that, you're an inspector.'

'Lawrence, I have to sleep —'

'He's nothing like you. How can he be? Nothing at all.'

'I know that,' she says, and she does, too well. 'You're imagining things.'

'Am I? Code-writing. The ability to transform the world into numbers. People seem to think of it as the great mystery of the new century. A talent dropped from heaven, like poetry, or fellatio. Have you thought of his life expectancy?'

'What?'

'They'll vacuum his gut every week. His diet will be balanced down to the trace elements. He'll have more spare hearts than a multiple road accident. And you're already ruined, my dear—' The words coming thick and sour. 'All those cheap drinks and filthy nights. They'll do for you.'

'Stop it.'

'Forget him, Anna. Close the case. He'll outlive you by fifty years, and he'll drop you in a heartbeat, a New York minute –'

'Stop.'

'You'll be an old fucker like me, while he's still fucking like a trooper. Do you think of that, when you think of him?'

She waits. I'm not crying, she thinks. Technically I am not crying. Nothing has left my eyes. And then she is, after all.

She closes her eyes. There is nothing but the sound of Lawrence's breathing, amplified by transmission. When he finally speaks again he sounds puzzled. He is a sleepwalker who wakes to the sound of weeping. 'Anna?'

'What?'

'Oh, I thought—' Unease, and the faintest bewilderment. 'For a minute there I thought I'd lost you.'

'It's alright.'

'No. Is it? What did I say?'

'Forget it.'

'No. I only rang to say—' She waits for him to

come to it, his voice messy with drink and incipient guilt. '—fuck it. I'm sorry. The things I say, I don't mean them, you do know that. It's the drink, Anna, the drink talking –'

'I know,' Anna says, and wonders, not for the first time, if she means it. 'Lawrence, I'm tired. We can talk in the morning.'

'Yes, of course. I am sorry, Anna. I am sorry.' His voice grows fainter. 'I wish I was better.'

'I know.' She is crying again. It isn't the kind he will hear, not tonight.

'I wish I was better for you.'

'Goodnight.'

'Goodnight, my dear. Goodbye, Anna. Goodnight.'

She dreams of human code and Lawrence Hinde and later still, in the smallest hours, of a house that is no longer her own. She closes the door on the world outside. There are the irises, tall as long grasses, the shelves of books, the photographs. All hers.

Her hair is wet. She raises her hands and finds it braided. It is the way she sometimes wore it at twenty, at eighteen, an hour's work every time. A Renaissance knotwork of shining black cords. She had almost forgotten the way it feels. The tautness against the skull.

There is a sound ahead of her. Burma? she calls. She can hear him hunting, finding his way by sight or sound or echo location. He sounds hungry.

She goes into the kitchen, opens the fridge. In the bright glare there is nothing. The refrigerator has no back. A corridor runs inwards, cramped as a ship's passage. Some distance away it stops at the inside of a second refrigerator door.

She closes the fridge. There is a tightness in her chest, a spreading excitement. One by one she opens the oven, the dishwasher, the cupboards. There are more than she remembers. Not all of them have passageways. Some have only wine glasses. Others open straight onto rooms. Not all of the rooms are empty. There are places full of childrens' toys, low lamplight, well-loved furniture. There are windows where other nights wait against the glass.

She thinks, where did all this come from? This isn't all mine. Who owns these places? But she knows. They are the homes of her clients. It is like opening old books. She recognises them all, she is wrong to have thought any of them ever lost to memory. Their homes are just as she imagined them. She goes upstairs, opening wardrobes and medicine cabinets. Her house is full of houses.

There is a glimpse of space inside the hearth. Anna kneels to peer in. It is a study, longer and deeper than her own. There is the flicker of the fire. The walls are faced with glass. There is music playing. It is nothing Anna knows. A man sits with his back to her. She crawls through. The flames lick along her belly and her thighs.

She stands, and finds Carl beside her. He nods

106

as if he has been expecting her. Together they watch the man in the chair. He has his head in his hand. His eyes are closed. He could be asleep, or listening. Anna thinks he is listening.

What's he like? Carl asks, and Anna says

I don't know. I really don't know him.

Come on, Carl says. *I'm not asking for the colour of his knickers.*

She looks at the Cryptographer. His eyes are open now, staring through the music into nothing. He has been working on paper, the sheets are arranged in some meaningful order at his feet, as if he is playing a gigantic game of patience. There is writing on his right hand, something noted down in haste, the ink blurred into the lines of his skin. Numbers in flesh.

There is a sensation at the edge of her mind, ticklish, near understanding. She reaches for it, hard, and in doing so feels herself begin to wake.

What is he like? she thinks desperately. What is it? And then she knows. He is like the figure with outstretched hands. He is like a man who is afraid of nothing. A man who no longer has anything of which to be afraid.

The Central Revenue of Limeburner Square is not a beautiful building, but then the premises of the Revenue never are. This isn't always the fault of the buildings themselves. There have been handsome tax offices, or at least places that were handsome until the inspectors moved in. After that the brightness goes out of them. There is an atmosphere that settles into the stone, a cheap accretion of anxiety and the minute observance of law. It is the smell of information kept too long. Of money gone sour. It is the last week of November, and the sky has fallen on London. Anna's Revenue looms through the mist like a bulwark of limestone.

Her office is on the thirteenth floor. Because of her seniority it is larger than average, five thoughtful paces long and four wide. Because people are still superstitious she also has the luxury of a window, a real one that opens. There are books, because she likes them. There are flowers when she can afford them. There are four items of graceless office furniture – one desk, three chairs – which is as much as she can stand and the least she needs to operate. There is an internal wall of sea-green frosted glass through which the shapes of people move, inspectors and clients going on their separate ways, anonymous and insubstantial as shadows.

Today is pay day, therefore there are flowers. Anna unwraps them, puts them in water. An inspector's ransom of red parrot tulips. Genetically natural. Or if not natural, exactly, then at least familiar. These are flowers her mother would buy. There are mornings when the man on the stall sells nothing Anna recognises herself.

She puts the vase on the desk and stands back. Her shoulders ache from driving, the road under mist, ordinary and dangerous, and she stretches, working the blood into the muscles.

The blinds are still drawn, and she goes to the window and fingers them open. At the Revenue's foot, the back streets of Amen Court and Pilgrim Lane are faint in the white air. The City is an abstract of lit and unlit offices. Upriver, the illuminations of the micro-city of Westminster are the brightest landmarks, distant circuses and squares laid out in faded neon and halogen.

Bright lights, she thinks, big city. She imagines their sum, the giant video screens and tiny glass-bulbed filaments. The delicate glass reservoirs of coloured phosphorescent gas. Electricity running through all of them, surfacing briefly as illumination. Soft Gold is different, she knows, but it is just as omnipresent. They might almost be the same thing, it would be easy to think so. The money and the power.

It is a fortnight since the dream of hidden rooms. Lawrence has been lying low, and will continue to do so for some time yet – Anna knows from experience – his shame eventually manifesting itself in a vastly overpriced delivery of roses, a lunch invitation on a tiny white card hidden somewhere among the buds and blooms. Carl has been conferencing in Paris, and his absence, coinciding with that of Lawrence, has left Anna in less familiar company. In a bar in Bow Sukhdev Hermanubis has taught her the rudiments of back-gammon, a game in which losing can be a strategy, his voice becoming less laconic over tulip-glasses of sweet tea and dishes of good Turkish *lokum*. In the West End she has gone dancing with Janet and Janet's friends and has liked it, has enjoyed seeing the older woman's face light up with laughter, the anger worked out of her under the cover of shadow and machinery rhythms. But she misses Lawrence just the same.

His absence throws her back on her own thoughts. More than that, it throws into relief what she might otherwise have hidden from herself for a little longer. That she is ready for John Law again. There is no more preparation to be done. She has been putting off the second meeting for some time.

She tells herself that it is the dreams, and this is true. It is years since her sleep has been so disturbed or the disturbances so vivid. She has never been so occupied with a client. She tells herself it is the thought of Lawrence, and this is also true to a point, because she knows that he knows her too well. He watches her too much, hurts himself in the watching. Sometimes he will divine sexual desire in Anna before she has even seen it coming herself. But not this time.

She doesn't tell herself it is the thought of Law's wife or child. She is not so ready to flatter herself with guilt. As if she would mean anything to a man as frequently desired as John Law. But she tells herself that she doesn't want to see him again, and this is a lie. It is an inversion of the truth.

She removes her hand from the blind. What light there is in the room falls away. She pulls back a chair and sits in the gloom. Her mobile is in her briefcase and she takes it out and sets it square on the desk, then leans forward, gazing down at it.

Lawrence, she thinks, if only you could see me now. Sitting here in the dark, squaring up to my telephone. You would laugh at me and make me laugh. Laughter would be a help with this. But Lawrence won't answer her, she knows, and there is another call to be made. She picks up the phone and dials. The voice that answers is masculine, mechanised, and smooth as glass.

'Good morning, and welcome to the SoftMark Corporation. You are currently being held in a queue and will be dealt with as soon as possible. Please choose from the following options or you may hold –'

Anna chooses. A musical interlude begins. It is the *Goldberg Variations*, a recording used recently in SoftMark advertising, so that the thought of the company is there like an itch as she waits. She holds the mobile away from her ear, her eyes resting on the flowers until the line clicks open. The new voice is female, American, and rattled, as if it is already having a hard day.

'Hello, you're through to SoftMark. I need a name.'

'Anna Moore, from the Inland Revenue.'

'Anna. Moore. Revenue.' The voice ticks off the

111

words as if they are on a checklist. 'Welcome, Anna Moore. How may I help you?'

'I'm looking for John Law.'

'Who?'

'John Law.'

'Oh, *Mister* Law.' The voice laughs, abruptly softening. 'Sorry, my mistake. We don't actually get a lot of calls for him, apart from crazy people. But you can't be crazy, can you, if you work for the Revenue? I'll just put you through to Senior Security.' And before Anna can protest the line gives way to another tier of music.

She closes her eyes. Behind the lids she sees the morning drive again. The road under fog. She thinks of desire, ordinary and dangerous. Then the music has stopped, and someone else is talking.

'Anna,' says the third voice, and this one she almost knows. It is mild, mellowed by a perpetual smile. 'Anna Moore, is it? We never got a proper chance to say goodbye.'

She opens her eyes. 'Terence?'

'That's right.' He sounds inordinately pleased to be recognised. 'How are you?'

'Fine,' she says, no longer sure whether she lies. 'I'm fine. And you're Senior Security?'

'Among other things, yes.'

'I thought you were—' and she tries to remember what it was she thought he was. A receptionist or a doorman? Or something more archaic. A butler or a commissar? 'I'm sorry,' she finishes, trailing off.

'What are you sorry for, my dear?'

'Nothing. How many jobs do you do, Terence?'

'One or two. We keep the core staff here very small. Very small. It makes things easier that way. It's a question of security. You'll be looking for Mister Law. He said you would.'

'Is he there?' Her voice small, narrowed down to the breadth of a wire.

'Oh no. He's at home. Hard at work at Erith Reach. His creative work – he hardly ever takes business home, of course.'

'No,' she says, obscurely hurt. 'Of course not. I don't need to see him immediately, anyway, but I do need to interview him again. Do you know how long he'll be away for?'

'Well, now.' Terence sighs. 'That would be hard to say. You'd have to ask him yourself. You'll have to ask when you see him. The thing is—' and he leans closer to the receiver, breathily confidential '—he left instructions.'

'I'm sorry?'

'These instructions. If you want to see him, I'm to give you the number for the gates. It's a daily number, mind you, and I can't give you tomorrow until tomorrow. I can only give you today today. But if you want to see him today, I can give you the number for today. Alright? Will you be wanting the number? Ready, are you?'

She drives eastwards, following the Thames through Whitechapel and Poplar. It is noon, and the river tunnels are still sunk in mist. Anna is a good driver, watchful, cautious, not too generous, but today her mind is not in it. She is thinking of the security man behind her and of what lies ahead, and on the Woolwich Road she runs a red light almost without noticing.

She is thinking of Terence. For someone so apparently conversational, she thinks, he is not a man who says more than he has to. He keeps what he knows to himself. She remembers their first meeting, the room of glass, the code under her feet, and tries to recall what the security man said to her then.

I trust him. And then almost something else. His face set, holding it back. Anna is a patient thinker, not brilliant, like Lawrence, but sedulous, missing nothing given time. South of the river it occurs to her that the man she met as a receptionist, and who is now Senior Security, could be all kinds of other things to SoftMark. Among other things.

She is thinking of her destination. Erith Reach. It is more a place than an address, or so it seems to her. If she tries she can remember what it used to be, a muddy district of cement factories, housing schemes and landfills, the dockyards long since gone. A place not in the city nor out of it, cut off from the pace of London by the great muscular arch of the Thames.

Now there is only the estate of the Cryptographer, three thousand eight hundred and fifty acres of land, seven hundred and sixty-three of water. Anna knows the figures, she is in possession of the facts. She has seen the society photographs, the vicarious images, *Homes of the Rich and Famous, Part One*. She has heard the rumours that the house has three postcodes, one for each wing, one for the pool. But she has never been inside. She has never even met anyone who has seen inside Erith Reach, so she thinks as she drives, and then realises she is wrong, of course. She has met John Law.

It is ten years since the Cryptographer bought the parish of Erith from London. Anna has seen the accounts. She knows how it was done. The lawyers authorised to compensate each of twelve thousand residents, the figures astronomical, not to be refused, the landowners and town council offered six times their market price. At the time the media were implacably outraged, Anna recalls, as if Law had got hold of something that should have been beyond the reach of money. As if he had purchased Limehouse or Mayfair. Which in a sense, of course, he had. He had bought up four and a half thousand acres of London.

Erith, which had meant so little to those beyond it before, became famous overnight. It vindicated those who had always distrusted the looks and celebrity of John Law, and gave a ready excuse to those who hadn't but were willing to make up for lost time. For months there were aerial photographs of the clearance work, environmental protests at news that the heathland was being forested, the marshes flooded, the tidal mud excavated, the few old buildings damaged in their relocation, brick by brick, to publicly owned areas. There was a venomous campaign for brine shrimps. The river was narrowed, the waters quickened, the embankments planted with promenades of willow and Dutch pollarded limes. And in the end, when the money had done its work, there was nothing left to protest about. There was only the most avid curiosity. A tantalising impression of greenness behind high walls. Of something lush with a river running through it, desirable, unattainable, and hidden at the heart of it, the silent figure of John Law.

She turns into a street of red-brick warehouses. Stops the car. To one side a peeling hoarding promises *Fret Maritime, Fret Arien*. Ten feet away the rows of buildings come to an abrupt end. A wall intersects them, unapologetic as a railway embankment. It is contoured, concave at the base, convex at the summit, a wave of chrome poised to break across the pavements below. Threatening, Anna thinks, her hands light on the wheel. She is not so naive as to be surprised. Where the road ends there is a gate, beside it a keypad inlaid with a lens. Anna gets out, types in her code, and drives on through.

An avenue of elms, their bare branches cross-hatching overhead. The crunch of gravel under the wheels. The hammer-chink of blackbirds complaining, and no sound – she stops again to listen – almost no sound of cars. The city is muted as the sea in a shell. It is the walls, she tells herself, some acoustic quirk or feature of the design, and

116

she goes on, slower now, the gravel begrudging her even that.

More than once she glances north through the trees. She has done it three times before she realises she is looking for landmarks, the familiarity of the river or the towers of the docklands, and that she can't find them. There is nothing but an obscuring line of hills, a cupola rising white among cedars, the view – when the elms give way to open land – of unobstructed sky, bright and pale and almost blue; the drive itself, freshly raked, like something from the turn of another century; and beyond the drive no people, no one anywhere, not that Anna can see, the empty greenness as full of possibility as a blank page.

She comes to a crossroads and stops again. What began as a tree-lined drive has now begun to take on the proportions of a private road. On two sides it continues back into the shadows of woodlands. To the north it descends between slopes of Bermuda grass towards a distant suggestion of water. Anna turns towards that. One of the few things she remembers about Law's house is that it has a private harbour. She peers forward, looking for the Thames, but there is only an ornamental lake, mist still clinging to its banks. The river is nowhere to be seen. Already she is late for her appointment. She is starting to wish Terence had given her a map, along with his daily code.

How stupid of me, she thinks. I seem to have lost London. A bubble of laughter rises up in her.

It is as if Terence's numbers have admitted her into another place and time, and she wonders if it is past or future, and what century John Law has chosen for himself. If I really lost my way now, she thinks, and the gate codes changed, I could be trapped for days. Except the walls are designed to keep outsiders out, not insiders in. So then I might escape to find that centuries had passed in my absence. Like in the stories, she thinks, nudging the accelerator, and as she does so two swans come out of the lake mist.

They fly low over the road, taking no apparent notice of the car below them. Their necks are liquid and flat as spirit levels. The windows are up, Anna can't hear the beat of their wings; their massive forms pass over her in complete silence. They look like creatures that should have died out long ago, Anna thinks, and also: they're like omens. And when she finally takes her eyes away from them there is a child in the road ahead of her.

It is a girl, standing very still, her face a pale O of surprise. She is wearing a buttercup-yellow puffa jacket that somehow serves only to emphasize her frailty. She is thirty feet away, twenty, before Anna can hit the brakes.

The wheels bite and lose their purchase. The gravel makes a sound like rain, *hishhhh*. There is a second when time crawls and the machine is utterly beyond her control. The earth rolls on under her. The child puts up one hand as the car reaches her. Anna feels no impact. It is a moment before she realises she has stopped.

'Are you alright?' she is asking before the door is open, while she is still struggling with the belt, but the girl only looks at her dumbly through the windscreen. 'Are you alright?' she says again, and this time the girl nods.

'Are you sure?'

'Yes.'

'Are you hurt?'

'No.' She smiles encouragingly. The expression fades as Anna leans back on the car. 'No, really. Look,' and the girl holds out her hands, palms upwards. 'See? There's no blood.'

'Oh. God.' Anna sits down properly. The bonnet is warm under her thighs, the air cold against her skin. The mist is drifting over, and she shivers, watching it come, like a crowd towards an accident.

'What about you?'

'What?' She looks back at the girl, seeing her properly. She is older than she first appeared, slight for her age, perhaps eight going on nine. Her nails are cut too short, painfully neat. Her hair is too pale to be brown, too dull to be blonde, but fine as blonde hair. Strands of it blowing across her inquisitive face.

'What about you? Are you alright?'

'I'm fine.'

'You look really cold,' the girl says, too solemnly, and Anna realises that she is, that she is still

119

shivering, and she is suddenly embarrassed by this child, so perceptive and caring for her, and whom she has so nearly harmed.

'Hold on.' She ducks back into the Revenue car. Her winter coat is in the back, thrown down between the seats with her computer case, and she buttons it over her expensive and inadequate work clothes. 'That's better,' she says, and when she smiles to prove it the girl smiles back, though her eyes are preoccupied.

'I didn't mean to walk in the road.'

'It wasn't your fault, I wasn't watching. I didn't think there was anyone around. Are you sure you're –'

'I'm fine,' the girl says, matter-of-factly. And then, as if reassured by her own innocence, she begins to talk. 'When I heard you coming I thought you were a lawnmower. You weren't saying anything Japanese though. Most of the time no one comes up here except the lawnmowers. Sometimes they get onto the roads and turn over, it's the gravel, it gets in them, and they start talking Japanese. Do you know any Japanese? I can say thank you, tidal wave and two kinds of raw fish. When they turn over you can help them and they say thank you very much in Japanese. It's good. I like it. Your car sounded like one of them. Except it wasn't speaking, of course.' She pauses momentarily for breath. 'What's your name?'

'Anna.'

'I'm Muriet.'

'Muriet. Where does your name come from?'

'I don't know.' The girl takes her hand away.

'Don't you like it? It's lovely.'

'No.'

'It's beautiful.'

'No, it's not,' the girl says quietly. And then, suddenly shy with envy, 'I like your hair.' And part of Anna is glad of the voice and the small face that goes with it. The way they make the child finally childlike, and herself, in contrast, older. Better.

'You shouldn't. When I wake up it looks like this.' She raises both hands to her head and draws them outwards, making slow-motion inward serpentine movements with her fingers, until the girl's face lightens with an edge of laughter.

'No.'

'It's true.'

'But I don't believe you.' Now Muriet is looking at her more curiously, her eyes green and bright. 'You don't work here, do you? Are you a trespasser?'

'No.'

'Oh. Nathan met one once. I was away, I was ill, I never saw it.'

'I'm here to see Mister Law,' Anna says, and the girl nods and glances away, as if Mister Law were the most boring thing in the world.

'What do you want him for?'

'It's my job. I'm a tax inspector. Do you know what that is?'

'Of course. We had one of you here once, too.

We get lots of different kinds of people. You don't look like a tax inspector.'

'What do tax inspectors look like?'

Muriet makes a face, a combination of pain, pity and amusement. 'Like Mister Cutler. He's the head groundsman. He's not going to be happy when he sees what you did to his lawn, either.'

They both look round. The tracks dissect the road and verge, twenty feet long. Anna becomes aware of the reek of burnt rubber. She swears under her breath, something vicious and Carl-like, and then wishes herself quieter, acutely aware of the child beside her.

'Nathan says he used to be in the services. He wears a suit all the time, even when he's burning leaves. We're trying to find out if he has a Parabellum.'

'A –?'

'It's a gun. Like the antrustions have.' The girl looks her over as if she is coming to doubt her. 'They're a kind of bodyguard.'

'You're a friend of Nathan Law?' she asks, trying not to think of Mister Cutler and the antrustions, whatever they are, and the girl nods.

'We're home-schooled. I don't live here,' she adds, reluctantly. 'My parents work at SoftMark. Nathan wanted me to be home-schooled with him. We were friends from way back. We have the best teachers. It's just us. Except it's December now, we don't have tuition in December. Only study time.' She looks up at Anna. 'Is your car going to work?'

'I don't know.' The thought not having crossed Anna's mind until this moment. And with the one thought comes another, the recollection that she is lost.

'If it does work, will you give me a lift? I'm supposed to find Nathan.'

'If I do, will you do me a favour? Will you show me where the house is?'

'Of course. We have to go there anyway.' And already she is opening the passenger door, climbing inside. Adjusting the seatbelt, making herself comfortable. Anna gets in beside her.

'Alright. Where are we going?'

Muriet points ahead. '—then around the lake. There's a kind of beach. You have to turn. I'll tell you when.'

The engine starts easily. The skid-marks diminish in the mirror. For a while Muriet is quiet beside Anna, the car steady under her hands, and she feels herself begin to relax into its routine of minimal movement and pressure. It is as if nothing has happened, as if the swans and the imminence of collision were all acts of Anna's imagination. Except there is the girl in the passenger seat, impatiently playing with the window, the seatbelt, the radio.

'Sit back,' Anna says, and Muriet does, leaning her head against the door. Anna thinks, it must be about twenty-five years since I was her age. A cautious girl on a river bank watching skaters. A quarter of a century, she adds to herself, and is surprised by the grandeur of the words in relation to her life. She wonders what she can have done with such a spectacular quantity of time.

Except she knows. She has become an inspector, a watcher of people. And always other people, never herself. She has spent her life in others' lives, hundreds of them passing her by. I am old enough to be this girl's mother, she thinks. And then; I am almost too old. And her heart turns over in its fleshy darkness.

'Here!'

'What? What?'

'Here, you're going to miss it!' But Anna turns with time to spare onto a smaller road, the gravel less well kept, the trees less formal, almost wild where they reach down to the lakeside. Beside her the radio idles between stations and she leans across and switches it off.

'You're quite a good driver.'

'Thanks.'

'Better than my dad.'

'Good.' Anna glances across at the girl. She is sitting up now, straight-backed as a child at its first piano lesson, her eyes on the road ahead. 'I hope you don't compliment everyone who almost runs you over.'

'I don't know, it's never happened before,' Muriet says so blandly that Anna almost laughs. 'Do you like it?'

'What?'

'What you do. Taxing people.'

'Well,' Anna says, and as she does so she finds that she is laughing after all. 'People do tend to see it that way, yes.'

'What's so funny?'

'Nothing. But funnily enough, you're the second person to ask me that in a fortnight.'

'You go down here.' Muriet points as the path forks. A rutted track runs down to a shingle beach bordered by pines. In the distance Anna can see someone standing by the water's edge. 'So do you?'

'Yes. I do.' She turns onto the track. The car leans into its suspension.

'Why?'

'I don't know. It's just a job.' Smiling for Muriet as she navigates between potholes. 'I like meeting people. Like you. I get to find out about them. How they live.'

'How do you do that just from taxes?'

'By learning their secrets,' Anna says, a little too loud with exertion. A little defensively, if she is honest with herself. She is not used to the clear questions of children. At the bottom of the track is a stony lay-by and she reverses the car and parks uphill.

'If they have secrets,' Muriet says, as the engine ticks into silence, 'then they don't want you to find them.'

'Maybe not.' Anna looks across at the girl, pale and grave in the car's hooded dimness. 'But my job is to find them anyway.'

Muriet nods. 'I don't think I'd like to be a tax inspector,' she says primly.

'What do you want to be, then?' Anna asks, but the girl doesn't answer immediately. She is looking out through the windscreen, perhaps at the figure on the beach, her eyes thoughtful and unfocused.

'I want to be rich.' She says it just as Anna thinks she has not heard. The words soft but decisive, the wind in the pines audible through them. And although Anna believes she understands money, and knows there are as many reasons to want it as there are reasons to keep secrets, the child's voice still shocks her. As if the need for something that needs to be desired is something she shouldn't yet understand or feel.

The sun comes out, uncertain and without warmth. 'There's Anneli,' Muriet adds more conversationally, and opening the car door she starts down the beach, breaking into a scrambling dash. Not looking back at Anna, calling out the name again as she runs, *Anneli, Anneli? Anneli!*

'Hello, you. Where did you get to?' Anna hears faintly. It is a woman's voice, soft and curious, and overlapping it the girl's answer, incomprehensible with distance and breathlessness. Anna leaves the car doors ajar and turns towards them. The woman and the child with the beautiful names. Feeling her own workday tiredness, her ordinary Anna-ness, the trudge of her feet drab on the stones.

'. . . trespasser,' Muriet is saying as Anna reaches her. They are both watching her, the woman slim as

126

the girl is slight. In one hand Anneli holds a navy bath towel. By her feet lies a small pile of clothes. '—but it wasn't. It was this woman called Anna.' The voice lowered. 'She's a tax inspector.'

'Is she?' Anneli widens her eyes, smiling. She holds out one hand, the gesture not only one of welcome but also of charity, as if she means to help Anna up some invisible incline. Her voice carries an accent, northern European, softened by absence. Her hair is shorn short and bright. Her eyes are smiling half-moons, blue irises seeded with some darker, indefinite colour. Her head is a sculpture. She has the kind of beauty that Anna only ever recalls having seen on screens or celluloid, in a Bergman or a Hepburn, angelic, unfleshed. Her hand is cold in the cold air.

'John was expecting you earlier. I hope you didn't have too much trouble finding your way. I'm Anneli.'

I know, Anna wants to say, and doesn't. *I know who you are. You're Anneli Law, the wife, the first true love, so people say. They say you used to be a pianist, a prodigy. Every night a young man came to hear you. No one knew his name until he sent you a roomful of flowers. Somewhere in the flowers was his proposal. You refused him for three years. You like sailing. You love pearls. You have been married only once, but you have left your husband twice.*

The knowledge of her knowledge hangs unspoken in the air between them, decorously silent, faintly uneasy. It is there in the way it must always be,

127

Anna thinks, between the Laws and the world. The world knowing everything, the Laws nothing. Like a weakness, she thinks, or an innocence.

'I'm sorry I'm late—' is what she begins to say, but there is a sound of splashing from the lake, drowning her out, and Anneli nods and turns away.

'This boy of mine will not come out of the water. Nathan!' She raises her voice. 'I would like you to get ready now.'

'Why?' The child's voice is faint, uneven with echoes and suppressed laughter. Out over the misty water Anna catches sight of a head bobbing, shocking in the winter landscape, slick and dark as a seal's.

'You know why.' And then; 'Nathan? I don't want to have to ask you again.'

'He's good at swimming,' Muriet says equably to the women either side of her. 'Last summer he bet John a million soft he could swim across the river.'

'Yes, well,' Anneli, her tone tightening. 'But he didn't.'

'They didn't mean it. It was a joke. They wouldn't really have done it.'

'I'll come out.' The boy's voice wobbles. 'But only if you come in. It's cold, though. So you can keep your clothes on. If you like.'

'Nathan,' Anneli calls out. 'You are going to catch cold. You will make yourself sick. And none of this is going to make Helen go away. Do you understand?'

Silence. The water overgrown with mist.

'Nathan. Nathan! I am going to count to three. If I don't see you moving by then, there will be real trouble. One. Two. –'

There is a cacophony of splashing from the lake. 'I'm moving! I'm completely moving!' Nathan shouts in mock terror. He sounds euphoric – ecstatic with the knowledge, Anna thinks, that no one can touch him, that he might as well be thirty feet up in the air as out from the shore – and beside her Muriet laughs openly, the boy's buoyant laughter coming back like an echo. 'Hey Muriet! Hey glitz-puppy!'

'Hey.' Muriet, her voice soft with smiling.

'Who's that beside you?'

'She's called Anna!' As if it is the best joke. 'She's a tax inspector!'

'Oh.' The splashing dies down. After a moment Anna sees that the boy has started to swim towards the shore, the water rippling ahead of him.

'Well.' Anneli turns to Anna, openly curious. 'You seem to have lured him out. Congratulations.'

'Maybe he's cold,' Muriet says.

'Maybe he is, but I think we're in Anna's debt all the same. You must be used to that. I wonder –'

There is a commotion at the shore. Nathan rises dripping out of the lake behind them, pallid with cold, skinny where his father is gaunt, shivering as his mother wraps the towel around him. Muriet bends beside him, whispering, incomprehensible, and the boy mutters back. Then for a moment there is silence, the women and the girl watching him. As if they are waiting for his explanation.

'It's colder out here,' he says finally, the words punctuated by the chatter of his teeth. His eyes skim lightly over Anna on their way from Anneli to Muriet. Anna guesses he is at most a year older than his friend, although he stands a full head higher than the girl. Already he is lanky, tall in the bones.

'Is it really?' Now Anneli has the boy in her arms her temper reveals itself more clearly. Not lost but effortfully held. 'Well, that's not terribly interesting, Nathan. I have to tell you it hasn't been worth the wait. Since we've been standing here we already know it's cold. We could have been at lunch by now –'

'It's fish. I don't like fish.'

'You'll eat what Rebecca makes you. Did you think it was summer out here? Did you think Muriet and Anna would be sunbathing?'

'No.'

'Is that what you thought?'

'No. I'm sorry,' Nathan says, but almost inaudibly, and if Anneli hears him she makes no show of it. She is drying him roughly, not only his thin arms and chest but each foot. The boy cowed, bracing himself against her hands. With slight unease Anna realises the other woman is close to real anger, and she wonders why.

'Did you think of us at all?'

'I said I'm sorry.'

'Not to me. To our guest.'

He looks up. His eyes meeting Anna's. Kennedy grey. 'I'm sorry.'

'That's alright.' Anna smiles, but the boy's gaze stays on hers, familiar as a photograph. She finds it hard to tell if he is angry himself or only curious. There is a shyness in his stance, the towel pulled together like a cape, although his eyes don't flinch. Anneli sighs and straightens.

'There, you're dry. Now get dressed, please.'

'Not here.' Finally Nathan's eyes slide away from Anna.

'Oh, such modesty. What is it, do you think you'll frighten Anna away?'

'No. I'm not a child.'

'Then don't act like one. Hurry up. I'll hold the towel for you. Quickly.' And then there is only the sound of the water, the boy dressing in abject silence, a boat horn on the river as it passes through Law's domain.

'Anna,' Anneli says. Her voice is softer now, more charming, confidentially-between-adults. 'I was wondering, since I'm already in your debt, whether I could ask a favour. I was meaning to walk back from here, but with Nathan so cold –'

'I'll drive you.'

'You're sure you don't mind?'

'Of course not.'

'She was lost,' Muriet butts in with mercenary eagerness.

'Were you?'

'Actually, yes.'

'I was showing her the way. She didn't know where she was. We almost had an accident—' and hearing the girl say it Anna feels herself blush, her skin warming in the cold sunlight '—but we didn't.'

'Of course not,' Anneli says without turning. Her voice absently reassured, as if Muriet has told her of a disaster averted years ago or countries away. As if Anneli herself were inattentive, Anna thinks, and she wonders whether she is, or if the lack of interest is just excessive politeness. Nathan reappears from behind the towel, spike-haired and sullen in jeans and sweatshirt. 'Are you ready?'

'Yes.'

'You didn't bring your keys? Phone?'

'No.'

'You should have, but at least now we don't have to find them. You know,' Anneli says, folding the towel, no longer attending to her son, 'strangers do get lost here. It's the landscape. John had it done so that no one would notice the city. He thought people would like that, it's what he likes himself. Which is typical of him.'

She takes Anna's arm, walks her back towards the car. I am a stranger, she thinks, but not a trespasser. Not the lowest of the low. She thinks, so this is what John Law does with his money. He makes cities disappear. The children lag behind, their voices ricocheting through the trees.

'It makes people imagine they don't know where they are. When we moved in I used to give garden parties all the time, wonderful nights, except that

132

the guests kept on getting lost. We could see them on the cameras, lumbering into trees, which was occasionally entertaining, but not much help. We don't have visitors so often any more. Not on that scale. Once we had a couple who slept in the woods for two days.' She leans closer. 'Actually, though, I think they wanted it that way. You don't look much like the last tax inspector we had here, by the way, he was much more high and mighty. And not nearly as pretty. Have you had lunch? You must eat with us.'

'No, I should –'

'I insist.'

'I really should see –'

'Anneli?'

'Well, if you should you must. John was telling me about your last meeting. If you follow the track back out and left. Yes, Muriet?'

'I've eaten cans of caviar and sausage dogs in a Rolls.'

'Have you really? And I thought you had such simple tastes.'

'No, it's a line from a film. We disguised it, you have to guess it.'

'No.' Abruptly short. 'I'm tired of games. Ask Anna.'

'I don't really know much about –'

'They've been studying cinema, I'm sorry to say. It's Hitchcock, isn't it? Turn right here. You'll come to a hedge, the house is beyond it. Is it Hitchcock?'

'It might be,' Nathan says from the Naugahyde depths of the back seat.

'No clues!'

'Clues? We don't need clues.'

'Yes you do. What is it, then?'

'I've eaten caviar at Cannes and sausage rolls at the dogs.'

'How did she know?'

'Anneli only remembers lines about caviar.'

'Thank you, Nathan. And was Mister Coldham a good tutor?'

'Good.'

'Super-wonderful.'

'Then we must have him back again.'

The voices distract Anna as she drives. They are casual, directionless, as if any enquiry might be meant for her, or as if she is not there at all. She says nothing herself, can think of nothing she would have to say. There is something exhilarating in only listening. The sense of a new place, desirable and incomprehensible.

Outside the midday sun is strengthening, burning off the last mist from acres of lawns. The river comes into view, a momentary brightness between plane trees, and the trees themselves, Anna sees, are London planes in every way, grown bulbous and gigantic on the polluted urban air. That at least, she thinks, is something Law can't wall away.

'We liked him.'

'Yes we did. Mister Coldhamsandwiches.'

'Muriet. Don't make fun of your tutors' names.'

'But they're always funny.'

'They aren't.'

'They are. Like Mister Pim.'

'There was nothing funny about Mister Pim.'

'There was. Because that's what he looked like.'

'Like what?'

'Like a Pim.'

'Muriet . . . what are you talking about? What do you mean? Stop laughing. You shouldn't laugh at people.'

'We don't always.' Another pause for thought, and then –

'Yes we do,' Nathan says.

'Yes, we do,' says Muriet. They sit close as conspirators. Anna watches them in the rear-view mirror. At the periphery of her driving vision she is also aware of Anneli, hands tight in her lap. Embarrassed over nothing, over the lightest of conversations and the presence of a stranger.

'What about Helen?' Anna says it for Anneli's sake. 'I didn't hear either of you laughing about Helen.'

No one answers immediately. The car, so packed with talk since the beach, feels emptied without it. There is the smell of Nathan's damp hair, of the bath towel folded on Anneli's lap, of the car's synthetics. Then, 'Helen isn't a teacher,' Anneli says, too brightly, all the playfulness in the car drained away, in its place nothing but a gathering silence, and Anna knows she has said the wrong thing.

I have assumed too much, she thinks. I have joined

in as if I know these people, as if I understand what remains unspoken between them. And I don't, after all. She risks a look in the mirror. Muriet is gazing out of the window with an assumed expression of blank television interest. Nathan is back in his corner, his face shadowed and indefinite.

'Is this yours?' he asks finally, his voice sharp. The question hangs uneasily for a moment before Anna realises it relates to the car, and is therefore addressed to her.

'Yes. More or less. I mean it belongs to the people I work for, but I've had it for years. Do you like cars?'

'Yes.' Without conviction.

'Me neither. I don't like cars but I like driving. And you don't like fish but you like swimming.'

'That's not the same. That's different. You're here to see my father, aren't you?'

'Yes.'

'Why?'

'It's not really something I can –'

'I'll ask him, then. He'll tell me. Do you know cryptography?'

'Yes.' Anna slows. 'I don't understand everything your father does or –'

'They should send someone who can. They should send someone cleverer than you.' He is still watching Anna in the mirror. His voice has turned fierce. He seems abruptly younger to Anna: not in the way Muriet became as she admired Anna's hair, but in the way adults become so. He is like a man

136

taking petty revenge while he can. 'You don't know anything –'

'Nathan?' Anneli says, calmly, the name a threat. 'Not another word.' And there isn't. The car lapses back into silence with an ominous finality. The hedge looms up, a curtain wall of yew carved in the shape of clouds, of boulders, the gravel road passing under its deep green arch – Anna can smell it through the air conditioning, aromatic and poisonous – and beyond the hedge she sees the house, its enclosing wings all titanium and glass, the upper floors obscured by cedars and umbrella pines. Lights through the evergreens. The sound of unseen fountains. The drive opening into a crescent of raked gravel.

'Here we are,' Anneli says, as if nothing has happened. 'Anna, thank you, you can park anywhere. Muriet?'

'Yes?' The voice no longer conspiratorial, shrunken with timidity.

'I'd like you to clean up for lunch. Take Nathan and make sure he does the same. Off you go, both of you.'

There is the double slam of car doors, the chuff of gravel. Nathan stalks across the drive, Muriet at his side, their heads bent together in conversation. As Anna watches, the boy shakes his head violently and Muriet turns away and trots back to the car. Anneli leans across her driver.

'What is it, Muriet?'

'I just wanted to say something. To Anna.'

Anneli sits back. 'Quickly, then.'

The girl bows closer to Anna. 'Thanks for driving me. I liked meeting you. I think you're cool,' she adds, as if there are others who do not, and then before Anna can answer she is retreating, the echoes of her footsteps in the forecourt beginning to fall over themselves. Calling after Nathan as he disappears inside.

'Well,' Anneli says, and then nothing. When Anna looks at her again the other woman is gazing out towards the house with an expression much like Muriet's, absently engaged. From somewhere she has produced cigarettes, a cheap, ordinary brand. She taps the pack against her palm. '—do you mind?'

'Go ahead.'

She nods, opens the passenger door. 'I'm sorry,' she says. 'About Nathan.'

'It's alright. It's not unusual. We're not every-one's favourite guests.'

'I suppose not.' She tears the foil seal, lights up. 'Do you have children? No. It's odd,' Anneli says, exhaling. 'I always wanted a boy. A golden boy. I didn't want him to be like me, I wouldn't wish that on a child of mine, but I didn't expect him to be so different. So hard to understand. He's good with secrets, like his father. And I married a man whose life's work is to stop people understanding anything. I suppose I got what I deserved. Did I?'

In the absence of an answer – it seems to Anna there isn't one she can give – Anneli nods, as if collecting her thoughts. 'Helen is my son's nurse.

Before he was born we were told there was a chance of diabetes. They showed us the most beautiful images. They were very proud of the images, but there was nothing they could do about the condition. Diabetes involves a large number of genes, apparently too many for any of the new surgery. It runs in John's family, this thing. Like the gift for numbers.'

She picks at the words, testing them between her teeth, like strands of tobacco, physical things. 'I knew that. John told me. We were hoping it might pass Nathan by, and then when there was no sign of it for years . . . it didn't start until he was seven. He's almost used to it now. It's severe, he has insulin with every meal. There's nothing else they can do for him, except show him their images. He knows how to medicate himself. He never complained. He took it well. He was always sensible, even as a baby. And quiet. Too quiet, people said, I never thought so.'

Her gaze has strayed back to the house, where it lingers, the sun catching in her eyes, searching out the mottled depths of the irises. To Anna it seems as if there is something possessive about her. A faint and unselfconscious anxiety, as if she is checking that the house is where she left it, or whether it is still true. The children are gone and there is no sound of them; only, somewhere out of sight, the measured, pendulous echoes of a game of tennis, incongruous in the spare winter landscape.

'What happened?' Anna says eventually, and

Anneli looks back at her.

'Happened? Nothing. He just changed. It started this summer. He began to avoid taking the insulin. He reduced the dosage. Stupid clever boy. John says he does it to test himself, and he'd know, they're very alike. Two months ago he nearly died. Muriet was alone with him, she was terrified, she didn't come to lessons for weeks. She's his oldest friend, his best friend. And so now we have Helen. He's not very happy about her, which I can understand, she's an efficient old misery. And Nathan does his best to make her life even more miserable, by hiding from her.'

'Which was why he was swimming outside in November. I didn't know.'

'Good.' Anneli lifts her legs clear of the car, into the sun, and stretches. 'Then apparently you don't know everything about us, do you? I wouldn't have told you, if you hadn't – well. Will you keep it to yourself? If you can?'

'Of course.'

'Thank you. Now, I'm keeping you, aren't I? You must want to see my husband. And I'm sure he'll be waiting for you.' She leans to crush out her cigarette, straightens, smiles down at Anna. The sun behind her.

They go in together. The doors are open. The hallway is cool, almost cold, the edge taken off the air but no more. Light falls through the high frontice, catching the old glass spheres of chandeliers (*three hundred Louis XIV gilt chairs*, Anna remembers. *Four hundred Victorian lampposts*) and a trough of water which cascades at one end from a fountain, at the other into a pool, so that the hall and the rooms beyond it are full of their echoes, the mutter of water following Anna as she follows Anneli inwards through courtyards and chambers, a colonnade overlooking the harbour, a wall made of aquaria, the fish arranging themselves into Mirós and Hirsts; a dining room where staff nod and step back from their business, as if the appearance of work were indecorous; a corridor of *gabbehs* piled thickly, and another of Persian carpets thin as parchment underfoot, the colours of gunpowder and pomegranates. A study at the end of it faced entirely with glass.

It is both like and unlike Anna's dream. Only now does it occur to her that she has seen the room before; that what she imagined in sleep was less a creation than a reconstruction, its details combed from half-remembered images and interviews. There is the hearth, set into glass. There is the smell of wood smoke and leather. There is the music, though Anna knows it. It is Berg, the *Lyric Suite*, one of the pieces her father would listen to in the early evenings, waiting to work; improving himself. An algebra of sound always on the verge of breaking into melody. If cryptography could be played, she thinks, it would sound like this.

Nothing is visible beyond the glass walls but spare woodland, grass lush under cedars. Anna's client sits in a worn armchair, facing the view, a pen and sheaf of paper propped in his hands.

141

Beside him on a folding table rests a tray, a glass of champagne, two pills, untouched, a covered plate, chopsticks. His eyes are closed. He could be asleep or listening. Anna thinks he is listening.

'John?' Anneli says, her voice low and warm, a purr, as if she is reluctant to wake the man, would like to keep him there. But the figure of the Cryptographer remains motionless, and his wife lays a hand on Anna's arm, lightly prohibitive, and goes closer, leaning beside him, repeating his name. Whispering it, the hardness Anna has seen and heard in her face and voice softening. *John? John. Love.*

He wakes abruptly, as if his dreams are about to catch up with him. Anna takes a step back into the doorway. The murmurs of the Laws barely reach her over the music's restless patterns and symmetries.

'Hello, you.'

'Hello.'

'Are you awake?'

'Yes.'

'Were you asleep?'

'I was dreaming.'

'Lucky you. Was I in it?'

There is the creak of leather. With one hand Law reaches out into nothing, and the music stops. 'You wouldn't want to be. Where's Nathan?'

'Playing.' Anneli says. 'Just playing. There's someone to see you.'

'Terence?'

'The Revenue.'

A muttered curse, something below the threshold of Anna's hearing, but heartfelt. She takes another step back into the dim mouth of the corridor, as if she has gone further than she intended, heard too much. I am the Revenue, she thinks, of course. The kind of people people have nightmares about. *I mean that as a compliment, you understand.* 'How many?'

'Just one.'

'Man or woman?'

'A woman.'

'Anna Moore.'

'I think so, yes. Some kind of Anna, anyway.' A pause. 'You didn't tell me she was attractive.'

'I didn't think it mattered. Does it?'

'No.'

'Then I shouldn't keep her waiting. Where did you leave her?'

'I brought her here –'

'Here?' John Law repeats, caught off guard, and he looks past Anneli to where Anna waits and stands abruptly, his sternness all but lost in ruffled embarrassment. 'Anna . . . come in. I'm sorry.'

'So you should be.' And she smiles, a bright, cosmetic expression, quicker than lipstick, professional. It makes her seem, if not at ease, then at least as if she knows what she is doing. She crosses to where John and Anneli stand, not quite together. 'The Revenue can't afford you sleeping on the job.'

He inclines his head, accepting the fault and the compliment. 'I was slaving away for them rather late last night. But I've dragged you all the way out here, the least I can do is be awake when you arrive. How are you, Anna?'

'I'm well—' *It's good to see you again*, she almost adds. The truth too close for comfort. Too eager to be known. '—and also late.'

'Are you?' He glances at the light outside and back, smiling, narrow-eyed, as she remembers him. 'You know, I would have had you down as honest, but not as a natural latecomer. Perhaps you had some trouble finding your way?'

'Perhaps I did,' she says, and in the background Anneli laughs.

'If it wasn't for Muriet we might never have found her at all.'

'Well.' Law brushes himself down. Imaginary disarray. 'You're hardly the first. What can we do for you now you've found us? Something to eat.'

'No.'

'You're sure? I can have something brought up, anything, within reason. You must be hungry.'

'She isn't,' Anneli says, as if she knows John will agree it is the strangest thing. 'I asked her.' She has acquired the expression of a woman who can't believe her luck, to have come across such entertainment.

'Is that so?'

'I'm fine, really, thank you,' Anna lies to them both, not intending to assert herself with her certainty, more out of habit than anything intentional. The inspectors of the Revenue do not eat with their clients. They do not become obliged, not if they are honest in their work: not if they are good. And

144

Anna is good. So she believes, of course she does.

'In that case—' John puts the tray on the floor, perches himself on the table, uncovers the plate. Under the cloth are sushi, a dozen of them, worked and bright and colourful as elements in circuitry. 'Or do you mind? I wouldn't want to distract you.'

'You won't.'

'What a shame. Take a seat. Or is even that too much to hope for?'

She takes the seat. Puts down her case, unlocks it, lifts out the dormant weight of the computer. At the upper edge of her vision she is aware of Anneli leaning over her husband, kissing him, one hand going to his face, but by the time she straightens in her seat the other woman is gone without a word. There is only John Law, his eyes on her, waiting. Like a cat watching shadows.

'It's good to see you again. You told me you'd be back. I half hoped you would be, but I wasn't sure whether to believe you.'

'You should always believe the Revenue.'

'Of course. But you'd got your money, after all. I'd assumed it was the money you wanted. It didn't seem like a strange assumption to make.'

'I suppose not.'

'I hope there wasn't any problem with the payment?'

'That would be rather unexpected,' Anna says, and realises, without real surprise, that he is talking too much. Too quickly, the way less assured clients often will when they are nervous. And sometimes they are nervous of nothing but the facts of their ordinary lives, Anna knows. And sometimes not.

'So it would be.' He is holding the chopsticks poised over his plate. Now he begins to eat, delicately, hungrily, talking intermittently as he does so. 'So it would. Then I wonder what it is, Anna, that you want from me now?'

'I just need to ask you a few more things.' She says it lightly, as she has been trained to do. 'There are still questions that need to be answered.'

The Revenue's phraseology. It comes to her automatically, a safety mechanism; questions without a questioner. Passive, as if there can be crime without criminals, mistakes without punishment. Law smiles faintly but says nothing, going back to his food, picking at it while Anna starts up the computer, waits for its clear light to settle.

'Ready?'

'Someone once told me that an inspector's first question is never the important one. Is that true?'

She shrugs, waiting. 'That depends how you answer it.'

'I suppose it must. Well, ask away.'

'How do you see your financial situation over the next five years?'

He laughs shortly. 'My financial situation?' Tasting the words, as if he could prise them from the air. 'It would take a great deal to change it. I suppose I consider failure on a regular basis, but I wouldn't deny that I'm successful. And success and failure are autocatalytic. They have a tendency to compound themselves.'

'Mister Law, I need you to be clear –'

'I know you do. The confessional need for transparency, I hadn't forgotten.'

'But I don't understand what you –'

'Yes, you do. Look,' and abruptly – hungrily, Anna has time to think – he puts down the chopsticks, takes the napkin, quick-fingered; grasps her hand, lays the linen over her palm, like a magician about to perform some prestidigitation – the Mystery of the Severed Limb – and now he is reaching for his pen, is drawing on the starched cloth, her hand convenient as a writing desk.

'What are you doing?'

'I'm showing you. This was still a kid's game when I was growing up. You too. A house to be drawn with one stroke of the pen –

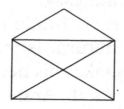

– and no going back. Do you remember that, Anna?'

'Yes.' His hand around her wrist. The pen tracing her skin through the cloth, ticklish, almost painful. It is only the second time they have touched. She doesn't pull away.

'The first time it seems difficult. To begin with, you might choose the wrong line. You might find

147

you've started something you can't finish. But everything comes to depend on those beginnings. Once you've accomplished so much –

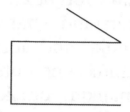

– then it is no longer possible to fail.'

He lets her go. For a second he seems to wait, as if he expects Anna to say something. When she doesn't he crumples the ruined cloth, drops it on the tray beside him. The gesture of a diner at a good restaurant. He is no longer smiling. 'From a certain point there is no going back. That is the point to reach.'

'You make it sound easy.'

'Inevitable. Not easy. I didn't say that.'

'The point of no return. Is that a quote?'

'Kafka.' But he shakes his head, as if something has troubled him. As if, Anna thinks, instead of proving his point to her, he has unearthed some doubt in himself, something better left buried. 'Not a man much interested in success. When he wasn't failing to write he was writing about failure. He'd like it here.'

'Here? Why?'

'Not *here*.' He smiles, the wrinkles fanning from the corners of his eyes. To Anna he looks older. Which is to say he no longer seems younger than her, or ageless. There is less glamour about him each time they meet. 'I meant here and now. I mean that people have come to appreciate failure. They find failure heroic, and they have no affection for success. They view it as a pitiful and woefully incurable psychological condition, a mental inability to be satisfied with the way things are and should be. A social disease. To be successful is to admit to a flaw in one's soul.'

'And are you?'

'Am I what? Flawed?'

'No.' She laughs at last, and easily, as if with old friends. 'Are you dissatisfied?'

'No.' He shakes his head. 'That would be wrong. I cherish the life I have. So many questions, Anna, and I've never asked you anything. It doesn't seem quite fair.'

She hesitates only for a second. 'Then ask.'

He folds his arms and sits back, mocking her, sizing her up like a photographer. 'Are you married?'

'No!'

'I'm sorry, was that too much question in your question? Would you like more sugar?'

She checks herself. 'No.'

'Good. Why aren't you married?'

'Why are you?'

'Questions for questions. What about family?'

'What about them?'

'What are they like?'

'Different. We're not close. I see my sister. How about you?'

149

'I've never met her.'

'I meant your family.'

'I know what you meant. I'm asking the questions round here. Do you have friends?'

'Yes, I have friends.'

'Tell me about them,' he says, and unfolds his arms. His tone has changed, there is something in it, a hint of seriousness, and she answers fast, not liking it, guessing what is coming next, the examination of lovers.

'You know, it's not true that you've never asked me anything before. You've asked me lots of things.'

'Have I?'

'Last time you asked me if I liked my work, and I said yes.'

'So you did.'

'And you asked me if I thought everything had its price.'

'And does it?'

'You seemed to think so.' There is a quality to their conversation Anna remembers perfectly, the quickness, the proximity of both laughter and anger. It is as if the words they say are less important than their rhythm, the grammar of emotion, which is like poetry, or music. Even so there is less intensity between them this time, and more warmth. It occurs to her that it is as if they have known one another for years, or as if they are passing strangers, who know they never will; who can say nothing or anything.

'Did I think that?' John asks. 'Some days I do.' He looks away, out of the far wall of glass, where the winter light under the trees is already softening to a form of dusk: just the way it did at SoftMark, Anna remembers, in the place where money is made without human intervention. When Law speaks again his voice is also fainter. 'I think I was hoping you'd convince me I was wrong.'

'Alright.' She lowers the tablet computer. Folds her hands on top of it. 'If that's what you want. I think you're wrong, I don't agree.'

He smiles, perhaps for her. 'Why?'

'Because I don't think that you buying an old tree off some octogenarian in Japan means everything has its price.'

'There are currencies even less substantial than mine –'

'I know what you're talking about, John. I know when we're discussing money and when we're not. Don't patronise me.'

'Do I do that?' He swings his long head back towards her, into shadow. Anna can just make out his expression of surprise. 'I don't think of you as someone to patronise.'

'I think you're talking about justice. You're saying there's always a price to pay. How often does that happen? When did you last see someone get what they deserve? What you're talking about only happens in bedtime stories. People get away with what they can, and they can get away with almost anything. It doesn't matter if you're talking about money or anything else. If no one sees them, no one can stop them.'

'You do.'

'But I'm hardly going to change the way they live. And God isn't a tax inspector.'

His laughter again, breaking through the conversation as if it has been there all along. 'Some might disagree. So you don't believe in Judgement? All that double-entry bookkeeping in the sky? Poetic justice?'

'No. Who would exact it, the poets?'

This time he doesn't laugh. 'People might exact it on themselves.'

'Why?' Anna shakes her head. 'No, what I see is that most people don't pay, most of the time. Not everything has its price, because not everything is paid for. Who would really want it any other way? Would anyone wish poetic justice on anyone except their worst enemies? And what could they do except wish it?'

'You make it sound simple.'

'Well, it is. That's what I think. If that's what you mean.'

She pauses. Now it is her turn to wait. John Law has come to rest hunkered forward, his head bent. Only when it becomes clear that he isn't going to reply does she lean forward herself. 'Is that what you mean?'

'I suppose it is.' Faintly. No one to hear it but themselves.

'John.' She bows her head closer, until their

foreheads touch. In the quiet she can feel the pulse trapped between his skin and bone. She can hear the synthetic thunder of an aeroplane.

'What is it?'

'Nothing.'

'What is it you think you've done?'

'Nothing. Not enough.'

'Is it the case?'

He looks up, baffled out of himself. 'Case?'

'In Japan. The code in the bodies of people . . .'

'Anna,' he says. 'Come on.' He is chiding, smiling as if he has seen her for the first time: and she has trailed off, knowing already that she is wrong, that Carl's story was never more than it seemed, the grossest public apocryphon, she is a fool to have thought otherwise even for a second. She is ashamed of the way it reveals her. 'I could help,' she adds, pointlessly, and Law laughs low in his chest, the sound feline, almost leonine. When he answers his voice is quieter, quizzical with thought.

'Are you my enemy?'

'What?'

'Greta says so. And Terence.'

'Terence? I thought –'

'Are you my enemy, Anna, do you think?'

'No.'

'Are you sure?'

She pauses only for a second. It is audible and definite as a rest in music. He sits back up, away from her. 'Nor am I.'

'I can help,' she says again, her ordinary voice

sounding louder than she means it, and Law makes a sound, almost kissing his teeth, frustrated and dismissive.

'No. All you can do for me is ask me your questions. And all I can do for you is answer them.'

'Alright,' she says, and then stops, the voice sinking in. So suddenly, unexpectedly insulting, it makes her feel nauseous. He gets up, stretching, walking stiff-legged to the nearest panoramic wall of glass. Looking out at the cedars, the tiered planes of their green boughs.

'You don't really believe in God, do you, Anna?' And again, she can't tell if he is deriding her or only asking her a question. She feels the hurt begin to rise up in her again, and with it its immediate antidote, anger.

'Why, do you?'

He doesn't turn round. 'The best mathematicians always believe in God.'

'Why can you never simply answer my questions?'

'Because they're not simply yours. You're only paid to ask them.'

'I see. Alright. Mister Law, why did you divert four million soft into an account in the name of your eleven-year-old son?'

'Ask me another.'

'With pleasure. What were you working on last night?'

He grunts an acknowledgement. 'It's not something I can readily explain –'

'Do you think you might find it easier in court?'

He lets his hand fall limply, and then simply stands, the glass behind him, the trees beyond the glass. 'I was working on a general problem in cryptography. A theoretical issue.'

'In the past thirteen years, have you neglected to disclose any personal income, or have you avoided paying British tax on any amount of personal income, besides that held in the Depository of the Gulf of Tartary in the name of your son, Nathan Law?'

He pauses, only for a second. 'No.'

'No.' She types, a tiny rhythm of percussion in the sparely furnished room. 'Are you sure?'

'I don't need to give sureties to the Revenue. Only my dues.'

She stops typing. Looks up, waits until he turns back to her. 'Then give one to me.'

'I'm sure. There are no more hidden accounts.'

She feels the anger go out of her all at once. For a moment it is as if it leaves her diminished. 'Lawrence was sure there would be,' she says dully.

'Then Lawrence was wrong. I don't need to hide my money from anyone.'

'But you did.'

'Once,' he says, quietly. And in the quietness Anna hears, quite clearly, that it would not have been his choice to conceal anything, if the choice had been his alone. 'Do you think I'm a liar?'

'No.'

'People do.'

'People don't hate you.'

'I'm not saying that. I'm saying they look at me and at their own lives, the things they work so hard to achieve. And they wonder how it can be possible, to honestly live such a different life.' He stops, as if giving Anna time to contradict him. When she doesn't he goes on, his voice harsher. 'They look for the means by which anyone could do it. The lucky fluke, the trick of it. They look for the lie. Perhaps you do too.'

'Not everyone wants to be you.'

'No. You don't, do you?' He comes back, sits beside her. 'I knew that the first time I saw you.' And then nothing. He watches Anna, taking her in. Her skin sheer from ear to collarbone, the hair coiled back. The curve of her neck, smooth and muscular, as if with some effort of containment. She is reading the computer screen in her hands, the volumes of information it contains. As if they could explain anything to her, anything at all.

'I don't have any more questions,' she says finally, and looking up at him she smiles, as if she means to apologise.

'I'm sorry,' he says, and because he means it she smiles again, and he is glad for her, even if he can no longer be glad for himself.

'No you're not.'

'No?'

'No one's sorry to see the back of the Revenue.'

'But I am. We're done, then,' John says, and Anna nods. 'You've made your assessment. Can I ask what it is?'

'My official assessment is that you've repaid the Revenue, including the full figure of punitive interest, and that to the best of my knowledge there are no more debts outstanding. That's all I have the authority to investigate.'

'And unofficially?'

Without answering she powers down the computer. Its light fades gradually under her hands. She doesn't reach for the case.

'Anna?'

'What?'

'Are you satisfied?'

'You know I'm not.'

'Then what are you going to do?'

She sits back, sighing long and openly. 'I'm going to go home, order a delivery dinner and open a bottle of wine. While I drink it I'm going to try and forget that I know you've done something wrong, and that I may never find out what it is. What else can I do?'

'You could see me again.'

She turns to meet his gaze steadily. 'And that would help, would it?'

'I didn't mean that.' He stops. As if he is taken aback, Anna thinks, ashamed, even, and she is surprised.

'Then what did you mean?'

'I meant,' he says, spacing the words, just as

they come to him. 'That I would be sorry not to see you again.'

'Why?' Anna asks, but already she knows the answer, perhaps better than John does himself.

'Why do you always have to know why?'

'It's my job.'

'This isn't your job any more.'

'Isn't it?'

'I thought you said you had no more questions.'

'I lied.' She reaches for the briefcase.

'See me again.'

'When?'

'New Year's Day. New Year's Day's night. The Winter Ball. It's not as formal as it sounds. Come. If you get here and change your mind, you won't even have to find me. Terence can send you an invitation.'

'Can he?'

'Anna.'

'I promised my family.'

'Liar.'

'Terence thinks I'm your enemy.'

'Anna.'

She stands. Feeling his eyes on her, not meeting them. Checking her coat, her case, absently involving herself in the mechanics of departure. 'Anna,' he says, for a third time.

'Alright,' she says. And she looks down at him, very still, as he takes her hand.

Afterwards, when she looks back at the investigation, it is at first relentlessly, exhaustively, as if

158

her recollections of what was said and done can be made to render up what was left unspoken. It is only as the days pass that she realises the case is over for her, just as it is for John himself. His repayment of debt has left her impotent. There is nothing more she can investigate.

As if it matters. As if what she ever wanted of him was money, or the promotion her prominent and rapid success might eventually bring. When she thinks of him Anna imagines she feels as her clients must have felt, the ones who have been most guilty, the frauds. He is a married man, a father. She knows how it feels when a family falls apart. But she wants to see him again, and not only him but the life he has surrounded himself with. The house sheltered in the trees. Nathan's laughter, and his echo at the shore, laughing back. Anneli. Even Anneli. It is him she wants, but not only him. She wants the people who have him in them.

Other things linger. There is a sensation of resistance she doesn't recall feeling at the time, a powerful resentment. As if she could never belong in a place like Erith Reach, a place and family so apart, and wishes them both destroyed. She has to catch herself, to remind herself that she doesn't hate John or the money he creates. She isn't sure if she will ever see him again. The invitation comes and lies unopened on the mantelpiece, an envelope of watered paper, rare and archaic.

And still, sometimes she stops whatever she is

doing, working on new clients or talking or alone with herself, the memory of the Laws coming to her as something desirable, painfully clear. When that happens it is often their grace that strikes her most. Their troubling beauty. Sometimes she dreams that she is there with them again, but always comprehending nothing, or not enough, always a sentence behind. Then it is all she wants, to understand their conversations and silences. It is a simple desire, not like love, nothing so complicated as that. Or perhaps it is like a first love. Like an obsession.

At nights she is restless, and in the days tired. She works late and achieves less than enough, her face sallow in the computer's faint light. Nothing is said, though the Revenue is aware: she is aware of its awareness. She falls behind, nods off over the lives of freelancers and industrialists.

Her life draws her back like gravity. It fills her with a vague dread, as if she is falling through the routine of days towards something not quite foreseen and terrible. She dreams of leaving, of walking out of her life into that of another, John's or her mother's. Greener grasses. One night, reading her father's boxed books, she turns a page to find no more writing, only blankness, an error in the printing, and feels a spur of joy at that most open-ended of open endings.

She cancels her monthly meeting with Martha, citing work, as one or the other of them will regularly do. Her computer fills up with the tiny icons of unopened messages. A monstrous haul of junk mail washes up from the Internet sites she has examined, even those she has never visited – *A Message from the Masters of Reverse Engineering!* – so that she angrily clicks them away. Eve sends unanswered communications which Anna's computer appends with urgent red flags. Lawrence sends flowers and a dinner invitation on a small white card.

She remembers no other dreams. The inspectors leave at six-thirty as the cleaners come in, the city closing down around them. A radio starts up somewhere. Music drifts out through the Revenue windows. The sounds of sirens, distant and inconstant, drifting in.

'Why?'
　'I don't know.'
　'Come on.'
　'I don't.'
　'First you extract seven figures out of him. Then you won't leave him alone even after he's paid. And now you're saying he wants to see you again?'
　'It doesn't matter.'
　'All that money, and you're saying he wants to see you? Why? You must be his worst nightmare. Unless there's something else.'
　'Carl –'
　'Maybe he likes it. Maybe he likes punishment. What did you do, tie him up with red tape? Whip him lightly with his primary records?'

'Leave her alone, Carl. She asked for advice.'

'And that's what I'm giving her. I'm telling her it's Freudian. What he really wants to do is fuck the Revenue over. He does want to fuck you, doesn't he?'

'*Carl.*' Sullivan raises her head ominously from her drink, hands closed around its warmth like vices.

'Alright. I'm just expressing my surprise.'

'Surprise? Jealousy, more like.'

'Surprise. And suspicion. Excuse me if I'm blunt as a cunt about it.'

'Mister Caunt, I am trying to eat my breakfast.'

'No, Mister Hermanubis, you're trying to eat my breakfast, as it happens. So does he? Anna.'

'No.'

'Does he?'

'I don't know.'

'Of course he does.'

'I don't think that's why he wants to see me again.'

'Then what is it?' Sullivan asks, softly curious, her voice weightless as the motes of snow that have begun to fall around them.

'I think,' Anna says, eventually, 'that he wants a witness.'

She comes bearing gifts. It is a white Christmas, the first in decades, the depth of the sky plotted out in snowflakes. All the way across London the streets are full of onlookers and distracted drivers, upturned faces.

She parks in a street off Belgrave Square and sits while the motor ticks down into silence. All morning she has been remembering the first days of winter, its onset, the time just before she met John Law. The recollections nag at her. The car in the frost. The train between stations. It is as if she can remember everything she has seen, everything she has said and thought, but not what she has known. She is not there yet. She doesn't know yet what she knows.

Martha's house is as she remembers it. It has been a while. The stone facade is the colour of fossils. There is a wreath on the door, the kind Martha might have desired as a child and might buy now she is not, a great lifebelt of holly with extravagant berries and unnaturally engendered clusters of sharp, perfumed flowers. The petals draw a bead of blood from Anna's hand as she reaches for the bell. She is still sucking her finger when the door opens.

'There she is!' says Eve, accusing and celebratory, as if Anna is a long-awaited means of transport who has arrived two at once. 'The most beautiful tax inspector in the world. Fashionably late as always.'

'Feel free to ignore her,' says Martha. 'She's been drinking since lunch. What have you done to your hand?'

'Nothing. Your guard-wreath attacked me.'

'Bad wreath. Show me? You'll survive. Do you still cook? I need to borrow you. Your mother can get you a drink, can't you, mother? What would you like?'

'Whatever you two are having,' Anna says, though

her voice, in contrast to those of her mother and sister, seems small and distant even in her own ears. They are both done up to the nines, all smiles, reflections of one another and therefore of Anna herself; and in their eyes Anna can see herself reflected. Not as herself – not as she imagines herself, at least – but as they know her. Sister and daughter. It is like being three people at once, Anna has time to think, and then Eve is retreating into the warmth, and Martha is taking her hand, leading her inside.

From the dining room comes the sound of music, masculine laughter. The kitchen is a microclimate of steam. Anna steps into it with the cold of the street still on her cheeks. The air has acquired flavour, as if its elements have been adulterated by trace elements of white wine, white fish, sweet herbs. Her sister has moved to the far counter, sorting through heaped vegetables. On the stove between them sits a kite-shaped copper pan broad as a dustbin. The lid trembles.

'It's turbot,' Martha calls. 'Whole. I thought to hell with it all, we'll have something special. Hope you're hungry.'

'Can I see it?' She is already reaching for the lid.

'Not yet, don't touch! It needs to cook through. It's a monster, actually. Huge, flat and ugly. Fish doormat.'

'Loch Ness roadkill?'

'Exactly. I've spent all day with it. You're an improvement. Here, can you do something with the salad? Take it away from me. You were always the better cook.'

'That's rather obviously not true.' Anna inches past Martha, takes up a knife, begins to cut. The steam is heavier at the counter, the taste of it more powerful. She closes her eyes for a second, the knife poised, comfortably stunned by heat and scent. Behind her at the stove her sister is talking, talking, just as she always has, saying nothing and everything.

'I found the recipe in George Sala, it's a hundred and twenty-four years old, isn't that amazing? He dressed the fish with capers. They're on the prohibited foods list now. They say the humble caper is dying out in its natural habitats. They're going to clone them, apparently, like world leaders and elephants. Mum flew them in for us. Not the elephants. She hid them in her washbag. Now she's complaining all her scent smells of vinegar. How are you? I missed our Friday. It's been too long, hasn't it? Why was that?'

'I can't remember,' she says, and at this still moment – John Law behind her, the dinner still waiting to begin – she can't, or doesn't care to. She grates the zest of limes, presses the juices into a bowl of oil, peels the frail skin from garlic. 'I'm sorry.'

'I didn't say it was your fault.' Martha lifts the lid from the turbotière with both hands. Peers tentatively in. 'Mum said you've been busy.'

'She means I've been ignoring her.'

165

'I know,' Martha says, and then, 'What's hap-pening with John Law, by the way?'

'I'm done with him.'

'Already?'

'I think so, yes.'

'You do work fast. What a shame, there was I thinking you'd grill him mercilessly for months on end. Slow-roasted Cryptographer, Revenue-style, complete with much dragging and many coals.'

'That's not what I do,' she says. 'That's not my job.' She is surprised by the bitterness in Martha's voice. She is not a bitter woman, though she is a surprising one, after all. Anna separates the pale cloves, crushes the fullest under the heel of her hand, the wet sulphurous pulp clinging to her skin. Takes up the knife. 'I don't eat billionaires for breakfast, either.'

'I don't know, maybe you should,' Martha says, turning casually from the stove, wiping her hands down on a towel. 'You know, I've got colleagues just like him. Mister and Missus Justices. The kind of people who think Fortnum and Mason is a convenience store. There are days when I think I'd like to live like that.'

'Why?'

'Why not? Don't you?'

'Not really.'

'We're different, then. I'm not greedy, I just think – imagine – it might make things so much easier. Never to have to think of money again. Wouldn't that be wonderful?'

'It's not like that,' Anna says. 'He's not like that.' Her voice is soft: fervent, if she could hear it, so that on impulse Martha leans forward and strokes her sister's face, meets her smile with her own more feral smile, curls the precious weight of Anna's hair back behind her ear.

From the dining room the male voice is audible again, calling out for more of something. It has an unfamiliar accent, Anna realises absently; West Coast American, not the Maine stolidity of Martha's husband Andrew; and before Martha has lowered her hand the realisation has come to Anna that something is wrong. That there is an absence in the house, a hollowness she should have noticed much earlier. Like the hole that a shadow will cast in fog.

'Who's that?'

'*That* is your mother's latest. She's been dying for you to meet him. His name's Max, he's in Luggage. He can tell you things you would never have believed about suitcases. You'll probably have to talk to him. Sorry about that.' She pauses at the stove, her hands still working, working. 'Not really much room for social manoeuvre, with only four.'

'Four?'

'I knew it,' Eve says from the doorway. Anna wonders how long she has been leaning there, a Sea Breeze not quite spilling in each hand, observing her daughters, drily critical. 'Of course I thought you might have realised. You spend all day understanding strangers, I thought perhaps you'd have understood your sister. But I guess not. And I did try and warn you, but you've been hard to get hold of. Silly girl.'

Anna puts down the knife. She is picturing the icons on her computer, ranks of minute, unopened envelopes. Her avoidance of her own life, which is inevitably avoidance of the lives of others. 'What's going on?'

Her mother tuts. Martha leans on the stove's edge, her weight on her arms. 'Andrew,' Eve starts, and immediately stops, uncharacteristically hesitant. 'Andrew and Martha –'

'What Mum is trying to say,' says Martha, 'is that Andrew and I have been having problems for a few months. I'm sorry I never got round to telling you. I kept meaning to. Anyway, Andrew has decided to spend some time alone.'

'Martha. When? How long?'

'He was gone most of last month,' Eve says. 'He came back for some things two weeks ago. No one has seen him since.'

'But his work –'

'He's left his job.'

'I didn't know,' Anna says. 'I had no idea.'

'Obviously, and you didn't ask.' Eve turns on her. 'I rather doubt you've asked your sister anything.'

'Stop,' says Martha.

'Have you?'

'Questioned my sister? No. I do enough of that all day.'

168

'*How are you?* is usually considered a civilised enquiry.'

'Stop,' Martha says again, but her voice is quieter when it should be louder; she sounds like me, Anna thinks with an involuntary shudder. Her shoulders, so much broader and stronger than either Anna's or her mother's, have pulled protectively together.

'Well,' Eve says. 'Congratulations, Anna. Would you like your drink now, or do you have any other indelicate surprises in store for us?'

No one answers. She takes the drink. The lid of the turbotière chatters and settles. Martha turns the flame off, turns towards them. Her face raw in the wet air.

'It's done,' she says. 'It's all ready. We should eat,' she says to both of them, as if it could be a question.

It is a disaster. For two courses no one talks except Max, Max who is in Luggage; and Max talks more and more, increasingly nervous of the silence, out of his depth before he knows it, his broad face damp with sweat above the vast piscine expanse of the main course.

Afterwards there are still presents that must be given and received. From Eve Anna gets a designer belt of microscopically articulated chrome, a length of shining metal that looks as if it might conceal a weapon. From Max-in-luggage – to whom she gives the music chosen for Andrew – she receives a vanity bag made of real pony-skin. And from Martha there is a slim parcel containing T. S. Eliot's 1936 *Collected Poems*, a near-perfect first edition, the pages ragged where they were paper-knived apart with carelessness, impatience or excitement almost a century ago. *For my sister, last of the bookworms,* Martha has written on the accompanying card. You do still read books, she asks, don't you? Yes, Anna says, yes, she still reads books.

The telephone rings as she is almost home, bringing her awake from the road as if she has been sleeping. On the radio singer after singer has been singing about love, and all of them badly, or so it seems to her tonight. She turns them down almost to nothing and pulls into a lay-by before answering.

'Well,' Eve's voice says. 'Are you sorry?'

'Of course I am. I didn't know.'

'I know, dear. Although in the circumstances I'm not sure ignorance is your best defence. Are you home? You don't sound home.'

'No.' The car feels too close around her. She clicks off the belt, opens the door. Balancing the phone in the small of her shoulder. 'I'm not there yet. There's ice. It was bad, wasn't it?'

'Exceptionally bad, yes. I've never seen a Christmas dinner so like the Last Supper.'

She gets out, stands under a bare canopy of trees. Beyond them the sky is clear, remote with stars. 'Is it a woman?'

'No. Do you know, I think I'd actually prefer that. A few years ago Martha thought he'd met someone back in Maine. It turned out to be nothing, or at least nothing important. But now I rather wish there was someone. I could understand that. And if she was in the States I could perhaps have tracked her down,' she says mildly. 'We all carry guns over there, you know.'

'Then what happened?'

'Money,' Eve says, blunt as money. 'He's been very good to Martha, financially, but something went wrong these last few months. She knew there were problems, but not how bad they were.'

There is a pause. The sound of a small room, of Eve alone in her daughter's house. 'I'm sorry,' Anna says. 'About tonight.'

'I know you are. Of course you are. Not that I thought we'd all walk hand in hand into the new year. We're family, after all. And when you get right down to it, it was Andrew's fault. But I've been thinking about it since you left. I have something to ask you.'

'What?'

'I want to know if you're seeing him again.'

'Who?'

'That man you were working on. John Law.'

A car goes past, too bright and fast. Anna leans away. For a moment she feels breathless, as if her heart is racing. 'You were listening, weren't you?'

'Well, I didn't see any sign on the door saying Private Conversation –'

'Well, it was.'

'Well, it doesn't matter now, does it? Are you?'

There is a low wall beyond the pavement. Beyond it steep undergrowth descends down a cutting into deep darkness. Anna sits down with her back to the foliage. She is beginning to shiver. Her coat is still in the car. 'Why?'

'Because,' Eve says, 'Martha said you got on very well with him. And that man has left your sister in trouble.'

For a second she is confused, not only by the phrase but by the circumstances. As far back as she can remember, Martha has never been in trouble of any kind that matters, has never slackened or weakened. 'What do you –'

'Anna,' her mother says, trying to be patient, foiled by the dual sharpness of frustration and embarrassment. 'It's not hard to understand. Andrew was a speculator. He speculated badly, he got it wrong, now there are debts to pay. The sums are impressively large by any standards, certainly big enough to swallow up the house, and Martha in it. She is a very good barrister, one day she might even become a judge, people say, but she has never been good with money, and bankrupt barristers do not become judges. Neither of them lived particularly frugally, they were always remortgaging, I can't imagine Martha would have an easy job digging her way out of debt at the best of times, and these are not the best. Andrew has taken most of their savings and done an uncharacteristically professional job of covering his tracks. Your sister needs help. She needs to buy herself some time. Are you still there?'

'Yes.'

'Do you understand what I'm saying?'

'Yes,' Anna nods at no one, the trees, the cold road. 'You're saying we can help her. Both of us,' but already she knows this is not what her mother is saying at all.

'Don't be ridiculous. Us? You don't care enough about money, and I don't care enough about saving it. We have no money, Anna, it's very simple. But there are people who do. There are people who don't care about anything else.'

'John isn't like that,' she says. 'Is that what you mean?'

'What do you think?'

'I don't know, that's why I'm asking, I just can't—' She bites down on her anger before it can slip away from her. In the back of her mind is a sensation of drift, half familiar. It is the slow-fast motion of her car in Erith Reach, with the child ahead of her. 'Are you saying that John Law should give us money?'

'Not *should*. *Should* is an awful word. *Could*. He *could* do it, if he wanted.' Tetchy with defensiveness. 'It's not as if he can't spare it.'

She tries to think, half listening to her mother's impatient breathing. 'What are you suggesting we do?'

'I'm not suggesting anything. I'm telling you that

the one time in your life when your sister actually needs your help, you're lucky enough to be in a position to give it. It's a fortunate coincidence that you know this man. I think we should make the most of it. For God's sake, Anna, all you have to do is ask him. Is that so wrong?'

'Yes,' she says, calmly, not quite calmly. 'I could lose my job.'

'But you won't.'

'Won't I? Does she know you're talking to me?'

'Of course not.'

'She wouldn't ask this.'

'No. But she's not the one asking.'

She squeezes her eyes shut. 'What about the banks?'

'Martha already owes them nearly everything. I don't really think asking them for more is going to work –'

'Then how can I ask a client?'

'It's easy. You just smile, like a good girl.' And then Eve sighs, as Martha sighs. 'But I know you won't. You're too proud, just like your father. So. What I would like you to do is give this man of yours a letter.'

'A letter?'

'Yes, a letter, you know? A letter, on paper, made of trees, in an envelope, written in ink. He'll like that.'

She opens her eyes. 'How do you know?'

'People say. I hear things.'

'I can't,' Anna says, but already she wonders

if she is right, if the opposite is not truer. The argument is already old and sour in her mouth, as if speech could leave a taste, a residue of guilt, a silt of anger.

'You don't have to decide now. I'll send it to you. You don't have to read it. You don't have to ask him. You don't have to say a word. All you have to do,' Eve says, her voice growing slow and measured, 'is give it to him.'

She has finished, Anna thinks. She has said her piece. And even as she thinks it her mother is saying *Goodnight*, and before she can answer the line has gone dead. Around her there is nothing left but the temporary grace of the empty road, the night dark as asphalt. The car open and waiting, the radio still on, whispering.

Two letters. One from John but not from him, not in his own hand. The other to John, not from Anna, but to be given to him by her. It is not exactly a correspondence, this communication through and for others. Just as what there is between them is not exactly anything. Not an investigation nor an affair, not friendship, not not. *Are you my enemy, Anna, do you think?*

The envelope with *Mister Law* in her mother's writing – scrawny, out of practice – she leaves on the floor by the door, beside the coats and the shoes and the flotsam of green and colourless bottles she accumulates for recycling every week. She ignores the letter as if it is something to be taken out, or thrown away. And perhaps it is, she doesn't know. It is not something she has decided, the choice is not something she is willing to make. She can't give it, and can't not. She doesn't want to know what she will do with it.

She has always liked the days between Christmas and New Year, the sense of waiting and completion. The nights fall early and the mornings come late, but this year the weather is often clear, the afternoons are frostily bright. There is nothing to do, and so she walks and meets friends and buys food on impulse in shops that she will never visit again, simple things, not only for the eating but for the look of them. A bowl of blood oranges. White eggs like flowers.

New Year's Day. She sits in the kitchen and reads Martha's gift. Eliot's desirably flawed brilliance. She likes it less than she remembers, the distaste for humanity reminds her too much of the Revenue, but she reads anyway, her sister's anxious voice following her through the pages. *You do still read, don't you?* And hers. *Yes, yes.*

When the Stranger says: 'What is the meaning of
   this city?
Do you huddle close together because you
   love each other?'
What will you answer? 'We all dwell together
To make money from each other'?

O weariness of men . . .
Exploiting the seas and developing the mountains,

Dividing the stars into common and preferred,
Engaged in devising the perfect refrigerator.

Three o'clock. The light is going. She puts the book away and goes upstairs. In the bathroom she undresses as quickly as she can and then showers as slowly as she is able, letting the warmth settle into her, loitering under it, the water coiling over her limbs and belly, the world vanishing into condensation, vaporised. There are children playing in the gardens outside, she can hear but not see them. *Snow!* The smallest voice of them is shouting again and again, though there has been nothing but frost for days. *Snow! Snow!*

She turns the water off, pads wetly to the mirror, wipes the glass. Her skin is pallid. Her hair needs cutting. Her eyes and muscles have settled into her default expression. She looks as if she thinks she has just misheard a question, and is too proud to ask for it again.

The invitation from John Law waits for her downstairs, still unopened. Anna doesn't need to read it. When it arrived she felt its thickness, embarrassed to be needing to do so. She held it against the light. And it is New Year's Day, after all, a hard date to forget. In a few hours it will be New Year's Day's night. She thinks there is still time to get ready.

She raises her hands to her hair, begins to braid.

★   ★   ★

She gets out of the car and the air is warm. It is January, London's coldest month, midwinter even in this century of climate change, but here it is April. She has driven twelve miles across the city, and it is as if she has stepped off a plane that has been flying south all night.

She realises it with her first breath, so that the second comes more sharply. It is not often that she finds money unexpected. She has examined its achievements too often, the repetitive ways people will try to put distance between themselves and the world. Now it surprises her, though, shocks her, a little, as if it could be wrong, and she wonders if it is, and why.

She thinks, it's only technology. In a year it will no longer seem like something supernatural, in five it will pass unnoticed. And as she stands there it comes to her that there is, in fact, something cheap about it: an old-fashioned, fair-groundish trickery. John Law's Marvellous Greenhouse Effect. It is false and delicious as good perfume. She breathes again, more tentatively, tasting the air, its odour of wet earth and thaw.

It feels like the proof of something. That money can do anything, change whatever it touches. Like Midas, she thinks. The king who changed the world to gold. The gold that changed the king. She wonders if that is true of money, after all, though it is not what she has always believed. It is not what she sees in her own world, where people are not immutable but are, still, stubborn-hearted, born into themselves. Ungolden. Where winter, despite everything, stays winter.

Here and there in the grounds she can make out torches, the flicker of flames; and guests, small groups, voices and laughter. Beyond the last curve of the drive the house shines intermittently, the crowds inside casting long and mobile shadows. The river is lined with lanterns and their reflections. There are vessels in harbour, a dozen or more, their rigging decked out with illuminations.

She has stopped on the verge where the drive opens out into its final arch of gravel. There are cars behind her and ahead, beautiful things in their way, all of them many times more expensive than her own. It is not something she usually takes the time to notice – it isn't something that occupies much of her thought – but nor is it usually so obvious. Impossible not to see that these transports – sculptured statements of intent, enamelled, chromed, fluid with intermittent light – will always be out of her reach.

She has never liked cars.

He's nothing like you, Lawrence said, weeks ago. And although Anna is no longer sure he was right in the ways that he meant, she knows it is true in the most mundane sense. In possession. She can see it now. The cars are a gentle reminder, an unspoken agreement of which she is not a part. She is different here.

No one is parked. The owners stand like Anna,

leaning on their rooftops, or wait in the lit privacy of their seats. Uniformed figures move along the cavalcade, bending at doorways, courteous. Anna can't make out if they are armed. She reaches back into the car, hunting for her card, the proof that she is admissible.

It isn't until one of the figures stops beside her – an impossibly beautiful boy in white driving gloves – that she understands: she has never met a parking valet before. It would be more pleasant in other circumstances; now it only leaves her with the sensation that there is no going back. She stands watching as her Revenue car is driven away from her with more skill than she is capable of exercising herself, and only when it is out of sight does she turn towards the house.

The crowd has spilled out from the hall of fountains, across the arena of gravel, as far as the light from the house extends. She remembers Anneli, slyly confidential: *Once we had a couple who slept in the woods for two days*. Other couples make way for her at the door. She checks herself, her clothes and skin, her mother's letter in her jacket pocket. Like a concealed weapon, she thinks, and puts the thought away, and goes inside.

A camera flash, like lightning. A deafening escalation of voices. Music – a quartet drowned out beside the fountain, a piano played, not very badly, somewhere in the adjoining rooms. The arms race of laughter. The brittle resonance of glass. Champagne, its whiff of gunpowder.

There is a moment when the impulse to step back, out into the night air, is almost overwhelming. Instead Anna makes herself wait, counting down thirty to nothing. She finds herself thinking of Lawrence: Lawrence, who would do this so much better than her. She wishes he was here. She wishes she was him.

Her senses adjust. The noise is deafening but not painful; it is an uproar that can be lived with. She finds herself remembering Carl's clubs, Janet's dance floors, which she has come to like, where nothing is said and music is unassailably pre-eminent. Here the atmosphere is less forgiving. Faces sweat in the ranked light of the chandeliers. Everyone is trying to say everything at once. Along the edge of the hall Anna can see an elderly man moving as if clambering through conversations, his face turned protectively to one side.

At the centre of the room two waiters have reached an impasse, their trays precariously loaded with champagne and kir, juleps, spilt ash, confections of caviar. Anna makes her way to them one step at a time and grabs a glass, finding too late that it is champagne, a drink she has never liked, though she wishes she did, as if liking it would better her. There is no sign of the Laws. Wherever they wait it isn't here, where the newcomers make their entrances and pause to be seen, singling out the known and the desirable.

Anna knows no one herself. There are only the people she almost recognises, the almost recognisably famous, some waiting with fixed expressions as if to overhear their own names, others around whom the crowd moves with fractionally added care, as if they might be breakable. She tries to remember the house beyond the hall. Some way ahead there are stairs, or so she thinks, a wide flight up to higher ground. It is something to aim for, at least.

She has made it through the first hall and halfway through a cavernous second before she sees Terence: and sees him before he sees her, so that she has time for a measure of nervous satisfaction at having caught the security man at his own game. He is observing the crowd, not as a professional would but as an older man might; avuncular – grandfatherly, even – and merry, smiling through his moustache at no one in particular. There is a glass of water in his hand.

His suit looks well cut, even here, but as a guest he is not convincing. He wears his clothes too much like a uniform, with too much care, standing too much to attention. It is only for a second, as he raises the glass, that Anna sees the outline of something worn under the tailored cloth. An unyielding edge and bulk.

She is surprised to be surprised. Since she is not yet drunk enough, is she brave enough, she wonders, to go up behind him, this man who thinks she is an enemy, leaning to whisper in his ear, *Hello*

Terence. Is that a gun in your pocket, or are you just pleased to see me?

She has no time to decide. Already he has turned, finding her face through the crowd, smiling welcome. Making his way to her with inconspicuous ease.

'You should try the cocktails,' she says as he reaches her, and he glances at his glass, back at her, and knits his brows.

'Family motto, I'm afraid. Smoke like a fish, drink like a chimney.'

'They must be healthy.'

'Oh, they are. Cheers.'

'Cheers.'

'Here's to a long life with plenty of trimmings. You got the invitation, then,' he says, and smiles the way she remembers; sweetly, apologetically. 'I wasn't sure you'd come. Not your kind of thing, this, is it?'

'Not really, no.'

'Too many people, is that it? Too much pressure?'

'Something like that.' Beyond Anna a young man with a glass in each hand throws back his head and laughs like an advert for good dentistry. Terence follows her gaze absently, as if what she chooses to see is none of his business.

'It's funny. I'd have thought you'd be used to it, doing what you do. I mean the pressure. How to survive it, how to apply it. But I told Mister Law he'd have a hard time getting you out of the

Revenue for this. Almost as hard as getting the Revenue out of Anna Moore,' he says, and sips. 'That's what I told him.'

'Can I ask you something?' she says, too loudly, her heart abruptly fast. The adrenalin spiralling up in her, like the arid bubbles in champagne. A waiter passes between them. She takes another glass. 'When did you stop liking me?'

'Now, why would you think that?' I've always liked you.'

'Have you?'

'Yes. It makes my job more difficult, that's all.'

'Your job being what? You never told me.'

'I never thought I needed to.'

'To protect John from his enemies?'

'Something like that, Inspector.'

'Just Anna.' And then, the knowing coming to her in the speaking. 'You're Terence Cutler, aren't you?'

'That's what it says on my moneycard.'

'Mister Cutler, the head groundsman.'

'I told you before,' he says, 'I do lots of things.'

His voice is still quiet – he is the kind of man who always speaks quietly, and who is always listened to. But for the first time Anna can make out something else in his eyes. A predictable, mercenary coldness: a reliable violence. She remembers talking to Muriet, the first time she came to Erith Reach.

You don't look like a tax inspector.

What do tax inspectors look like?

184

Like Mister Cutler. Nathan says he used to be in the services.

She was wrong, Anna thinks. We don't look like this. He's nothing like us. I'm nothing like him.

'I'm not his enemy,' she says finally, and Terence Cutler shrugs.

'He doesn't think so, either.'

'Then why –'

'You know, sometimes my employers are their own worst enemies. Sometimes I end up having to protect them from themselves. A hard job I have with this one. And now you.' He drinks his water. 'A lot of people think the worst of him. The way they go on, you might have thought he kills people for a living.'

'I don't think that.'

'Well then, that's good, isn't it?' He is watching her again, his head cocked as if in measurement. 'There was a man here looking for you.'

'Who?'

'A Mister Finch. Friend of yours?'

'No,' she says. 'No, I don't know anyone called –'

'Because he's no friend of ours. The girl was after you too, Muriet. Couldn't wait for you to get here. Mister Law told her you'd come. I didn't believe him, but he was right, wasn't he? I've lost money on you tonight. Not that I suppose I'm the first.' And he smiles again, this time with something approaching candour.

'Where is he?'

'Here and there. You might try the balconies, or the casino rooms. But you'll find him, I'm sure, I should think you'll be good at that.' Genial accusation. 'Very professional, I should think, very businesslike. One other thing,' he adds, as she is turning away.

'What?'

'Look after yourself, won't you?'

'Why?'

'No offence. It's just advice.'

Her skin crawls. 'It doesn't sound like advice.'

'Don't take it badly. Upstairs,' he repeats, and nods her onwards.

The steps are no less crowded than the entrance halls. At the top guests have clustered like tourists at an observation point. They point out those below, as if recognising famous heads of hair, wealthy baldnesses. A woman in pearlised leather leans out too far, snatching illicit photographs. *I mean*, she says, *why stop at Fall? Would summer be too much to ask?* And: *We don't have fall in London, dear*, says the woman beside her. *We only have Autumn in London.*

Out of sight in the adjoining halls a clock is striking, seven, eight, nine . . . an hour later than Anna expects. She wonders where the time has gone. She has done nothing, found no one except Terence; and Terence Cutler, she thinks now, she would happily have never met at all.

She turns from the stairwell, sweating, the railing firm against her back. There is a quality to the atmosphere she is only now aware of, an element just at the limit of her senses; the subliminal electric hum of endorphins and adrenalin.

Her heart is going too fast and she takes a breath to steady it. The warm air cool against her face. She wipes her cheeks with the back of one hand, wishing for mirrors. Two women passing smile without stopping.

Beyond the hallway she can see the upper rooms, the largest chambers, like John's study, faced with glass. The crowd up against nothing, as if it might topple out into the dark –

She can see Anneli. She stands out from her visitors, listening to something said, not quite laughing in response. Her hair is up, and in it there are diamonds, even from two rooms away Anna can see them, their brightness out of all proportion to their size. She looks happy, it seems to Anna. But the longer she looks, the more ambiguous Anneli's face becomes, until, if Anna imagines her mouth away, it is no longer clear if the other woman is smiling at all.

Something whacks against her hip. Muriet is beside her, leering maliciously, a glass in one hand, the other still curled into a fist.

'What was that for?'

'You're late.'

'For what?'

'For everything.' Then with less reproach, more sympathy, 'You missed all the best food. Nathan ate ermine. Do you like ceviche?'

'Not if you're going to hit me with it. Muriet, have you seen Nathan's father?'

'Why?'

'I have to give him something,' she says, one answer out of many. The first that comes to her.

'A present?'

'Yes,' she says, 'a kind of present.'

'He was inside talking about money, then he was outside talking about snow, then he was outside with Nathan. I don't know after that. He doesn't like parties. Nathan says he used to like them but he doesn't now. I saved you some ceviche,' she says elliptically, as if to continue on a brighter note. 'Nathan says it's something like fish. Why did you take so long?'

'I had to get ready.'

'You look better.' She reaches for Anna's hand. 'Come for a walk? I'll show you something nice.'

'Alright.'

'Good. Not yet,' she says, 'Anneli wants you first.' And holding on to Anna she leads her away through the milling of the crowd.

They are seen before they are in speaking distance. Anneli's face lights up with pleasure, relief, or some admixture of the two. 'Anna!' she cries as they reach her, and the guests around her look up with forced goodwill, like diners disturbed at table. 'I thought you weren't coming.'

'Of course she came,' says a woman in livid red brocade. 'Who wouldn't?'

'Anna works for the Revenue,' Anneli says, as

if it is an acceptable explanation of antisocial tendencies, and then, as those around her express or feign varying degrees of interest, 'Anna, this is John Tissier, the ex-Minister for Defence, his partner Jane – Jane Luther, the economist – Aslan Saad, the mathematician. Professor Saad was just asking how we could stand living here.'

The mathematician shrugs without embarrassment. He is young, heavy-jowled under a caul of sweat. Anna looks down, imagining Muriet's expression, wanting to share in it, but the girl is gone. 'I was making a legitimate point.'

'You were being incredibly rude,' says the ex-Minister for Defence mildly. 'The way you always are. It must be something to do with numbers, do you think? Numbers and company don't mix. Is your husband incredibly rude, Mrs Law?'

'So rude no one can find him.'

Laughter, more polite than genuine. Through it comes the mathematician's voice. 'It has everything to do with numbers. My rudeness. As you so call it.'

'As we so call it?' When the woman in brocade laughs her eyes narrow to affectionate slits, as if she is with old friends. There is a cigarette in her hand, motionless, burnt down to a ram's horn of ash. 'What would you call it?'

'Curiosity. Numbers are always telling. For example, there is the number of people living in this house, and the number of rooms they inhabit –'

'Eighty-eight, I read that somewhere,' says the ex-Minister. 'Is that correct?'

'But such *handsome* rooms!' Jane leans in on her hostess, 'Do you know, they always remind me of 1600 Pennsylvania Avenue –'

'Would anyone like another drink? Anna, or are you on duty? Jane, what'll it be?'

'The moon and stars and everything in between.'

'How about something in the meantime?'

'Martini.'

'And how many is that?'

'Mind your own business. People in glass houses –'

'Eighty-eight rooms,' repeats Aslan Saad, ponderously insistent. There is a shine to his eyes which suggests he is not quite harmlessly drunk. 'And three inhabitants. It is the mathematics of inequality, if you will.'

'It's not only us here, of course,' Anneli says. When she speaks nervously it is too quickly, her accent comes through more strongly. The diamonds she wears glitter, bored, strung onto the strands of her hair. 'There are the day and night staff, the guards, all of them have rooms here if they need them – the children's tutors in term time. We don't really live here alone. Not alone.' She turns to Anna, shivers for effect. 'Homes aren't made to be lived in alone, are they? The homes of the single are a little scary, I find. No one is to know what they get up to.'

More laughter, no less uncomfortable. *But I live*

alone, Anna thinks, and doesn't say, though to Anneli she doesn't need to; the knowledge of her mistake is there in the other woman's face, the way it falls in the moment before she is aware of herself. She turns to her other guests.

'I'm so sorry. I'm afraid there was something I needed to discuss with Anna.'

'Taxes?' Avidly.

'You'll have to excuse us, Aslan, please, Jane, it was good to – John –'

'*I told you*—' Anna hears, as Jane Luther turns away, but what she told her partner Anna will never know, can only guess. They are already gone, losing themselves in the crowd, and the young Professor too has almost vanished, as if he was barely present at all; only his arm is still visible, like the smile of the Cheshire Cat, reaching between faces for the nearest tray.

'Creep,' Anneli says after him. Her voice is low and warmly venomous, her head bent, and the naivety of the insult so unexpected from her that for a moment Anna thinks she must have misheard. Anneli, seeing her surprise, finds a smile. 'It's what Nathan and Muriet call them. The Creepy Cryptics.'

'Who?'

'People like Saad, who attach themselves to John. I don't know how he got in, he certainly wasn't invited. I should probably tell Terence. They always creep in somehow and they're always cryptic, as if they know something about us we don't. So. It's a kind of joke,' she adds, absently helpful, stirring the ice in her highball. 'I'm sorry. To use you as an excuse.'

'No.'

'Yes!' Anneli says, urging the apology on her. 'Because I'm always apologising to you, aren't I? And asking for favours. You've been very kind, in the circumstances. Are you enjoying yourself?'

'Very much,' Anna says; an easy lie, the expected one, but Anneli is shaking her head.

'Actually no. That's not what I meant.'

'Then what –'

'Your work.' Shrewdly smiling. 'I meant your work. But I know you're not, really. You're just doing your job, aren't you?'

'Oh. But my work here is finished. I'm not here as the Revenue, I'm really only here as myself . . . John must have told you—' she says, but Anneli is waving her away.

'I have another favour to ask you. It's a question. Would you mind?'

'Not at all.'

'Do the wives always know?'

'I'm sorry?'

'Do they know?' Anneli's voice is conversational again, light and insistent as dancing, as if she is saying nothing. 'When their husbands lie to the Revenue? When you meet the families of your clients, the loved ones, all those significant others, do they lie to you too? Do they know that they should? I suppose it's a simple question. I'm asking if I should know.'

The lights go out without warning. At the same moment, as if synchronised, there is an explosion outside the glass rooms. The sky is lit with suspensions of gold, so high up they might be atmospheric phenomena. There is a second burst, a third; hollow cubes, spheres, pyramids. The reports echo across the landscape. The shapes drift northwards over the river, collapsing into their own reflections.

Fireworks, someone murmurs in the dark, in the tone of voice with which they might have said, *It's alright, it's nothing. Go back to sleep.* Even so there is a groundswell of voices, a sound both desultory and expectant. Above the explosions the distant fin lights of airships are visible, zeppelins holding their positions at high altitude, their proportions ghostly and martial in the pall of smoke.

She becomes aware of the glass in her hand. She is holding it too tightly, the long bulb giving fractionally against her fingers. Delicately dangerous. She relaxes her grip. 'Are you saying John lied to me?' she says, and Anneli laughs as if the slight, dark figure next to her has said something charming, though her voice is falling over itself, no longer fit for public consumption.

'No! I reserve the right to hypocrisy. If I knew he was lying – if I knew how to phrase my lie – then I'd be lying to you. But I don't. There's something wrong, it's not just us, but I can't . . . I

193

hardly see my husband now. There, now you know. It's been worse since you arrived. I did wonder if he was seeing you, but it's not that, is it? He works day and night, but he won't tell me why. He tells Nathan.' Her voice twists. 'He tells *Nathan*. But he doesn't tell me. So you see, I only wanted to know, to know –'

'Anneli,' Anna says, and at the sound of her name she looks up. The fireworks illuminate her face in neon primaries. It is the first time Anna has seen her physically less than beautiful. She has begun to cry, her features are worn down by misery.

The crowd murmurs. Something is falling from the airships, spiralling out through the light of the fireworks until it seems to fill the whole sky. The first flakes reach the glass rooms and melt into nothing. *Ah!* someone says, like a child. *Snow!*

'I'm alright.'

'Are you sure?' Their voices hushed, hurried.

'Yes, I'm alright.'

'You should sit down. I'll get you –'

'*No*. I just need an answer.'

'I can't help you.'

'Can't,' Anneli says with some ferocity. 'Or won't?'

'Can't. I don't know what he's done.'

'Promise?'

'I promise.'

'Oh. Good.' Anneli sighs back the tears. 'How very good it is to be disappointed, sometimes. I don't know why I asked you. Because there's nothing as frightening as not knowing, and you seemed as if you might. Because I like talking to you. You're much too nice to be what you are. You're good at being spoken to, did you know? Has anyone ever told you that?'

'Don't wipe your eyes. Here.'

'Thank you.' And then, inconsequentially, 'We never make love any more. Not for months now. I suppose it must be to do with money. Everything else seems to be. Can you imagine the money he would lose in the time it takes to make love?'

'No. I could calculate it for you, if you like.'

'Christ, could you?' She laughs on cue. 'Please don't.'

'What did you mean about Nathan?'

'What?'

'What did you mean, when you said –'

The lights go up as abruptly as they were switched off. The night draws back out of the glass rooms. Snow is falling against the roof, settling by dint of quantity in the warm night air. There is a half-hearted chorus of applause. The more assertive guests push towards Anneli, a hand on her bare shoulder, her neck, a word in her ear. She shakes her head questioningly at Anna.

'You said he tells Nathan?'

'Of course, because Nathan understands. Numbers run in the family – didn't you know? Didn't I tell you?' she says, as if to say, *Really, inspector, don't you listen to what people say? Don't you know anything?*

'How long has this been happening?'

'—not long—' Anneli says, distracted, smiling general acknowledgement, and Anna thinks, not long at all, no; only since last summer; but this she doesn't say.

Instead she remembers the boy's face, stepping from the lake water towards her. The drip of water from his limbs. His expression, raw, as if intruding to the bone. Fearful, it seems to her now. His voice fierce, not like the father, but like the mother.

You're here to see my father, aren't you? Do you know cryptography? You don't know anything.

'Can I talk to him?'

'What?'

She has to raise her voice. Already Anneli is almost gone, the crowd eagerly pressing in between the two of them. 'Do you mind if I talk to Nathan?'

'Of course not! Though I'm afraid he might not want to talk to you—' And then a man with the physique of an opera singer is throwing his arm around her, *Delightful!* he is whispering, *Fire and ice, the best of both worlds, how like you both,* and there is nothing left for Anna to do but step away, the guests jostling her along, abetting her departure, as if they are glad to be rid of her. She looks round for Muriet, searching for her diminutive form or narrow face, taking another drink from an adjacent tray, as if it were something to hold on to, but there is no sign of the girl, and the need for air and breath rises in her until she can't stand the room any longer.

She makes for the nearest door. Beyond it lies a stairless upper hall hung with worn black basalt glyptographs. She passes through into rooms where people are talking about their histories and love affairs, the nature of the teeth of sharks, the latest public fall from grace, rooms where they are talking about their immortal souls, rooms where they are dancing in ones and twos, rooms of candelabra double-coiled, like hunting horns, rooms of sculpture in pools of illumination, a room with a sliding door indistinguishable from the glass around it, a balcony beyond it with a view of the harbour and the river, jigsaws of light on the water, the night air full of the smell of fireworks, which to Anna has always been the smell of change and autumn, of fall and revolution, and after tonight always will.

The door slides shut behind her. The noise of the house is immediately gone. It is as if the crowd Anna has made her way through has ceased to exist: as if the winter ball were nothing but acoustics – laughter and music and viciousness – and silence could switch it all off, like a light.

Her eyes begin to adjust to the dark. The balcony is one of many, a ziggurat of terraces, each tier cascading evergreen vegetation. Each terrace runs the length of the wing and turns the corner southeastwards. Along the way there are alcoved benches, most of them empty, only the more secluded occupied. A black man in a dark suit leans alone at the railing nearby. There is the wink of his cigarette or cigar. She cannot make out John, if he is here at all.

She closes her eyes and breathes as if coming up for air. The snow has already stopped, real-unreal, though the atmosphere is cooler with its passing. The boardwalk is damp with melt.

'How do I look?'

She opens her eyes. There is no one beside her. It is like ventriloquism. The black man is still staring out, giving no indication of having spoken. But there is no one else close enough to have done so, unless they are on the terraces above or below, out of sight.

'I'm sorry,' she says to the man at the rail, 'did you say something?'

'You were looking at me.' This time she sees his lips move. 'So how do I look?' His voice is London black, accented with money and education and something African, a residual elegance and richness.

'Handsome, in a drunk sort of way.' She says it bluntly, her supply of etiquette all but exhausted, immediately regretting it, so that she is grateful when he smiles, his head nodding with intoxication.

'My drunk or your drunk?'

'I'm not drunk yet,' she lies.

'Then it must be mine,' says the man, and now

that he turns to face her she can see him properly. His features are angular, the skin very dark. His hair is oddly cut, chopped, unkempt. There is something faintly familiar about him, as if he is one of the almost famous. Under Anna's gaze he turns his cheeks, once, twice, like a man shaving, then looks away. 'It's a fine night.'

'Yes, it is.'

'Maybe all the nights here are fine ones.'

'Maybe,' Anna says. They stand for a minute, strangers looking skywards together, like tourists in a cathedral. 'I don't think so, though.'

'The grass is always greener. Do you agree? And the stars are always brighter. You know,' the man says, 'I know you.'

'Do you?'

'Yes indeed. We've met before.'

'Really,' she says, and he grins, pleasantly flirtatious.

'You think we haven't met?'

'I'm sorry, no –'

'Have we not had the pleasure?'

'No.' Smiling too now, despite herself. The man has raised himself on one forearm, hunting in his jacket.

'Here,' he says, and Anna takes the card, turning its ridged copperplate to the harbour lights.

TUNDE FINCH
QUACK DOCTOR – ANTIVIRUS
SPECIALIST – CRYPTOGRAPHER

We work in the dark, We give what we have,
Our doubt is our passion, And our passion is our task.

'Tunde Finch,' she reads off neutrally.

'Tunde, please.'

'Tunde,' she says. 'I've heard about you.'

'Good things, I hope?'

'I was told you were looking for me.'

'And now I've found you,' the man is saying, 'or we've found one another. Either way, better late than never.' But Anna is no longer listening. Her mind is doubling back, running ahead. The man's voice echoing back to her.

Anna Moore, is it? A pleasure. I missed who you were with –

'SoftMark,' she says, 'October.'

'Right.'

'You were in the hall—' *the hall where money is made, without human interface* '—the shareholder reception.'

'Right again.'

'I didn't remember you, I'm sorry –'

'Hey. I'm used to it. But I remember you.'

'Do you work for SoftMark?'

'No!' He laughs. 'I'm a shareholder, for my sins. Sometimes it buys me as much as an hour before I'm escorted to the door. My great advantage is that the Laws never like to create a scene if they can possibly help it. If they could buy invisibility, you know, I think they would. No, I'm what you might call an activist.'

'You were talking to John—' but Tunde laughs even more, infectiously, deep-voiced, *tee-hee-hee*.

'No. I've never talked to Mister Law. Or I mean Law has never talked to me. I've introduced myself many times, but somehow we've never talked . . .'

His voice drifts into silence. He looks away from Anna again, anxiously back towards the harbour lights. The expression doesn't suit him, Anna thinks, though the lines of his face accommodate it easily, as if anxiety is something he has come to accept over a course of years.

'Anna,' she says, and holds out her hand, so that Tunde Finch shrugs himself out of himself to take it.

'Anna Moore. I know.'

She holds out the card between two fingers, offering him back to himself. 'So you're a cryptographer? You're everywhere tonight.'

'So it seems.' He doesn't take the card. She pockets it.

'And a Quack Doctor, whatever that means.'

He laughs again, good-natured: likeable. 'Quack is a term for useless data, used by the unscrupulous to overload company systems, inflicting damage, weakening defences. I am a quack doctor. I heal the damage and the weakness. And, as my card says, I work in much the same way with viruses.'

'You're a computer hacker,' she says, and he smiles without teeth.

'Hacker to my friends, cracker to my enemies.'

'What's the difference?'

'A cracker breaks systems for profit or pleasure. A hacker does so only in order to highlight weakness. I think of myself as a professional hacker.'

'And are you?'

'Sometimes, yes. There was a time when I used to write viruses myself – I have that in common with Mister Law – and I took pleasure in it. But now the companies I worked against invite me to work for them,' Tunde says. 'And I accept their invitations, when the price is right.'

'And the rest of the time?'

'The rest of the time is mine, and in that I run an Internet society, an affiliation of professionals and enthusiasts in my field. We call ourselves the Masters of Reverse Engineering.'

'MRE.' She drains the last of her glass. 'Funny. I know that name too.'

'Then congratulations are in order,' Tunde says, still smiling, though the humour has gone out of it. 'You're one of the few.'

'I was looking for information on John. I almost visited your website.'

'So Mister Law has brought us together more than once. Our fora often hold discussions of his work.'

'The Masters of Reverse Engineering. It's quite a name. Should I be scared?'

'Not unless you have a particular phobia of overworked and under-exercised computer programmers.' And then with abrupt sobriety, 'But we should all be scared, since you ask.'

'I see,' Anna says, as if she does. Anneli's voice coming back to her. *They always creep in somehow and they're always cryptic, as if they know something about us we don't.* 'And what do you do with all this mastery?'

'We are dedicated to the wider application of the hacker philosophy. Which is to test, to eliminate weakness, and thereby to strengthen.'

'Fair enough. That doesn't sound so bad.' She leans beside him. Below them the terraces slope away like gigantic steps. 'I don't think I've ever met a philosophical hacker before. Or even an unphilosophical one.'

'You've met me before.'

'I meant in my work.'

He nods again, slow, it is almost a bow. 'We are something of a black market.'

It takes longer than she would like for her to understand. Longer to answer. 'I don't remember telling you what I do.'

'No.'

'What else do you know about me?'

He clears his throat uncomfortably. 'I'm sorry if you find all this disconcerting. I make it my business to know Mister Law's business. That happens to include you. At SoftMark I tried to discover who you were. Unfortunately I was asked to leave before I could do so. When I found out that you worked for the Revenue, that you have some authority, I thought perhaps you might be able to help. I tried to contact you, but you never answered – possibly my address for you was incorrect. Then, when I acquired the guest list for this evening, I came across your name again. I thought that if I could meet with you, speak to you, that you at least might listen –'

'Listen to what?'

'To what we have to say.'

'We?'

'The Masters –'

'Of course. Actually, I'm not sure –'

'Anna, how much thought have you given to what Mister Law actually does? To cryptography?'

'Much too much. That means no thanks, if it's all the same to you.'

'But it isn't all the same to me. May I – please – may I explain?'

'I have the feeling you're going to anyway,' she says, and the second cryptographer sighs, studying her until she has to laugh out loud at his earnestness.

'Cryptography is a beautiful science.'

'Is it really?'

'Yes. It is the science of concealment, and concealment can be very beautiful. Cryptography can take an alphabet and fold it back on itself, again and again, like origami, until the letters become numbers and the numbers binary. It can hide the blueprint for a gun in a conversation about snow, the pattern of lights on a train, the genetic structure of a flower. But it can also undo these things. The study of concealment also concerns discovery. It is the science of the codemakers, but it is also ours. It is the responsibility of the codebreakers.'

His voice is soft and rapid, his face dogged with incipient disappointment. He doesn't look up at Anna as he talks, as if, she thinks, he is afraid she will stop him somehow. That he will look up to find her gone.

'Sometimes these professions are the same. Often these people are less than enemies. We are willing or unwilling partners in a cycle of invention. And this is because the only way to make a code stronger is to know its weakness. And unless the code is broken, there is no way to know for sure what its weakness will be. It is a paradox – the only way to truly know a code is to break it. Without us, the hackers and breakers, there would be no more codes. There would never have been a second code if no one had broken the first. But the history of cryptography tells us that wherever there is a weakness there will be someone to discover it. Whatever their motivation, there is always someone who will try. And there is always a weakness.'

He looks up, patiently earnest, hopeful, pleading, his eyes white in the dark. 'Do you understand what I'm saying?'

'Yes,' she says. 'No. I'm sorry.'

'It's alright. I'm telling you the first rule of cryptography,' Tunde says. 'The first rule is that no code can be made that cannot be broken. There is no such thing as the perfect code –'

'Anna? Aaaa-na!'

The voice is childlike, sing-song, floating up or down from the terraces above or below, it is hard to be sure which in the dark. The sound cuts Tunde off. He glances away sharply – as if he were a trespasser, Anna has time to think – and she reaches for him, the alcohol singing in her blood.

'Wait. Tunde – I am listening. I want to understand. Tell me again –'

'Call me.'

'No, wait, you don't have to –'

'Call me,' he repeats urgently, pushing the card back into her hands, the hands into her body, and then he is stepping back from her, walking quickly away along the terrace.

'Tunde!'

'There you are.'

She looks up. At the railing above is Muriet's face, disembodied, peering down. 'What are you doing?'

'Nothing,' Anna says. 'Talking.'

'Who to?' Sharply curious. And before Anna can answer, 'How did you end up down there?'

'I don't know.'

Muriet clucks her teeth. 'Wait. I'll come down.' Her face retreats out of sight. 'Don't move!'

'I won't,' she says, though only to herself, since no one else seems to be listening; and she doesn't,

206

standing quite still, the drink a dull ache at the back of her skull.

She kneads her eyes shut and imagines that the pain recedes. In the dark she finds herself thinking of the cold, inching back over the walls of Erith Reach. Soon it will surely be winter again, just as it was the first time she was here. The gravel begrudging her progress. The women by the water's edge. Nathan's laughter.

It is something she has never grown accustomed to, the effect her profession has on others. She has never been at ease with their unease: not like Carl, or Janet, who has learned to take such relish in their loathing. But she wonders dully now whether it was her presence in itself that frightened Nathan, or whether she was more incidental than she seemed. She is piecing together what it might have been that could have scared him into silence as he swam towards the people on the shore. Something shared between father and son. A secret composed of numbers. Unmentionable, unthinkable.

It doesn't seem to her hard to imagine, now. She wonders if she has not known all along. But then she is a slow thinker, Anna, suited to her work. Not brilliant, only sedulous. It is her talent to miss nothing, given time.

The night's conversations come back to her haphazardly. She screws up her eyes, trying to make some new sense of them, but they are voices raised in a small room, echoing, unintelligible, indecipherable, pulling, nagging at her, saying her name again and again.

'Anna. Anna? Anna –'

'What now?'

The harshness of her own voice surprises her. Muriet is beside her, caught off guard in her eagerness. There is a bamboo platter in her hands, ludicrously ornamental, covered by a folded cloth.

'I brought you food. They kept it for you. They didn't want to but I made them. And then you left and I couldn't find you. I think it's still cold—' Her voice diminishing, crestfallen. 'You don't have to eat it if you don't want to.'

'No,' she says feebly. 'I do.'

'It doesn't matter. Here. Are you alright?'

'Yes.'

'Do you want to sit down?'

'No, no.'

'Are you angry with me?'

'No.' She takes the plate. 'I'm sorry, love. It's nothing to do with you. I've drunk too much. And I was thinking of someone else.'

'It doesn't matter,' Muriet says again. And then, the edge of curiosity creeping back into her voice, 'Who?'

'No one.'

'It can't have been no one, when you said it was someone.'

As if it matters, she thinks. As if it matters what I say. An inspector with nothing left to inspect, only good at being spoken to. Like a child, and with no one left to listen but a child.

She uncovers the plate, begins to eat. The ceviche is cold and delicate as snow, the flesh sweetened with vinegar. 'I was thinking of Nathan, and Nathan's father.'

'Oh. Are you angry with them?'

'I don't know.'

'How can you not know if you're angry?'

'It's a long story.' And then, before the girl can ask the inevitable, 'This is good.'

'Really?' She beams. 'Nathan said it was toxic.'

She is happy for the chance to laugh. 'I see. Toxic. And so you saved some especially for me?'

Muriet shrugs. 'Have you finished?'

'I'm finished.'

'Good. Now look. Aren't they brilliant?' Muriet says, and Anna follows her gaze. In the harbour a dozen sailing vessels lie still at their deep-water moorings, rigging belling with faint and desolate intermittence. In the half-light it is difficult to make out their scale. The largest are more ships than yachts, the nearest more than a hundred feet from bow to stern, the mainmast half as much again in height.

'That one's Nathan's,' Muriet says – breathes, as if the vessels are horses that might be startled – and for a moment Anna doesn't understand, the question is on her lips, before she realises that, of course, the nearest ship is Law's own. It is like seeing John himself for the first time – something spoken of so often it has become almost unbelievable. The yacht with thirty-seven rooms, some of which will play you music, so people say. Anything, you just have to ask.

'Isn't it beautiful?'

'Very,' Anna says, but without the conviction the word requires. Beside her Muriet stirs.

'I think it is.'

'Oh no, it is.'

'That's what I want. When I'm rich I'll have that.'

'What will you do with it?'

'I'll take Nathan. I'll take him and we'll sail away into the sunset.' She recites the phrase as if it has been learned by rote. As if the words have capitals, Sail Away.

'I was looking for him,' Anna says, and Muriet groans.

'You're always looking for someone.'

'What's wrong with that?'

'Anna,' patiently, 'people are trying to have a party.'

'Maybe I want to have a party with Nathan.'

'Well you can't, because you're having one with me.'

'We can be a party of three, can't we? Have you seen him?'

'I don't think so.' Muriet undoes her hair. Tails it, untails it.

'You don't know if you've seen him?'

'I think I've forgotten,' she says, and then, less discontentedly, 'Come on.'

'Where are we going now?'

'Nowhere. You need to walk.' She starts off eastwards, Anna falling in beside her. Making small talk, the boards slick and dark underfoot.

'What will you do when you reach your sunset?'

'Whatever we want. We'll have supplies. Food, medicine, computer games, money.'

'Like the Owl and the Pussycat. All wrapped up in a five-pound note.'

'What?'

'Nothing. It sounds like a good plan.'

'You can come too, if you like.'

'Really?'

'You can be my personal tax inspector. Except there won't be any taxes. You'll have more fun that way.'

'You're right, I will.'

In the dark her laughter sounds deeper, as if she has been sleeping. For a moment she says nothing else. She is feeling better already, the food and kindness have sobered her, her drunkenness is on the ebb and her headache with it. She can feel the girl beside her as they walk, fixedly imagining her world. Off with the sunsets.

They have come round to the back of the north wing. There are no more alcoves here, and no people that Anna can see. The wind is beginning to pick up, finally blowing the London January in across the river, and Muriet moves closer. Like a cat seeking warmth, Anna thinks, and her thoughts run on to the rhyme again, and to John's son, owlish, bone-thin, and the things his

211

father tells him.

'What about Nathan?' she says. But carefully, which is to say she is no longer only asking questions. 'What will Nathan be?'

'Whatever he likes. He knows everything.'

'No one knows everything.'

'Of course not, it's a figure of speech. But he knows how to sail. He knows how to read stars. He knows how to make code. His father taught him. He knows everything about numbers.' And then, almost as an afterthought, 'He knows you want to talk to him.'

'Does he?'

She feels the child shrug without seeing it. 'He knew it as soon as you came here. By the lake, he knew it then. He doesn't want to talk to you.'

'Did he say what I want to talk to him about?'

'What Mister Law tells him.' She states it matter-of-factly, as if the things Mister Law might tell are as uninteresting as evening conversation. They are at the railing now, side by side, leaning in jasmine.

'What did John tell him?'

'That's funny, you calling him John. Everybody else calls him Mister Law.'

'What did Mister Law tell Nathan?' She is stilted with impatience.

'I don't know, he didn't tell me,' Muriet says; not mischievously, but as if she is willing to be entertained. 'And if he did, I wouldn't tell you.'

'Why not?'

'Because it's a secret.'

212

'Not secrets again!'

'Yes. And you know what? Everyone should have secrets. And you ask people too many questions.'

'Maybe I do. Alright then, can you keep a secret?'

'Probably.'

'If I didn't have to, I wouldn't ask anyone anything.'

A stop. Muriet's face turning in the dark, astonished as the moon. 'But that's your job, finding out about people. It's what you like, that's what you said. Really?'

'Really.'

'Oh.' Muriet goes quiet. 'Don't you like your job any more?'

'Sometimes. I end up knowing a lot of things about a lot of people. It can be hard work, finding secrets, and even harder keeping them.'

'I know.'

'How?'

'Because of Nathan,' Muriet says, speaking her thoughts, her voice running on into the night air.

'Because of Nathan. It should make him happy, though. Sharing things with his father. He must be proud.'

Silence. It seems to Anna that there is a new edge to Muriet's expression. An element of reluctance or unease, as if something has happened to the conversation, the discussion of sunsets, which she almost understands, but not yet, not quite.

'It doesn't make him happy?'

'No.' The voice shrinking. 'It's cold. I want to go in now.'

'In a minute,' Anna says: and if a stranger were watching her at that moment he might notice the way she looks down at the child. It is an inspector's look, not cold or unkind or cruel, but soft and searching and definite. Like a surgeon locating the jugular.

She is an inspector, after all. She has been interviewing Muriet for some time: she knows it, even if the child does not. She has spent a third of her life in the acquisition of information, after all, it is what she knows, and without any doubt she knows there is information here to be acquired.

There is at least one more secret she would like to find, and to keep, if she can, if she could. Not for the Revenue, because she is not here as the Revenue. She is here as herself. She would like to understand John Law for herself.

'I talked to Anneli. She told me why Nathan was swimming that day.'

'She doesn't know why. Why?'

'Because of Helen.'

'What else?'

'The way he hurts himself.'

'He doesn't *hurt* himself.' Righteous indignation. 'That's a stupid lie.'

'That's what she said. She said he changes his medicine.'

'Yes, but –'

'She told me he started doing it last summer.'

214

'*Yes*, but it's alright because he knows how to do it, it's an experiment, he understands all about it, he measures everything –'

'Muriet,' she says, 'he could have died.' And it is true, of course. A true blackmail, though truth doesn't make it feel any better. It only makes it more effective.

Even so there is a moment when she thinks she has misjudged her timing. Seconds pass before the girl looks up, her face startled into woefulness. 'What will you do?'

'I'll find out what's upsetting him.'

'Will you make him happy again?'

She almost says yes. It is on her lips to do so. 'I can't promise that.'

'Will you try? Promise to try.'

'I'll try,' she says, 'I promise. Where is he?'

'Hiding,' Muriet says, and doesn't add, *from you,* as if that at least should be obvious.

'Will you take me?'

And she does: though this time, when she leads Anna away, she doesn't take her hand, but only walks ahead of her, as if shy to be seen with Law's inspector. They go back in silence, up through unlit rooms, backtracking, trying at locked doors, the crowd muted if audible at all, the floors and wings of Erith Reach changing, as if other architectures have been purchased and reassembled inside its walls, Frank Lloyd Wrights, le Corbusiers, French and Tuscan palaces, the child at Anna's side muttering to herself like an old woman in a cellar with a dropped key, *where was it, here was it, no this way*, and finally stopping at a door, opening it, peering in, and inside a long room full of slatted boxes, as if someone is about to leave or to arrive, a lifetime's supply of unopened possessions – small as books, big as trucks – and among them, sitting on them, a gaming board propped between them, are the people Anna is looking for: the man and the boy, looking up at the same time, with the same intent surprise.

'Anna,' John finally says, not as if she is wholly unanticipated, a pair of dice still in his palm, so that it is as if he has been waiting for her advice on the game at hand. She sees that they are playing, not chess, as she would have expected, but snakes and ladders. It is almost comical to see them there, with the old, simple game on its old, battered board. One of them is winning. One of them waits on the head of a snake.

'I didn't mean to—' Anna begins, not even sure what it is she has meant not to do, but Muriet drowns her out, loud with unhappiness.

'I didn't tell her, she just knew. I didn't bring her,' she cries, disregarding the evidence standing over her, and who in fact she is now trying to hide behind, her hands gripping Anna's waist. Only Nathan doesn't say anything. He gets to his feet, quiet and deathly pale, moving to stand in front of John, putting himself between his father and their visitor.

There is a second, a lull, when Anna feels a

missing piece fall into place. It is to do with the way the players looked as she first saw them from the doorway, before they noticed her arrival. She recalls the way John was watching his son. In her memory he is waiting for the boy to make a move he has already foreseen himself, it is very clear, an after-image. In a game of so much chance and little skill it is not a good move, Anna thinks, not something to be proud of for more than a moment, but even so, there is pride in the way John watches his son. Pride, pity and love, so that Anna, remembering, finds quite suddenly that she knows the answer to her question. She knows who John Law is rich for. The money hidden in the name of the son because it has always been meant for the son.

Then they are all talking at once. 'It's alright,' Muriet is saying to Nathan, 'she doesn't mean anything bad—' and again Anna is trying to say something – is it meant to be something as ridiculous as *Hello?* – to the man who has now risen from his seat, and who is saying her name again, conciliatory, she can't hear it, she can only see it, *Anna,* like a smile. But it is Nathan's voice which cuts through them all.

'You don't know anything! You don't know, you don't know!'

It is a chant, a child's catcall, mocking, celebratory and fearful. Anna looks up from him to see John turning back to his son, startled.

'Why are you here? Why did you come?' Derisive

vehemence. 'We don't want you here –'

'Nathan!' John says. 'That's enough.' But Nathan turns back on him, half as tall, twice as fierce.

'She shouldn't have come.'

'Anna? Why on earth not?'

'She's not your friend!'

'But you knew she was invited, didn't you? I thought you said—' And then, his eyes clearing, 'Is that why we've been traipsing around up here for so long, ignoring our guests? Because of Anna?' He laughs into his son's wounded silence. 'Are we hiding from the tax inspector?'

'You can't talk to her.'

'But I can. I invited her.'

'Why?'

'Because I like her. And I talk to who I like.' The jaw locking onto the repetition, the reined-in temper showing through the accent. How cruel we can be to children, Anna thinks. How kind they can be to us. 'She's my guest, Nathan, and you'll do me the favour of treating her like one.'

'She's not!' Nathan cries. 'How can she be your guest when she's not even your friend . . .' But his voice is failing. His eyes are unsettled. He looks as if he has been punished for something he doesn't understand, Anna thinks, and she feels Muriet's hands loosen around her.

'Come on. Nath.'

'What?'

'We've got to go now.'

'Why? No.'

'Come on.'

'You don't understand –'

'She's alright.' Muriet, whispering. 'She's not bad. Not really bad.' And after a moment Nathan looks up at John, as if searching for clues or instructions.

'Go on,' John says, quiet now.

'She's not your friend,' Nathan says for a third time, defeated, not looking at his father any more, and as he goes, Muriet trailing beside him, it is John's voice that comes back to Anna. *Are you my enemy, Anna, do you think?*

They wait until the children are gone. The door leans ajar behind them. Some trick of acoustics brings the sound of a piano, far distant. Someone is playing Rachmaninov, flourishing his phrases, showboating. All hands and no heart, Anna's father would have said, though it is a music her mother has always liked. She wonders if the pianist is Anneli.

'I didn't know if you were coming,' John says with abrupt awkwardness. He stands where the children have left him, looking in the direction of their departure, as if not sure what to do with himself now they are gone. 'I hoped. But when I didn't hear from you –'

'Well,' Anna says, 'here I am.' Which can hardly be a lie, she thinks, but is nevertheless an omission, a kind of untruth, since she suspects that John has been more than hopeful of her attendance. He has

219

been sure enough to put money on the chance – if Terence Cutler is to be believed – which he isn't, Anna thinks, though he isn't the only one to deserve little in the way of trust: and she shivers. Not at the thought of Terence or of John, but at the smooth and pervasive presence of deception.

She looks up to find his attention on her. He is studying her face as he always does – so intensely it is as if he might see her better than she sees herself – and she turns away, as she also always seems to do. The room is larger than she would have expected from its echo, a warehouse of an attic stretching into shadows, its landscape of crates softened by dust.

'Here I am,' she says again. 'But where am I?' and he laughs, following her gaze.

'To tell the truth, I'm not quite sure. I haven't been up here in a while. I'd hazard a guess this is where all the gifts go.'

'Gifts?'

'From people, you know. Corporations. Governments. And there are the things Anneli buys for us. She used to buy lots of things, when we were first married. Not so much now.' His face has fallen a little. He turns back. 'I'm glad you came. I've been thinking of you. How are you?'

'Fine.' She circles round to the boxes on which he and his son have been sitting.

'Good,' he says, and again, already he is searching for conversation, 'Good. I wanted to tell you I had a call.'

'What?'

'A message. From your mother.'

'Oh.' She sits down, stretching her legs. A tiredness settles over her, as if the evening has already lasted into the small hours. For a moment, like déjà vu, she has the sense of being an outsider again in a place with strange laws. Like the travellers in old stories, she thinks. Visitors of the Sidhe. Unfortunate guests. 'I didn't know she was going to do that. She didn't tell me.'

'It's fine.' He pauses. 'She sounded impressive.'

'That's one way of putting it, I suppose.'

'You're very different.'

'Thanks.'

'I didn't mean it like that. You said it yourself, once.' He hesitates again. 'She said you'd have a letter for me?'

'Did she?'

'Something about your sister, and a loan.'

'I don't want to take your money.' She says it quietly, she could be speaking to herself.

'Are you sure?'

'Yes.'

'Really, it's not a problem—' Eager, hurrying, forgiving her insult. 'You don't have to say anything now, I'd like to, it's an easy thing for me –'

'I don't want your money, John.'

'Alright,' he says, and stops. 'Okay.'

The silence grows between them, thick as dust, until she can't bear not to break it. And then he has done it first.

'It used to mean a lot to me.' He is smiling again, not at her now but at the goods around them, the halls and ziggurats of crates. 'Nathan's the same. More of everything, that's what he wants. He's never gone short of anything, but it's always been the same worry for him. Everything coming to nothing.' He trails off into the waiting silence, edgy, searching already for a way to break it again. 'If I was even ten years younger I wouldn't believe you could say no to an offer like that.'

'You're very close,' she says, and is glad when it pulls him up short. Wrong-footed, he looks back at her.

'Who?'

'You and Nathan.'

'Yes. We are, yes.'

'He means a lot to you.'

'He means everything to me. Anna –'

'You shouldn't have told him about the code,' she says, and waits for the time it will take him to answer.

'You know, then,' he says finally; almost, Anna thinks later, with relief. 'I wasn't sure. When did you –?'

'Oh, John. It doesn't matter, does it?'

'To me.' He sits down opposite her. The board still between them. 'It matters a little, to me. What are you going to do?'

'I don't know.'

'Will you tell the Revenue?'

'I don't know.'

222

'What would they do, do you think –'

'John,' she says, the name a refusal. The anger reaches her finally, as if the alcohol has dulled its progress. Her voice trembles, and it shocks her. It is not how she would ever speak to a client, and she wonders when she stopped thinking of John as that.

'I'm sorry. Really I am. It's in no way certain.' Encouraged, the animation creeping back into his face. 'Nothing's happened yet. It may be that nothing will –'

'The account in Nathan's name,' she says, not to stop him, although it does. 'You set it up years ago. You knew something was wrong then, didn't you?' She watches him, trying to be sure of his answer, but he won't look at her. 'A box full of real gold. And you didn't tell anyone. Didn't you tell anyone?'

He shrugs it off. 'There are people who would have found out anyway. There are others who worked it out for themselves, but most of the time no one listens to them. It isn't pleasant to distrust money. Look – I never said my work was perfect. People wanted to believe it, and I let them. It was what they wanted, it was what I wanted. But cryptography isn't a perfect science. The night I invented Soft Gold I thought I'd done something so near perfect, that no one would ever – no one would find the measure of the nearness. But I was wrong. I've known it for years. But I did think – I believed I had –'

After a moment he runs a thumb quickly across his mouth, along the upper lip where the sweat has settled. 'They could be wrong, though. I've tried to break it,' he goes on, half to himself. 'And always failed. That's to be expected, of course. The advantage will lie with others, and the less alike we are the better for them. I can't think of everything. It's what I can't think of that will be the end of it. It isn't that everyone thinks of everything, only that someone will always think of something. One day, someone will find the measure by which my work falls short, and they'll work at it until the numbers crack. There's no shortage of people who would love to see it happen. There are those who want to break Soft Gold just because it's there. It's their golden mountain, and they'll never give up until they . . . they're not fools, either. Not all of them. I've watched them. They're becoming more organised. They write to me. I try not to read the messages, but sometimes they get through. Have they talked to you –?' And when she doesn't answer, 'Anna, listen, I've been working on this for years, a decade or more now, and I think I almost have it. I could stay one step ahead, if I knew what they meant to do. What I mean is, I've been perfecting a new design, and if – if you could just let me have a little more time –'

He is stuttering, stumbling over the words. If she didn't know him it would surprise her. She knows too much about lies not to understand what he is doing to himself. 'Why did you tell him?' she says, and he grins with unhappiness.

'Ah, no. You've got it wrong, that wasn't how it was. It was worse. I was working all night. I must have fallen asleep. When I woke up he was reading my notes. He'd already worked it out for himself. He was proud, he wasn't worried. It was only later he realised what I was doing, and what it meant—' He looks into her face, searching. 'I swear it. Anna. Please. Try and believe me.'

'That's the second rule.'

'What?'

'The second rule of tax inspection. Never believe the client,' she says, still angry, too angry, and he frowns, angry a little now himself.

'Is that what I am?'

'It's what you were. And you lied, John, you lied to me all the time! And you knew what it was doing to him!'

'I knew, and I knew what it would do to him if I gave up. To him and to uncountable others. I never meant to hurt anyone, I thought I could give them something –'

'Oh, don't. What about Pandora? How good was that for the uncountable others?'

'Anna, that was decades ago, I was just a child then –'

'Like Nathan,' she says. 'A child like Nathan,' and watches as he folds.

'I'm trying to make things right –'

'Right? Who elected you to decide what's right?'

'No one. Anna, don't be like this –'

'What about the right to know? Is that not right enough for you?'

'It wouldn't help. It would be the worst thing. This is business, not politics. What should I do, then, what should I say? "I'm sorry to announce that mistakes have been made. Please don't be alarmed. Remember your savings will always be safe with SoftMark, where the new millennium is now available." Money is trust, Anna, that's all. Break it and you have nothing.'

'It wouldn't have to be like that.' She shakes her head, driving herself on, willing him and his conviction away, though she is tired of it already. She wishes they could stop. 'I knew there was something, but I couldn't be sure. I wouldn't let myself realise. I never thought you'd be so stupid, that you'd do anything so –'

He stands, as if no longer able to sit beside her. 'Please. It's nothing yet. Nothing's certain. There's nothing yet to be afraid of.'

'Why didn't you tell me?'

'I didn't know if I could trust you.' He stops beside her, not touching. 'I thought I could, but I wasn't sure. I don't know now. Anna.'

'What?'

'Can I trust you?'

It takes a while for her to consider it. A minute to find it in herself to laugh. The anger in her winding itself out to a hollow ache.

'What is it?' John says, and reaches for her, his hand on her shoulder, her neck.

226

'It's funny. All the time I've known you, and I was asking myself the opposite. Maybe it was the wrong question.'

'What was that?'

'Whether I could trust you.'

She gets to her feet. At the periphery of her vision she can sense John's presence. It is almost threatening, as if in his bewilderment he might try to reach out and stop her. As if he might box her up with the uncountable gifts. She is abruptly aware of how much bigger he is than her, and how alone she is, whenever she is with him: how alone they always are, together. And I am the threat, she thinks, after all.

'What are you doing?'

'I have to go.'

'Why?' he asks. And then, 'Not like this.'

She puts her hand to his cheek. He doesn't close his eyes, as she would have done herself. She holds his face as if she could memorise it. But he looks so unlike himself – lost and ashamed – and it is not how she would choose to remember him.

'Thanks.'

'For what?'

'Everything.'

'Anna,' he says, as if he is asking for something, though she has no idea what, and she wonders if he does, either. Later it occurs to her that it is only her silence. As she reaches the door he calls her name again, and then she is out, walking fast, not looking back as she passes down through the stairs and halls of Erith Reach, descending through the places she has been led, the rooms full of laughter and idle revelation, the courtyards of secluded lovers, the mutter of water, the corridors with Miró walls, the letter in her pocket like a weapon, the crowd casting long and mobile shadows, the valets waiting in white gloves, the car warm and dark as a head. And still, creeping in, insistent, indelible, following her out into the ordinary traffic of the city night, there is the smell of gunpowder, which to Anna has always been the smell of Autumn, of Fall, and after tonight always will.

All night she lies awake and listens to the aeroplanes. Her thoughts are measured in flight paths. Every hour or half hour she is stilled by a sound like something opening, as if the sky has slid apart. Each time, as it fades, there is the soft rush of the motorway: calming, tidal. The airport is less than two miles away. It is something she ceased to notice years ago, so that its sounds come to her now like recollections. They remind her, not of John or of herself, or of what either of them has done, or of who has done who wrong, but of others. Millions of people, more than could ever meet, and more profit and loss than could be accommodated in the thoughts of anyone. The uncountable lives.

The lives that touch her go on without her. Eve sends her enigmatic flowers two nights before Martha calls, low with gratitude, to thank her:

228

and she accepts both the thanks and the news that Martha's debts are paid as best she can, with a shadow of guilt but without any real sense of anger or surprise. Less expected is the news that Carl has been promoted over her – his face on a February morning alight with a surplus of joy – but the politics of the Revenue seem distant, and her failure leaves her only with a curious sense of relief, as if a grip has loosened on her of which she was never wholly aware.

It is spring before she sees Lawrence again, at a small restaurant east of the Angel. He is quieter than she remembers. At the time she thinks it is because of the apology he never gives again, the discomfort of it, and only the next morning does she remember it is because she talked so much herself. Lawrence patiently listening while the food grew cold between them, his keen eyes following her as she talked and talked and said nothing, more grateful than she can allow herself to know that nothing is all he asks of her.

And in April she calls Tunde Finch. She has kept his card for months, conveniently forgotten in a pocket, but the thought of him is harder to put out of her mind. She leaves a message for him finally, distracting herself into doing it, half hoping for no reply, but he calls back within hours, his voice urgent and eager.

Their meeting – on an unseasonably warm night broken by rain, when every street smells of wet dog – is less than either might have hoped for. He looks diminished, Anna thinks. Almost wretched, as if Erith Reach gave him some dignity he lacks out in the real world. There is a rash of eczema across one side of his neck, rising up under the hairline, which he scratches or touches as he talks, as if for luck. Their conversation is stilted as they walk along the river from the Tower to the Needle.

'You like him,' Tunde says, the Thames at his far side turning seawards, so that if Anna looks at it too often it is as if they are walking backwards, like people in bad dreams.

'Why shouldn't I?'

'No reason. I like him too.'

She slows her pace. 'Really?' she says, and he smiles, but thinly, this time. No longer quite so likeable himself.

'Alright. You've got me. But I do respect him. I admire his talent. You know, back in the 1950s, the first computer programmers used to play a game called Core Wars. What they did, you see, they made organisms out of numbers. Then they would see which one could take over a computer. That's how viruses started. That's what those early programmers were making, they just didn't know it yet. Soft Gold is a virus too, a tame virus. Mister Law has been playing Core Wars for a long time now, and he's been on a winning streak. An admirable streak, but nobody wins for ever. Nobody would permit it. It goes against the public grain. I'm not the one who's going to hurt him.'

'Then who is? Do you know?' she asks, and he

shakes his head, perhaps only declining to answer, the street lights beyond him wrapped in iron vines and monstrous fish.

'Do you remember Bill Gates? "I'm waiting for the anticlimax." That's what he had to say about failure. He knew it comes to everyone in the end. Mister Law knows it too. They say he can't break his own code. I've always wondered if that's true. They say so much – they talk so much they never listen. It changes without human intervention, have you heard that one? That's supposed to be a strength. But I think it cuts both ways. If no one knows how Soft Gold will change, how long before they realise if it changes for the worse? Will he know, do you think? Anna?'

But Anna doesn't answer, and when the second cryptographer asks her what she has done, who she has told, what she intends to do, she has no answers to those questions either. No answers and no excuses, so that his face falls and his voice becomes edged with disappointment – but not, she thinks later, surprise – the gulls above them rising, riding the air, their mewling like an animal mimicry of laughter. At the next Underground station he leaves her without saying goodbye, head down, hands buried in his pockets, shouldering his way into the Westminster evening crowd, and she never meets him again.

Each morning her office waits for her. It seems ugly to her now, thoroughly unlikeable, half her life and no part of it. A room with a distant view of people, thereby well suited to its purpose.

She keeps the blinds drawn and takes up smoking. It is a habit which has never attracted her before, but now she finds she likes it. It reminds her of Anneli. The selfish little acts of cigarettes, the way their use measures out time.

What will she do? Who will she tell? Nothing and no one. It is not a decision she makes. It does not feel like a choice. The sun creeps through the blinds, across her neck, in beads of light.

It is the thought of John, waiting for her betrayal. It is the glimpse of his desperation. She wishes she could talk to him again, but she cannot bring herself to do so. It feels as if it is already too late. She would tell him that she is only in possession of the facts, as she has always been. That she has a secret to keep, and that she always keeps her secrets. And that she loves him. She was ready to love him before she ever met him. She would like to tell him that.

There are days when she attempts to lose herself in her work and others when, as far as she can recall, she does no work at all. The smoke idling from her hand, the thought of John coming to her repeatedly, a dull ache of recollection or imagination, each time different but the same, like variations in music. She spends her days waiting, just as in her thoughts he is always waiting: for her, or for her to act for him. Or waiting as he has always done, she sees now, for a price to be exacted. A man waiting for the fall.

II

FALL

It begins in small ways, in the smallest hours, when there are few to notice and there is little to be done. It shows itself minute by minute, in ways that are easy to doubt, like night weather, rain that might clear by morning. And it happens quietly, and so far from anywhere, that for some time it is as though nothing has happened at all.

On the island of Copper, in the overheated Quonset huts of the Nikolskoe research station, wearing nothing but unwashed thermal underwear and a 'From Here You Can See Tomorrow' T-shirt, Matti Pellinen is dreaming of sober men as she inputs data from the Aleutian Abyssal Plain – its sunken cliffs and isles and spires. It is only in passing that she registers the moment when her screen shudders, the graphics distorting along their peaks and troughs. It is, she thinks, as if a williwaw, an Arctic squall, has passed through its electricity.

On Ebon, where twenty of Anna's cigarettes will buy more albacore than a man can eat, the Reverend Toke Tsitsi, Minister for Internal Affairs, checks his savings late at night – it is his personal remedy for insomnia – and has no one to tell (or at least, tells no one) when he finds he has been credited with twice the gross national product of his country. It will come to seem a small thing by morning, though it doesn't yet appear so to the Reverend, as he waits for light in sleepless joy.

On the lightship tender *Mimir IX*, east-north-east of the Ross Ice Shelf, Jan Luettringhaus is watching twentieth-century films as the clock turns through midnight, his face blue in the laptop's light, Oates's famous last words going round and around his head (*I may be some time, I may be some time*) until he longs to call his sister and ask her if he sounds mad yet: so that when he tries, and finds his account terminated, he knows no better than to blame the sea and the life that has brought him to it. Forgetting that it is money that makes the world go round, and money that will bring it to a stop.

In the days that follow there will be other stories, better ones, as stories go, as if there is comfort in the betterment, or grace in the improbable. On Nauru – so the story goes – the burden of national debt is lifted by Jacky Chong Gum, a quick-thinking state accountant working on her first job through the night. In Alice Springs, Bapp Walker Muir, a farmhand of no fixed address, spends thirty-seven minutes as the richest person ever born inside the southern hemisphere. In Magadan, Siberia, a modest high-school student makes eleven hostile takeover bids for leading German football teams, answering questions only as the Emperor Siberius.

There are people who turn on their computers to find personalised messages – *Happy Birthday Nikos From the Dateline Virus – Welcome to the Fall* – and whole towns where nothing happens at all, as if a storm has passed them over. And as it seems to do so the world turns on, longitude by longitude, into the new day.

It is 22 September, 2021. A Friday, autumn in London and Westminster, fall in New York, though on Nauru and Ebon there is no such season, and on Copper there are no trees which would give such a thing meaning. Later there will be those who search the date for motives, and contrive to find them, though history can lie in this way, through its endless accumulation of fact. (It is the first day of the Revolutionary Calendar, the first of Vendémiaire, Year One; the first morning of the People's Republic of China; the name-day of Jonah, who lay hidden in the belly of the whale.) There will be theories, contagious in themselves. (That the virus was made in America, the last place on earth it will reach. That it was propagated by John Law, a man grown deadly tired of waiting. That it was written by a twelve-year-old in Mecca, a ten-year-old in Jenin, two children in Lucknow.) And as the truth dawns, hour by hour, or falls, as night falls, there will be accusations, and with them the search for justice or at least recompense and most of all for those responsible: and in their lengthening, mystifying absence, for somewhere else to lay the blame. For scapegoats.

237

That comes later. At first there is little of anything. By design, the International Dateline crosses some of the least populous areas of the earth. There are too few people to notice the scale of what is happening. For the most part, as the virus goes about its work, there are only doubts, warnings from unrecognised addresses, the small talk of the Internet, a sporadic mutter of telephones. Unread queries and questions sent across the empty miles of the Pacific and the Bering Sea. The Chathams and the Gilberts, the navigation stations, bare hills of ice plant and speargrass.

It is four hours before midnight reaches Tokyo. By then rumours have already begun to precede the events themselves – the whisper that something has gone wrong with money – but then there are always rumours, foreigners say so many things, and at nine o'clock the stock exchange opens its five ponderous western doors to the glittering pollution of the Nihombashi rush hour.

In the minutes that follow the index begins to fall. It happens slowly at first, in thin trading, unpleasant but never unexpected – the brokers grimacing over their plastic-adorned *bento* breakfasts – the pace of change only accumulating as unease crystallises into fear.

By the time the floors are closed it is already too late. It is as if, through money, time has slipped backwards. In less than two hours, the world has been set back scores of years. The faces broadcast, later wiped out, sagging with the understanding that something has gone wrong, and so critically wrong that decades have been swept away, like ships and houses by great waves. Whole lives, if lives can be measured in money; and they can, since they are. In greed and generosity and desire.

The faces are not the first Anna knows of it. All morning and on into the afternoon she has been interviewing clients at the Revenue, a parade of similarly abject men in similar second-best suits. She eats late and alone in a sidestreet café, not far from the green plot by St Paul's where she once sat with Lawrence.

It is a fine day, the sky above the dome all mares' tails, and the café is one she likes, both for its giant tarnished urn of tea and for the fact that she has never met anyone from the Revenue there. It is a place where no one knows her as anything more than a customer.

She is thinking she has time for a walk, a long short-cut along the river, her reports can wait, when she hears Tunde Finch. His voice drifts down around her, disembodied, too close for comfort, and she looks round sharply, as if to catch a ghost.

The café is as good as empty. An old woman in old clothes talks to her cup as she draws it towards her. An unshaven man in an Underground uniform leans at the counter, waiting to pay the waitress, his face set idly towards the television. The TV –

single-function, pensionable – hangs from a cradle of bars in the stained corner above the entrance. Anna has to stand up before she can see the figure on the screen.

The second cryptographer is seated in a bucket chair, talking to someone out of sight. He is wearing a dark suit – the same one, Anna thinks, that he wore at Erith Reach. He stops talking only when the interviewer interrupts him with questions, though for a few seconds Anna is too surprised to understand what is being asked or answered. It is a shock to see him again, or perhaps it is that Tunde looks so shocked himself, as if his feelings could be transmitted across the waves.

The cameras have closed in on his profile, Anna can make out the rash by his hairline, the rough skin inadequately brushed with make-up. 'Not sleeping,' he says, in answer to a question Anna has missed. 'I wouldn't say that. I would say incubating.'

'But what do you mean by that, incubating?' The interviewer is professionally terse, her impatience verging on the accusatory. She looks as if she is having the day from hell; which she is, of course, though in that she is not alone. The camera draws back to encompass them both.

'It means, well. What I mean is, by incubation, it has probably changed since its arrival –'

'And this would have been months? Or are we talking about longer than that? Can you be specific?'

'No. Months, or yes, it could have been years,' Tunde's face bright under the studio lights, his voice stuttering. 'To have spread itself so widely, to have infiltrated systems like, like this – we do know there must have been a long period when –'

'You say infiltrated systems, but it seems to be only Soft Gold which is infected. Only that currency, which is something you have been predicting would happen for years –'

'Yes, but – I see what you're implying – but people have been trying to break Soft Gold ever since its inception, and no one has ever come close –'

She understands ahead of time, which is to say before those around her. Her first thought is for herself, since she has done nothing these last months: has taken no steps to save what she has, such as it is. She has never exchanged her Soft Gold for possessions. She has only been waiting, all this time, has felt drained to invisibility by expectancy, all year, as if she has taken on the nature of Law's money. And now it is too late to save herself anyway.

This is it, she thinks, here we are. She is surprised to find she isn't scared. Instead what she feels is the first faint stirring of guilt. And overlying that, and stronger, a sense of primitive relief, as when rain comes.

'They was dear little things,' says the old woman to no one in particular, her gaze lingering on Tunde's neck. 'Scratch and Sniff, that's what we

241

used to call them, but we meant it nice. Scratch and Sniff, what with the eczema and the rhinitis.'

'Quiet a minute, Lucy,' says the waitress, wiping her hands on a cloth, and Lucy sighs and goes quiet.

'. . . But if a system with Soft Gold installed cannot operate commercially,' the interviewer is saying, 'then the unbreakable code has been broken by default. Hasn't it?'

'I don't know.' Tunde looks lost, as if unable to convince himself of what he has spent so long trying to convince others to believe. 'It could be that the code has been corrupted. The reports seem to suggest that something has gone wrong with the transaction process, that accounts are miscalculating figures of Soft Gold as they are received. In that case it may be the gate mechanism in the Soft Gold program which is infected, and not the money itself . . . but this isn't yet proven, it isn't something I can confirm. What the Dateline Virus has most clearly corrupted is the atmosphere of trust any currency needs to operate. Trust is the weakness here. There are things that not even John Law can encrypt –'

He pauses, tries to sit upright, the bucket chair working against him. Behind him the channel logo has been replaced by a new headline, SOFT GOLD MELTDOWN, the middle word intermittently obscured by Tunde's hair. 'Tunde Finch, MRE, on the Dateline Virus crisis,' the interviewer says with finality, and the cameras swing back to

242

her, Tunde left behind, as he always is, Anna thinks distantly, the bearer of bad tidings, the shot messenger, his voice carrying on for a few seconds before that of the interviewer overrides it.

'Worldwide, emergency measures are being taken to combat the Dateline Virus, with experts suggesting that by bypassing tomorrow's date hardware may be immunised against the threat. But the success of the operation is not yet clear, and with an estimated three and a half billion computers in use globally, many efforts are a race against time. Administration in Britain is reportedly already being hampered by the knock-on effects of the virus itself. Later we hope to talk with John Law, the creator of Soft Gold – the soft money that comes with an "Unbreakable" guarantee – and in a moment we will be discussing what can be done before the virus reaches Britain at midnight tonight. But news is still coming in of the catastrophic financial fallout occurring throughout Asia and the Pacific Rim, and the damage is already being felt here in London, where Soft Gold has now fallen seven per cent against a basket of soft currencies, and images of events further east have caused widespread shock and anger.'

'I always said, didn't I?' says Lucy.

'What are they talking about?' says the Underground worker. 'What are they going on about now?'

'Lucy,' says the waitress, anxiously, glancing at the man. 'We're trying to listen.' But Lucy is no longer prepared to keep her peace, and pats the table for emphasis.

'I always said. Don't trust the Electrics.'

There is a moment of silence. Outside a heavy figure in a City suit goes past at an ungainly jog. Then the spell is broken, and the Underground man swears blackly under his breath and makes for the door, his moneycard in his hand, the bill for his tea left unpaid, the waitress shouting after him, distraught, as if he has left her herself, the old woman serenely watching them both. The screen above them cutting away to other, remoter pictures, the footage of the stock exchanges – Sydney and Jakarta, Hong Kong and Tokyo, Pusan, Taiwan, Surabaya, Singapore. The floors first alive, then emptying, the cameras moving silently between the bloodbaths.

Outside the traffic is slow, metal shouldering past metal. There are sirens, light and panicky in the distance, just as there are any other working day. As far as Anna can tell there is nothing yet out of the ordinary, though she looks for the expressions of the drivers all the same as she dodges between their company cars and limousines.

It is three uneven London blocks back to Limeburner Square. By the time she gets there she is out of breath, and one of many. A queue of people starts on the Revenue steps and degenerates into a crowd somewhere inside the fountained atrium. There is a sense of anxiety, as there always is, here, but also of expectancy, an eagerness which is out of place in the Revenue's grey halls. A pregnant woman in a gold sari sits watchfully, a numbered ticket in her hand. A man with dreadlocks and no shoes is asking for his money back.

Anna is apologising her way through when she catches sight of Carl by the elevators. He is stabbing the buttons repeatedly, his executive suit rucked up, as if he has been grabbed by the scruff of the neck. Beside him a younger inspector is making himself as insignificant as possible. Only as Anna reaches them does Carl look up, his face foul with anger.

'About time.'

'I only just heard.'

'Bollocks! You could have gone for lunch in Outer fucking Mongolia, you'd know by now. It's only been a fucking hour. We need you here. Look at this.' He nods backwards at the crowd, his forehead creasing in a snarl. 'The receptionists have gone into hiding. There was a lawyer in here demanding a rebate. A *rebate*! What do they want?'

'Money?' she says, but it is as much a question as an answer. It occurs to her that the crowd looks more lost than anything, as if most of its members would like someone to tell them what to do.

'Well they're not going to get it here, are they? Who do they think we are?'

'We don't get paid enough for this,' says the

younger inspector, with unobtrusive sullenness, and Carl goes on, oblivious.

'And what do they expect us to do? What is wrong with this fucking button?'

'Or explanations,' Anna says to one question of five as the doors hiss open.

'Then they can join the queue. Get in,' he says briskly, and she does. 'Not you, Goater.'

'Why?'

'Because I want to talk to Anna in private, you lanky strip of piss.'

The doors ease shut. Through the plexiglass Anna watches Goater's aggrieved face fall away. Carl is adjusting his jacket beside her.

'Ambitious little cunt. It's people like him who give us a bad name. Where's your computer?'

'Upstairs.'

'Take it down to Tech. They want to delete tomorrow.'

'Tomorrow?' she says, and, understanding, recalling the news report, 'Will that work?'

'How the hell would I know?' He is still smoothing his jacket, grimly working out the creases. 'We'll find out soon enough, won't we?'

As they ascend his face calms. London and Westminster spread out below them, tinted blue through the glass walls. 'I can't believe it,' he says eventually. He licks his lips, stretches them back across his teeth, a monkey grin, humourless. 'No, I can't. Can you?'

She shakes her head and wishes it were true.

If she had told Carl – if she had warned Martha or Lawrence or Eve – what would have happened then? She looks out at the city – the City of Money – its roads and towers, the empty thoroughfare of the river. Nothing is yet visibly out of place. She wonders if John is here, and if the world has changed because of him. If such a thing could be so imperceptible, here of all places.

If he is here, she thinks, he is at Erith Reach. If he is there, he is watching his life unfold around him. She wonders if he cares, or not that, exactly – of course he cares! – but she wonders if he cares enough to fight for it.

It used to mean a lot to me.

He must care. She wishes, suddenly and guiltily, that her first impulse had not been to come to the Revenue. But it is too late now.

'How the mighty have fallen,' Carl says out of nothing, and Anna looks back at the oddity of the phrase, the echo of her thoughts. 'That's what they used to say. All those clichés. The harder they come. Too big for his boots. What goes up. Riding for a fall. They're all just different ways of saying the same thing, aren't they?'

'Are they?'

'You tell me, you're the one who reads. Riding for a fall,' Carl says again, lingering over the phrase. His voice has turned meditative, and amused. There is a warmth to it. 'That's what he's been doing, isn't it?'

'Who?' But she already knows who. She understands, abruptly, why Carl wanted to talk to her in
private.

He shakes his head, leaning against the far wall,
watching her down the length of his sharp face.
'All this time I thought he was—' He makes an
odd gesture, finger and thumb narrowing along
parallels, a mime of exactitude. 'Living the dream.
The biggest and the wettest. But he wasn't, was
he? Not if he knew. If he knew it must have been
terrible. Do you think he knew?'

'Of course not,' she says. But Carl nods, as if
she has given a different answer. She has an abrupt
sense of claustrophobia, of having walked stupidly
into an undisguised trap. She wishes she were back
in the café, where no one knows her. This is how
it must feel, she thinks dully. This is how it is, to
come here as a client.

They are approaching her level, decelerating.
She wills it closer, *Come on*, her stomach sinking
into her guts.

'They'll kill him, you know,' Carl says. His eyes
are darker than she remembers. She wonders if he
has started wearing contacts.

At last the elevator stops. The doors don't open.
Carl stays where he is, leaning comfortably. His
new office is floors above. 'Don't think they
won't.'

'Why?'

'Because he's there.'

The doors open. She steps out backwards.

'They'll kill him,' Carl says again. 'And if they don't, I will. I want to see you later. We need to talk!' he yells as the doors close, and then he is gone, rising beyond her.

'The world should never change at midnight. It's uncivilised. It's hard to maintain the appropriate hysteria after dinner. I find I'm getting used to it, you know, already. It's a talent I have for adjusting to the unthinkable. I'd like to go to bed, in fact, but I don't think it's allowed, is it? I'm really too old to be sitting at my computer at all hours, waiting for my life savings to turn into pumpkins.'

'Stop complaining.'

'I don't see why I should.'

'Because you're not too old for anything. You're only sulking because they closed your bar. And you haven't got any life savings. That's what you always told me.'

'Oh, well. Everyone has something. Everyone has something to lose. My neighbours have been sharing their sorrows with one another for hours. Mister Myhrvold has a plan to sue John Law on our behalf and invest the damages in pigs. He says pigs don't get viruses. Which I don't think is quite right. And Justine came down to cry on my shoulder. She's the pianist. She also did something very exciting to my computer. A gifted woman.'

'How nice for you.'

'No, everyone seems to be complaining, except you, Anna. Why is that?'

She shrugs, as if the line might convey motion. She is balancing the mobile in the hollow of her shoulder, the live plastic warm against her bone. On the tablet screen two news bulletins are playing in overlapping windows, the sounds turned down, anchors mouthing like actors in silent films. On one a countdown is in progress. On the other a man in Alexandria is burning an effigy.

The man's anger has already faded. He looks embarrassed to be caught on camera. The effigy is faceless, vaguely masculine. It could be almost anyone.

'The point about complaining,' Lawrence says, 'is that it maintains the illusion that something can be done. Besides, it's not as if anyone has anything better to do.' There is a sound, a faint clink on the line. Glass against glass. 'Anna? Are you still there?'

'Yes.'

'Oh, good. Why are we whispering?'

She glances up at the office door. Through the glass panels figures are visible, blurred and surreptitious, passing between offices. The Revenue is hushed but not silent, neither empty nor occupied in the manner to which it is accustomed. In the adjoining offices inspectors are gathered around their computers, Carl and Janet and Mister Hermanubis, as well as the younger generation, the newer recruits who talk to Anna with guarded respect, if at all. A year ago she would have joined them. Now she goes quiet as they pass. It is eleven fifty-two. Eight minutes to midnight.

'Anna?' Lawrence says again.

'What?'

'Do you remember my grandmother?'

She tries, smiling, accepting the offer to think of other things. A frail woman, fine-boned as Meissen, poised at a café table. 'You've got a photo on your desk. I don't think I ever met her, sorry.'

'No, you didn't, did you? Probably all for the best. You would have hated one another. She was a tax inspector too when she was young, in Essen, in Germany. Very loud. Another drinker, I'm afraid. And when I was young she used to tell me – as bedtime stories – what it was like between the wars. The years when money became worth less and less, until it was nothing but the paper it was printed on. Not money at all. The legendary wheelbarrows of banknotes. I used to have terrible nightmares about it all.'

'Well, that's one thing, I suppose.'

'What?'

'There won't be any wheelbarrows now.'

'She used to say it was like a delirium. People didn't believe their money was falling. They thought it was a conspiracy, that all the other currencies in the world were rising. The first sign of madness, you see – that nothing had changed except everyone else. It sent everyone a little mad. That's what she used to say. What time is it?'

She checks the screen. 'We've still got a little while.'

'Have you talked to him?'

She doesn't pretend not to understand. With Lawrence there is no point. 'No.'

'Don't you think that you should?'

'What would he have to say to me?'

He sighs impatiently. 'If you called him, you might find out.'

She doesn't reply. She doesn't mention Carl. Everyone, it seems, would like her to talk to John Law. For a moment she wishes she was at home, between her own four walls, with Burma to warm her and ask for nothing. It is too late now, though, and here there is at least a sense of power. The illusion, as Lawrence says, that something might be done.

'I've been thinking.'

'Of seeing him?'

'Of leaving.'

'Leaving what?' And then, as it comes to him, 'My God. The Revenue? Don't be ridiculous. Why? Since when? What else could you do?'

'Raise pigs?'

'Anna, you shouldn't just laugh about it –'

'Why not? There are other ways of making a living.'

'Of course,' he says, but not as if he believes it. 'Oh well, of course there are.'

'This isn't everyone's idea of the perfect job.'

'It's perfect for you.'

'No,' she says. 'It's not.' And to herself: It was. And I was perfect for them, but not any more. I am not the person I expected myself to be.

'Well,' Lawrence says, uncertainly gentle, 'if that's what you want. I'm sure you'll make a wonderful pig farmer.'

'Thanks.' She checks the screen. 'It's time.'

'So it is. I'll open the champagne.'

'I never liked it.'

'I know. Should we link hands, then?'

'I don't think I can reach that far.'

'I would very much like something to hold onto,' Lawrence says, not entirely steadily, and then just as Anna is about to reply she finds she can no longer hear him. From the interior of the Revenue a shout goes up, an angry excitement, as if an argument has broken out, and beyond the open window of the office the bells of St Stephen's Tower begin to sound. A carillon, reversed and repeated. A ring of twelve, old and dark as grime, toll following toll out across the miles of Westminster and London.

One way or the other, music always reminds Anna of childhood. Most often it will be her father who comes back to her. The spread of his hands, the set of his face (which is like Lawrence's. It is not something she denies to herself.) It still seems to her an odd thing, that for all his love of music she can never remember him singing. As far as she knows he never did so – but doesn't everyone sing sometimes? – nor learned to play an instrument. His pleasure was in the listening.

Sometimes it is different. Sometimes she hears a verse of a song, certain hymns or traditionals, and it is Eve she remembers. When that happens it is not her mother's face that comes to her, but her voice. Her memories of Eve are not of a woman listening – her mother never sat still for anything – but singing.

The songs were always the same, old and grim as fairy tales, like the stories of Lawrence's grandmother. Anna has never known where they came from, who wrote them, though there was a sameness about them: it doesn't seem impossible that her mother made them up herself. And Eve's voice was poor, though it was kinder then, in the days before she lost her way in her marriage, before the years when she slept alone and woke bitter. Less harsh than it has become. And perhaps because of this, it is not the music of the songs that Anna still remembers, but their words, which always seemed to be about love or money, money or love.

> Well money has its own way
> And money has to grow.
> It grows on human blood and bone
> As any child should know.
> It's iron stuff and paper stuff
> With no life of its own
> And so it gets its growing sap

254

From human blood and bone,
Blood and bone.

As if in a different life, she remembers being sung to sleep. The sensation of slippage and descent. Her mother's voice. Lightness, darkness.

She wakes at her desk from dreams of childhood, knowing nothing of where she is or why, only alert to the fact that something is wrong, out in the world. This time there is no doubt about it.

The office is bathed in light. The blinds rule it with shadow. A foot from her face the mobile lies keeled over on one side, the power still on but fading, the display dim: Lawrence's number selected, ready to be dialled. The room smells of gin and, more inexplicably, of cigars. A water cone lies on its side in a thin pool of neat spirit.

Her eyes are dry. She closes them again. For a while she stays like that, listening. There is a pain in her neck, not entirely unpleasant, just enough to stop her falling back into sleep. The sun comes and goes, as if clouds are passing rapidly across it. But it is earlier than the light suggests, she can hear it in the familiar routines of the building around her. And already there is something out of place.

Someone is singing. The voice seems unfamiliar, though it comes to her that she wouldn't be able to put a name to it even if she knew it: the inspectors of the Revenue do not sing as they go about their work. The singer pauses – there is the bony rattle of a keyboard – then goes on, graceless but serious, somewhere in the rooms beyond the partitioned walls.

Do you think you've hit bottom?
Do you think you've hit bottom? Oh no.
There's a bottom below.
There's a low below
The low you know.
You can't imagine
How far down you can go
Down.

It is a change of sorts, though not one she would have expected. All day she notices it, and for days afterwards. As if it could fill some vacancy, there is suddenly music everywhere, in the most unexpected places, often awkward, most often unfamiliar. It is almost like a celebration.

In Limeburner Square an old man takes up residence by the fountains and plays the violin every morning for hours, unaccompanied, asking for nothing, so that people are at a loss for what to do about him. On Saturdays an ice-cream van begins to work her neighbourhood, playing its xylophone fragments, out of season and out of tune, something she hasn't heard in years. In the Revenue itself there is a discordance of radios and web stations, each one at first broadcasting news, and each giving way to music as the days pass. The interview rooms and locked repositories echoing with a dozen warm ghosts of Elvis, a tuneless drift of Madonnas, the austerity of plainsong. Mister Hermanubis singing in the corridors.

It is a benign kind of madness, Anna thinks, remembering what Lawrence told her: though his words are brought back to her soon enough in other, more malignant ways. Three nights after Soft Gold falls she comes home to find the study window broken, glass winking inwards underfoot. It takes weeks for her to be sure of everything that is gone. A box of rings she never wears, a Venetian mirror she ceased to like years ago, the best clothes she has always loved. No books, an oversight for which she is pathetically thankful. And somehow – she tries to imagine it – the refrigerator, with nothing spilled or left behind.

We're the lucky ones, Janet says. And Anna says yes, they are lucky, though she isn't sure if it is true, or if true what difference it makes. The information they have received and the measures they have taken work – their own accounts, the accounts of the Revenue, are not corrupted by the broken code – but the damage is already done. Day by day Soft Gold is worth less, its value dropping through benchmarks and plateaux and barriers as if it has suddenly discovered gravity. As if there is some end in sight from which it cannot be separated.

There are other currencies into which people can put their trust. They do so desperately, sometimes doubtfully, but most of all bitterly, in sorry anger, like believers who have lost their faiths through personal loss. Nor is it only Soft Gold they have ceased to believe in. In the last week of September the dollar becomes tender again, and by October, under emergency measures, the Royal Mint reopens its production lines. The world becomes more physical, or so it seems to Anna, its desire for wealth rooted again in touchable things. Metal stuff and paper stuff. Fridge-freezers and Venetian mirrors.

There is only that one day when the world seems without money, the twenty-second itself, the first of Vendémiaire. And even though it is an illusion – even though money is not something that can be uninvented or lost – it is not something Anna forgets. The music never far away, the streets crowded, the shops shut up; all as if for some festivity. A smile on a stranger's face, a young woman seen in passing, the expression a peculiar twist of fear and exhilaration, as if the worst has happened and has turned out to be only another day in that life, after all. The gloom of loss one minute, in one place, and in the next a sense that a weight has lifted. That money itself has lifted, brightening, like weather.

For a week the Laws refuse all entry to Erith Reach. Every day, at some hour or other, Anna catches sight of the scene outside the gates, broadcast live or recorded, the choicest moments to be interspersed later with other news. The coverage seems to her monotonous, though people watch it – she watches them watching – rapt, like webcam junkies. It is as if they are waiting for something, and as the days pass it begins to worry her, as if they must know something she doesn't. Like animals, she thinks: but it is an inspector's thought, and she stops herself before she can consider it again.

For the most part those who assemble under the overhanging walls are protesters, sightseers drawn to the centre of things, or the journalists themselves, each camera dumbly recording the ranked ordnance of competing media. But each day there are other figures too, sometimes in uniform, more often not. They arrive alone or in pairs, speak briefly at the gate intercom, and leave as quickly and quietly as they arrive.

The government has opened an inquiry – has opened several, it seems, or at least relaunched the same one several times – and there is a police investigation into the virus. But neither inquirers nor investigators have spoken to Law. There are reports that he has talked to no one, that even the police are waiting for the privilege of an interview, and the public anger (which has always been there, squat, ugly, envious, waiting for its chance) is tempered only by the sense of public satisfaction. The belief that the Laws' refusal is proof in itself. Evidence of a guilt which is only to be expected, and has only to be defined.

★ ★ ★

It is late when she dreams that she sees him. She is going through the house, checking the doors and windows before bed, leaving on lights downstairs, setting music to play in the kitchen, as she has every night since the break-in. Already it has become a ritual, comforting, disembodying her for sleep, and by the time she comes to the bedroom and begins to undress she is not wholly awake. She goes to the window, the last in the house, naked in the dark, feeling for the cold flange of the lock, and then she sees him.

It is one of those London nights when the rain is endless and the street lights are brightened by the reflections of water, all light and noise. He is standing across the street, on the sloped concrete where the driveway of a house crosses the pavement, under the shelter of the road trees. He has no coat and his clothes and hair are wet, she can see them shining, and in the faint glitter of the downpour his figure and those of the trees above him seem the only real things.

She knows it is him, it is the paleness of his face, and also the way he holds himself. He stands as he stood the last time she saw him, like a man grown ashamed of his own height. There is not even a moment when she thinks it is anyone but him. There is no jolt of fear at his presence. Instead what she feels is happiness – that he has come to her – and sadness, as if in the way of dreams she has understood that his apparition here is an omen, a sign that something terrible has happened to him, out in the waking world. But she is half asleep, and she does not remember that it already has.

Her hand still rests on the lock. She raises her fingers, pressing them out against the glass, *Hello*. At the motion he looks up. He doesn't wave back, doesn't smile, but after a moment he stirs himself, shakes his head, says something – to her or to himself, she can make out only the motion of his face – and steps forward across the road.

And then she is running, to dress herself, to open the door for him, to bring him in. Knowing in some part of her – it feels like her heart, although the heart does not know or feel – that he won't be there.

And of course he isn't. There is no one outside. There is nothing waiting for her but the cold, waking her. The chill of the rain creeping in around her, like something looking for something.

Law Missing

She is in transit when she sees it. The traffic is slow – she has started off late in a futile effort to avoid it – there are protests planned for later in the day, a march of forty thousand from the City to Westminster, neither the first demonstration that month nor the last – and the morning rush hour has been reduced to bad-tempered, crawling tailbacks well outside the city's access tunnels and ring roads.

By noon she has reached Piccadilly, one arm

resting on the sill of the open window, her foot touching absently at the accelerator when the cars ahead will allow it. Her thoughts are on John – on the twelve months in which she has known him, which looking back seems to have been a period of years – when she glances up at the gigantic news hoardings overhead. And there he is, and a yawn dies in her throat. There he is again.

Under the headline, above the scrolling lines of news, is a picture of him. It is one of the media's limited stock, familiar to Anna as it will be to those in the streets around her, well taken but already several years out of date. It shows John in evening dress, turning to speak against a background of night. His face is at ease but his eyes are attentive, as if he is on the brink of registering the presence of the photographer. Reproduced on such a large scale there are details visible that Anna has never noticed before – a suggestion of trees and open air, a blur of discoloured torchlight in the distance – and as she stares up at the screen she is almost certain that it is an image of Erith Reach. The green palace behind high walls, desirable, unattainable.

The news has tickertaped through to its end. She puts both hands on the wheel and sits quite still, waiting for it to begin its progress again.

*** NewZRoom! Five minute updates, next news in 297 seconds *** 1210: Soft Gold creator disappears *** Officials call at home yesterday, find John Law missing *** Family

262

confirm Law gone for days ∗∗∗ No note discovered ∗∗∗ More as it comes ∗∗∗

Anneli's face at the winter ball, her misery lit up in the dark. Nathan's expression at the shore. John in the room of unopened gifts, calling after her.

A horn sounds, long and angry, bringing her back. She finds that she is shivering. The Westminster air is cold against her face and arms. She puts the car into gear, her hands blunt and mechanical, and moves.

Her mobile begins to ring as she steps inside the Revenue. She knows it will be Carl before she answers. Ever since their conversation in the elevator she has been avoiding him, and events have made it easy to do so, since the Revenue has been a controlled experiment in disaster all week, its computers no longer to be trusted, its inspectors fully occupied by the complications of work and their own lives, and most of them, besides, not naturally disposed to running errands between competitors. But it is different now. Now she almost wants to see him.

'Anna,' he says, his mouth full of audible food. 'Don't hang up.'

'I'm not going to.'

'Good. You heard, then. Where are you? Business lunch again, is it? You might have sent me a postcard.'

'I'm right here.' She cradles the phone, case and

263

coat in one hand, the other outstretched to stop the nearest elevator doors as they begin to close. She steps into the crowded space, two subordinates making way for her in the confined space.

'The prodigal returns. You know, I was beginning to think you might have left us.' There is a wet sound of swallowing. 'Can you find your own way up, or should I talk you through it?'

'Fuck off.'

'Temper temper.'

'So it's true. Twentieth,' she adds to the inspector beside her. She can feel him listening as he selects her floor, straight-faced, and she turns away towards the wall.

'Something's true, that's for sure.'

'What does that mean?'

'Wait and see.'

The floors chime by. She doesn't hang up. The workers around her thin out until no one is left but her. At the far end of the line there is no sound, as if Carl has stopped eating, stopped breathing, almost, though she is aware of him still being there, the simmer of his impatience.

'Alone yet?' he says, finally.

'Yes.'

The swallowing begins again. 'That's what it's like,' Carl says between mouthfuls. 'Up here – you get a bit of space to yourself. Nice, isn't it? You should get promoted some time. Give it a try.'

'Spare me the career advice. You were wrong about him,' she says, as the doors open. She steps out into an empty corridor. There is a smell to it, of new carpets and old furnishings – oak and brass, transported from one Revenue building to the next, like relics – that reminds her of the last time she was here. Years ago, the day she was summoned before the Board.

'I'm never wrong. Turn left, the door's open. When?'

'You said he couldn't go under if he tried.'

'Did I?' His voice coming to her twice, a call and its echo. 'I did, didn't I? But I didn't know him then.'

'You don't know him now.'

'And I didn't mean six feet under.'

She sees him as he sees her. He is sitting on his desk, facing the doorway, mobile in one hand, spork in the other, a tin tray of noodles balanced precariously on his knees. He is not a large man, and the breadth of the desk and the clasp of his knees diminish him. He is wearing a dull, expensive suit that makes him seem older than he is. He is framed by the room and the window behind him. Like an icon, Anna thinks, or a caricature. The Revenue Mandarin: artless, heartless, all-devouring.

There is nothing else on the desk except a single sheet of paper. Beyond the window London is spread out southwards under a sky full of rain. Carl puts the phone down carelessly, points the spork precisely towards the door. 'Close that. Do you want anything?'

She shuts the door. Though the office is very large there is only one chair, behind the desk on which Carl sits. Anna goes to it, lays her coat across it, puts down her case, Carl turning to follow her.

And I didn't mean six feet under.

'You look like you could do with some coffee. I hope you're sleeping alright.'

'I don't want coffee.'

'You should. It's better up here. You'd be surprised.'

'Is he dead?' she says dully.

'You tell me.'

He isn't smiling. He is not, in fact, laughing at her. His voice – the coarseness of it – no longer quite goes with the way he looks. It is as if the wind has changed while he has been talking, and he has been stuck with the same old sneer, the redundant chip on the shoulder.

It is not something she has noticed before, but then she has seen him less often, these last months. Up close his face is drawn, as if he is determined not to look tired. He looks older in the flesh, it is not just the suit doing it to him. Most of all he looks as if he belongs here. Briefly she is glad for him, and then she pities him, and is glad only for herself.

He puts down the tin tray, picks up the sheet of paper, holds it out. 'Here. Go on, it won't bite.'

'What is it?'

'They found it over at SoftMark.'

She takes the sheet. It is almost blank. Along one edge a copy machine has blackened the paper with

266

a negative blur of light. Beyond that margin lie six short handwritten lines.

She goes cold, her heart falling inside her. 'They said there was no note.'

'It's not that. That's not what it is,' Carl says, and then, after a moment, 'Well. I don't know if that's what it is.'

She sits down by him on the desk. Side by side, as they used to wait on the bench in the square each morning. After all the time she spent investigating John she is surprised to realise she has never seen his handwriting. It is different to the elegant copperplate on the invitation to the winter ball. This script is so small it is almost unreadable. Crabbed, as if afraid to take up more paper than it has to.

> *How different we become under the hammer.*
> *How malleable we are. Hard to tell what will*
> *become of us, hard to explain what we each eat*
> *and sleep under. My life has become a weight.*
> *I have done things I never expected. Now I find*
> *that somewhere in them I have gone wrong. I*
> *wish I had*

She reads it through twice, the first time instantaneously, and blindly, so that she has to go back and start again.

'It doesn't look like he finished it,' Carl says, obviously, but as if it is a question.

'No.'

'It could mean anything.'

'Yes, it could.'

'It doesn't say he's going to do anything. Alright?'

She puts the page down on her lap. Smooths it out. The dream comes back to her, if it was a dream. The apparition under the trees. She is on the verge of tears, and she closes her eyes, stopping herself.

'Anna?'

'I'm okay, I'm fine. Give me a minute.'

'Right.' Gruffly he busies himself beside her. There is the sound of a drawer opening and shutting. When she looks up he has produced tissues, a small packet of them primly wrapped in plastic, their fabric decorated, ludicrously, with the faces of celebrities and politicians. 'Here. I used to keep these for interviews. Don't worry, they came free with something. Amazing how many clients cry over money, isn't it?'

'Thanks.' She unfolds a tissue. The face on it is familiar, though she is slow to recognise the features. It is John's guest, the ex-Minister of Defence in the rooms of glass. She is grateful it isn't John himself.

It must be something to do with numbers, do you think? Numbers and company don't mix.

She presses her eyes into the softness. When she is done she balls the remains. There is an oversized chrome bin on the far side of the desk, and she throws the wad and misses. Beside her Carl snorts with familiar derision.

'Keep the day job.'

268

'I am,' she says. 'I'm here, aren't I? You want me to find him, don't you?'

He cleans his teeth with his tongue, thoughtfully, extracting the last of his meal. 'More or less, yeah. I want you to bring him back.'

'Why?'

He nods with satisfaction. 'That isn't a no.'

'It doesn't mean yes.'

'It should,' he says. 'Alright,' and opening one hand he begins to enumerate reasons on the blunt tips of his fingers.

'One, he's been gone four days. He was supposed to be away on business, but he isn't. You might have thought a wife would call the police, but no. This wife didn't call anyone, she didn't see anyone. She let him go. If you ask me, I'd say that means she knows something.'

'Maybe she's ashamed. Maybe she thinks he's left her. Left everything,' she says, not really believing it herself, not quite knowing why she says it – because the way Carl thinks is so crudely accurate – and he laughs.

'Don't be stupid. Money men are like prostitutes. They always say they're going to give it up. They never do.'

'And you'd know.'

'Don't judge me,' he says, his voice altering fractionally, the wrong side of cordial. 'And I won't judge you. Anyway, it doesn't matter why he's gone. What matters is we get him back. Four days makes him an officially missing person,

269

which, when the missing person is him, means the police are involved. Unfortunately they're having problems. The Laws have let them in now, but they still won't talk to them in words of more than one syllable, and SoftMark are worse – they never give information to anyone if they think they can get away with it. So we've been asked to assist. We're the last government body which had—' he licks his lips, as if in thought '—personal contact with Mister Law. You're the last representative of the government to have done so. That means you'll be helping the police in their investigations. There's a Detective Inspector Mints you need to talk to. He'll keep us informed, you'll do the same. Got it? Then – this is the second thing – there's the government inquiry. There are important people who want to talk to Mister Law. They're having trouble under-standing the shit he's left behind. They don't know a lot about codes and viruses, and they're hoping he can explain things to them. So you'll be acting for the Government, just like you always have.'

'What about you?' she says, and when Carl smiles it sets her teeth on edge. She had almost forgotten how easy he is to dislike, and how little he seems to care.

'Me? I'm just passing on instructions from above. But since you ask, I've spent the last week calculating the time I've lost because of him. Time as money, I'm talking about. Eleven years, one hundred and thirty-seven days, seven hours. That's a long time. That's a life sentence. So I want to talk to him too. Me, the Detective Inspector and Her Venerable Majesty's Government. But I'm first.'

She puts down the note beside him on the desk, carefully, stands up, picks up her coat. Carl gazing up at her, curious, expectant. 'So?'

'I'm finished with him.'

'No,' he says, 'you're not.'

'I'm not doing it for you. Send someone else.'

'Who?'

'Anyone. Goater.'

'Goater!' He barks laughter. 'I wouldn't send that bastard to find the arse-end on a dog. No. Your objection is duly noted, but we all want him. We're relying on you. You're the best we've got, Anna, you do know that, don't you? You are going to find him.'

It is only later that she admits, and only to herself, that he is right. It doesn't matter who has asked her to find him; it is almost incidental that anyone has asked her at all. But it will be for the Revenue that she does it now, because it is they who have asked. And because she is still a part of the Revenue. The Revenue is still part of her.

But he is wrong, too. All these years, she thinks, and Carl doesn't know her well enough to understand it. Her head in her hands at the study desk, the sound of sirens in the dark outside, so ordinary as to be almost imperceptible. Or at least, she thinks, it is not what he said. Perhaps he thought it didn't need to be mentioned; that she could want to find John for herself.

For two days she does nothing. She knows where to begin, but she has no desire to go to Erith Reach again. She finds she does not want to see Anneli, and the thought of Nathan fills her with a loathing of herself, as if she is somehow to blame for what has happened. It is how he will think, she is sure of it. She remembers how it is at that age, when there is less rightness and wrongness to things, only sameness and difference. She thinks, how different it must be for him.

An inertia takes hold of her, and she lets it come. It is easy to do nothing, in fact, because for several days there is nothing. No orders or information, the media only endlessly repeating what they have (old news and older photographs) with a kind of grave relief, as if, after all, they are glad that Mister Law is gone. His absence leaving the world less exciting, but safer and more equal. The police do not contact her. There is no call from the Detective Inspector, nor from Carl, as if he is content to have sent her on her way. And then the rumours begin.

He is seen in Kristiansund, at an amateur performance of Schubert. He sits in a cheap seat with an obstructed view. Coat on, collar up, though it is a church hall, and unfortunately cold inside, so that he is not alone in these precautions. Afterwards he does not applaud but leaves in silence, watched – a local journalist has already been called – walking slowly, like a man carrying something. As if he is carrying the music away. As if it could be spilled.

He is recognised on an improbably diverse selection of web fora under elaborately meaningful pseudonyms, lurking at the borders of conversations about three-dimensional games, the Japanese syllabaries, the portraits of Zorn, the orchids of Bhutan. In York Factory, Manitoba, he is the man at the door of a rented room who receives an order (rice and ribs) from a courier of the Middle Earth Chinese Delivery. On Anticosti he is the visitor who plays cards – for good, hard cash – with three workers of the Anticosti Lumber Company, and wins, though he has a tic as he takes his dues, a flinch, as if he has been hit.

For three nights he is the only guest at a waterfront hotel in Benjamin Constant, Brazil, where he speaks to no one except the maid who cleans his drab room. (*Thank you so much*, he says, or so she says. *Muito obrigado*, once, and nothing else.) *Like a cup*, she says, knowingly; or so the news translations say she says. *He was like a cup dropped once. Not broken, but weakened.* He is a figure photographed indistinctly in a square in Pointe Noire. Sitting bowed, as if gravity has become too much for him, eyes closed in the fierce October sunshine. He is a body trawled from the mouth of the Sumida river. White as the flesh of a fish, unencumbered of all identity.

Monday, New Vine Street. Detective Inspector Mints brings her weak tea in a cardboard cup and

273

sits down next to her, as if she might require sympathy. He has a small, unhappy face, prominent at the forehead, receding towards the chin, mouth pursed in a permanent expression of disapproval or disappointment.

'I'm sorry about this,' he says, so that for a second, as she drinks, Anna thinks he means the tea. He puts a heavy file down on the table and opens it, as if it is not something he honestly expects to enjoy. 'We're back on paper records this month. It's supposed to be safer, what with everything, but we're all a bit out of practice at it. It's not helping, I'm afraid.'

'It's alright,' Anna says, putting down her tea. 'I'm sure it's fine. There's certainly a lot of it,' she adds, pulling the file towards her, since the policeman seems reluctant to say or do anything more; and he blushes.

'It shouldn't have happened like this. It would have been different if we'd got to the family earlier. The longer he's gone, the harder it is.'

'You've done this before?' She opens the file at random. The uppermost sheet of paper is an inventory of shipping and aircraft registered both under John's own name and on his behalf by representatives of SoftMark. The list reaches the bottom of the page and, as she turns it and the next, keeps on going. Someone has been crossing off the items one by one with a red pen. They haven't got very far, and the pen is running out.

'That's why they had me take the case. I've

been lucky with missing persons,' he says with modest matter-of-factness. 'I've always got them back, even the deceased. But it's not the same. It's different with someone like Mister Law,' his voice changing, nostalgic, defensive, dropping. 'It's a lot harder.'

She turns the pages carefully. Shipping, contacts, real estate. 'I would have thought it'd be easier, in some ways. Everybody knowing he's missing. Everybody knowing him.' Beside her the policeman sighs.

'No, they just think they know him, that's all. They haven't met him, have they? No one's actually met him. They just see a few old society pictures, and they think they know him. It doesn't help. It's only been five days, and we've had over fifteen thousand sightings. And that's just here. It's not helpful. All we're doing now is adding them to the list. And that's not even the problem.'

Pictures. Nathan a grinning infant, not much larger than the pigeons that surround him. Anneli at the wheel of the famous yacht, John leaning behind her in sunglasses. His arms around her, the light in her hair as she smiles. All at sea.

'So what is the problem?'

Mints picks up her tea, glances at it, puts it down reluctantly. 'Well, money,' he says.

'He can afford to hide.'

'There is that, it's true, but I meant it differently. It's what I always did, you see. Missing people need money. It's expensive, more expensive than most of them expect. Keeping moving, keeping fed, somewhere to sleep every night. So I waited, and in the end, if they were still alive, they always used a card. You would have thought they'd have realised, but they hardly ever did. Sometimes they want to be found, of course. Sometimes they're addicted to it.'

'Maybe he'll make the same mistake, then.' An acetate binder, John's passport inside, pressed open to his photograph. 'Maybe he wants to be found.'

'Yes, well, whatever he's paying with it won't be his cards.' He nods towards the file. 'They're all here. He left them all behind.'

She leafs through until she finds them. Eight moneycards sealed in more acetate, credit and currencies, John's skinprint reproduced on each. The infamous icon of Soft Gold.

'It all costs something. He'd have to go a long way, and it doesn't come cheap, to get away from the kind of mess he's left behind. And that's not helping either. That's slowed things down right along the line. Crime's up eighty-two per cent on August. Funds are down. All in all, he couldn't have planned it better.'

'But he didn't.' She looks up. The way he says it makes her. 'Plan it.'

He glances at her doubtfully, as if he might have said too much. 'Well, that remains to be seen. There's the house, after all. And the family issues.'

'Issues?'

He smiles for the only time. Prim pleasurable regret. 'You mean you didn't know. The Laws divorced four years ago. I'm sorry, I would've thought you might have picked it up, during your own investigations . . . but no one knew, of course. His passport has him married. No one had a clue. Not even the child. Otherwise, well, everyone would have been in on it.'

She goes dizzy. There is the aftertaste of the tea in her mouth, sweet, like rust. *Oh,* she thinks, *Oh, Nathan.* Beside her Mints goes on and on, disappointed, disapproving, querulous.

'Not very admirable, is it? It's the families who suffer. That's what I tell the ones I find. Half the time it's the families they're running away from, but still. "You should think of your family," I tell them. But they always are, that's the funny thing. Mister Law's no different when it comes down to it. He's been transferring assets to them for years. The London estate's in her name. Erith Reach – you might have noticed that. I expect that's why they divorced. There was something in the son's name too, wasn't there? Something a bit improper, if I'm remembering it right.'

'Are there other accounts?'

'Oh, I'd have to assume this is the tip of the iceberg. Wasn't that why your people got involved? You see, the way I do it is to look at things as an impartial observer. An impartial observer might say he knew something was going to happen.

An observer might think Mister Law was putting his house in order. Providing for those he knew he'd have to leave behind. It might seem quite a coincidence, all this. Because why would he have done so much, if he didn't know what was going to happen?'

'He wasn't planning it,' her voice shallow. 'He was planning against it. He was scared.' And Mints frowns, doubtfully, understanding nothing.

'Scared. Yes, I suppose he might have been. Anyway, we don't know anything for certain.'

'Does he know yet?'

'I'm sorry . . . does who know what?'

'Nathan.'

'Who?'

'Nathan, the son.'

'Oh. Well, I wouldn't really know.' He leans towards her. 'It's not your fault. There is so much to know about him, isn't there? It makes it hard to know where to start. It's really very hard,' he says, and leaning back he picks up the tea, finally, and drinks it down.

Kennedy eyes. She can't remember where she first heard that of John. It isn't something that she would have thought of herself, the image of an American President killed two decades before her birth, but it has stayed with her because, once heard, it is exactly right. The lids at their extremities downturned, wry when he is grave, unsmiling when he is smiling. The corners folding slyly into old mirth. The sockets deep-set, harrowed by exhaustion.

Now he reminds her of Kennedy again. She remembers where she was the moment she heard his money had been broken, what she was doing as the news came through that he had disappeared. Kennedy moments. And if he is found, then there will be that, too – when, and how. There will be other things she is unable to forget. His life has become as inescapable as her own.

At Pont Street she looks up and finds herself about to turn head-on into one-way traffic. She has been driving as if in fog, lost in self-doubt, with no idea of where she is going or why.

She has to stop. Her palms slip on the wheel as she looks for a place. There are double-reds along the roadside and she pulls into an alleyway instead and sits in the soiled space between service entrances. An air vent mutters and chugs overhead. There are cigarettes in her bag and she reaches for them instinctively, as if she has always needed them.

Divorced. *You didn't know?* And she didn't. In three months of investigation it isn't something that even crossed her mind. She should have been told. They should have told her. With a little twist of rage she remembers the accountant, Mutevelian, in the halls of SoftMark. *Well. They should have sent A1.* Mild, as if she was saying nothing at all.

How could she have missed it, how could she have been so stupid? But she knows how. It is because they lied to her, if only by omission, counting on the burden of facts for concealment. It is because she wanted to trust John, because trust was something he inspired. And most of all it is because she forgot the rules of tax inspection. Chose to forget them. Never believe the client. Information is the inspector's greatest weapon.

She shakes her head. The cigarette has burned down to ash in her hand. The trapped air is full of the smell of it, like medicine or insecticide. She starts the engine, lets it warm. Turns again in the narrow space.

It is a foul night, so cold and wet that there is no room in the house that will stay warm. She works late, not wanting to stop, blinking in the computer's stale light. Punishing herself, though she is not sorry to do so. In the light of all that has happened she is not sorry for herself.

She looks for the rumours, weighing them, saving to disk anything that has even a remote resemblance to fact. Already the theories have multiplied and interbred, acquiring depth and detail from one another as they are passed from site to site, professional, amateur, conspiracist. Now it is the John in Canada who has died, his remains washed up on the northern shore of the Hudson Strait. Now the John in Japan is alive again, a figure glimpsed in traffic on the bridge across the Inland Sea. The early sightings have already begun to be accorded precedence, as if age has made them legitimate; and the stories which come in their wake make them seem so. Documents and photographs of aliens and celebrities. John Law And Elvis Presley Seen In Sardis, Pennsylvania. John Law And Wife Eat With The Dead. John Law Lives Underground On Mars.

Nodding off, her eyes closing despite her. Beside her, coffee cooling in an uncleaned glass. She comes awake shivering, sweat cold on her face and breasts, with no sense of how long the night has gone on without her.

The computer has gone into screen saver. She touches the keys and the Internet reappears. She has fallen asleep in front of an amateur John Law photo-gallery. *You've found Rick's Crypt! Knock yourself out. I'm still under construction, so stay tuned and please come again.*

There are only three pictures posted. Anna knows them all by heart. John at fourteen, dour against a social rehab unit background, a foreshadowing of his own son. At twenty, boarding a private flight, sleek and sure as an athlete. At thirty-five, in evening dress against a background of night.

She clicks the last shot. Sluggishly it fills the screen. It is the most familiar of the three, the image rendered everywhere in headline proportions with the news of the disappearance. It is not something she should need to see again. But it is a good photograph, full of skilled intention. She has always liked it for that. The way it captures John as he turns, unprepared, if only for that second. The sharpness still forming in his eyes.

And until it does, he looks happy. That is what she likes most of all. It is something she has never seen in the flesh. His face so relaxed in happiness.

She leans closer for the details. There are the trees, just where she remembers them. The edge of a cloud in a night sky. It is cold, she can see John's breath hanging in the air. There is the torchlight, ghosted by some trick of photography. Odd, she thinks, that there should be this one flaw in a picture which is otherwise so well composed. The illumination is misplaced, discoloured, floating out beyond the trees. The clouds are only visible where the light catches their edge.

She comes awake. Her scalp contracts. She right-clicks on the photograph, scrolls down through icons to the image of a magnifying glass. The photo flickers and returns, less well resolved but twice as large, the screen framing John's face and breath. She drags the picture down until nothing of him is visible.

Almost impenetrable darkness. The cloud is broken only once. Through that the light comes. It is not reflected from below or ghosted by the camera. There is no trick to it. The colours – red bleeding into pink, curtains of faint electric green – are unfocused but not unformed. There are columns of light, huge as clouds, hidden in the overcast sky.

Rain smatters at the study doors. Her eyes ache in the way she knows will soon spread back into her head. She saves the image on the screen, turns off the power. Leans back.

She wakes stiff, with the feel of the keyboard a dull throb in her fingertips. For some time she sits on the edge of the bed, propped on her arms, head down, sleep leaving her like a hangover. Outside the world is green under a clear sky, and the lawns and the last leaves on the trees look heavy and lush, as if it is summer again.

She pads downstairs. She has forgotten to leave the radio on, and for once the house lies in silence. On the kitchen counter last night's coffee sits where she left it, scummed with a faint iridescence.

She pours the leavings away, brews a fresh measure, switches on the news. Two experts are discussing Lord Lucan and plastic surgery. Their voices are mild, never raised. They are comforting as shipping news. She doesn't need to listen to know they will end up talking about John. For days there has been nothing but him, one way or another. In his absence he has become more famous than ever. It is as if half her own life has been given over for public consumption; as if she is watched, somehow, by figures always just out of sight. She has not forgotten – has not let herself forget – that it is what she wanted, once. Knowing no better. Not to watch, but to be watched.

'In other news, the first lawsuits against John

Law have been lodged in seven cities across Japan. Civil actions against both Mister Law and SoftMark, the company responsible for Soft Gold, are expected to run into the thousands in the coming weeks, and courts in Britain are preparing themselves –'

She hasn't got round to a new fridge. All week she has lived off takeaways, cold in the morning, hot at night, eating the same thing twice a day until the accumulation of tin trays – fragile, rancid – has begun to depress her. Now there is fruit instead, each piece more than she can afford, and surprisingly cheap pastries from a Jewish shop on Lower Marsh. Duck and walnuts, salt fish and green mangos.

She turns the radio down low, wraps two pies in a paper bag, takes them out with her to the car, and eats them as she drives, east to Westminster and onwards.

The twin city has changed again. The curious sense of festivity has already begun to fade. One shop in two or three is still shut up behind chain links or grilles. Some look more permanently closed. There are crowds, as there always are, but they are in the wrong places now, as if they have lost some natural instinct for navigation. The high streets are empty, but Hyde Park is crammed with onlookers, grimly patient under the trees. Anna can't make out what they are waiting for. Someone to say something or something to happen.

At the Tower she crosses the river. There are

traffic warning boards overhead, the first lightless, the second flagging the roads clear to the east. She is thinking, not of those ahead, but of her first days at the Revenue. Shadowing her mentor. Lawrence, teaching her.

Try to remember that you're not only dealing with numbers.

His voice warm beside her. The smell of something on his skin. The sweetness of him, like cologne.

What else am I dealing with?

Alright. There is a man in a small country. For nineteen years he puts away everything he can. In the twentieth year there is a run on the national stock market. Suddenly everyone is investing, everyone is an expert. The man's neighbours become rich overnight. So the man invests his own savings, and immediately the market turns. People lose their homes, their land, everything goes to the loans they have taken. And our man loses everything he has ever made. What does he do?

He goes mad? As if it is a question. Lawrence laughing. At the time she didn't like that. That he would laugh at her. That night she will go home with him for the first time, drink with him into the small hours, falling asleep on the study couch. Waking to find him standing over her. Naked, his cock aching, thick as a bruise.

Of course he goes mad. Wouldn't you?

Maybe. I don't know. Would you?

We're not talking about me, thank God. We're talking about him. What is he going mad for?

Money. Shrugging. *Just money*. And Lawrence shaking his head, so serious that she wishes he would laugh at her again.

Not just money. Never just money.

Beside *Fret Maritime*, *Fret Arien* she stops the car. Over Erith Reach the sky is a bleached, spent blue. There are perhaps two dozen people waiting in the street. Three police officers stand apart, talking between themselves. No one looks Anna's way as she gets out, but a woman in a linen suit watches as she approaches.

The walls are disfigured. There is the outline of writing, faint neon colours, the messages already scrubbed to illegibility. The chemically sweetened smell of urine. A thin, dry gruel of shit. A wide dent in the gate, as if someone has unsuccessfully tried to ram it open. Beside it the keypad has been staved in, the cyclops eye of the camera broken and blind.

She walks back to where the police wait. They turn together, two men and a woman. They are similar as siblings, their faces professionally benign, giving away nothing. She has already taken out her cards, has begun to explain, when the female officer cuts her off.

'You have reason to be here?'

'Yes – actually, yes. I'm here with the Revenue. I've been in touch with Detective Inspector Mints, at New Vine Street –'

'Mints.' The woman's voice is scoured, stony, with no connection to her expression. One of

the men takes Anna's papers. 'You have iden-
tification?'

She hands over her cards. While the woman
checks her skinprint against a handheld computer
the third officer unhitches his mobile and begins
to speak into it, his voice so muted that Anna can't
make out what he says. There is only the sensation
of being talked about, instinctual, unpleasant.

'Alright.' The policewoman holds out Anna's
cards, glancing back at her colleagues as she does
so. 'Problem?'

The officer with the mobile glances up, shakes
his head. 'She's expected.'

'We can't spare anyone to go with you,' the
woman says dourly. 'And the house is some way
from the gate –'

'I've been here before,' Anna says, and the officer
raises her eyebrows as if unable to believe she has
been interrupted.

'—so try not to get lost. Are they ready?'
she says, and the policeman with the phone
nods. 'You'll return to your vehicle. When the
gate opens drive on through. Go straight on,
turn left, third right and straight on again. If
any civilians try to follow you in you'll stop
and wait until we've dealt with them. Is that
all clear?'

Yes, she says. It is all clear. She walks back to
the car, gets in and waits. The two policemen have
moved in, clearing the crowd back, but the gate
stays shut. The dashboard clock ticks softly. She

has never realised it made any sound at all. She shivers in the cold, stale air.

There is a tap at the driver's window, so close it makes her jump. She looks up, expecting the policewoman to be there beside her, and finds to her relief that it is the woman in the linen suit.

She opens the window. The woman's face is bent close and smiling. 'Hi,' she says, East Coast American. 'You going inside?'

She says something in reply, not as much as yes, though it is apparently enough.

'Are you a relative?'

'No.' She glances back at the policemen, the gate. 'Excuse me, I have to –'

'Business, then,' the woman says. It is a statement, not a question. 'Do you mind if I ask you a few things?'

'I'm sorry, I –'

'Just a few things.' The woman leans closer, still smiling, the edge of her head inside the window. Blocking it. Anna can see her hands now. In one is a mobile, in the other a dictaphone. 'How long have you known Mister Law?'

'I don't –'

'You don't know him. Okay. Are you with the police? No.' Keen, smiling eyes. 'The government?'

'No. Yes – look, I have nothing to say. If you could just –'

'Who were you hoping to speak to? Not the Laws, right? What is your reaction to that?'

'No,' she says, not replying but refusing. Her hand is on the window control. It would only take a second to close. But she has a sudden image of what would happen. The woman not stepping back, but leaning in, still smiling. The glass closing against her neck.

'Anna Moore!'

The policewoman's command echoes in the narrow street. The journalist's smile falters. She withdraws her head and straightens up with an expression, not of guilt, but of wry regret. Beyond her the policewoman waits. Ahead the gate stands open. Anna closes the window, starts the engine, and drives in.

No one follows her. The figures of the policemen diminish in the rear view. She turns first left, third right. The house is closer than she remembers it, the distances lessened by familiarity, and there are no figures – no Muriet – to help or hinder her. Before she expects it she is passing under the yew hedge, the foliage still cut smooth as moss, the gravel still raked as it opens out into its ultimate crescent.

The house is closed up, the doors locked, the harbour empty. The glass walls of the upper floors have been polarised, shutting out the light. A helicopter mutters overhead. Anna has been knocking for some time before she notices that there is an intercom to one side of the doorway. A second security lens, unbroken, half concealed by lintel and creepers.

She presses the button. There is no accompanying sound. Nothing echoes back from inside the house. Through the glass she can make out the fountain, the pool, the trough of water.

A light blinks on beside the lens. There is a crackle of static but no voice, only a sigh, something that might be mechanical or human. The click of a lock as the doors edge open. She steps inside for the third time.

The chandeliers are unlit. Furniture is stacked against one wall: a pair of old brass telescopes, massive as artillery; a pile of carpets, ten feet deep, like something from a folk tale. There is no sign of life except, in the pool, the nosy faces of pond fish, butting at the surface.

The house feels deserted. And then she remembers, understands, that it always felt like this. Even when they were all here, John and Anneli and the children going about their private lives, even when the hall was filled with guests and the swell of talk and laughter. It always felt like a place where life had grown beyond living.

She walks through to the second hall, stops by the foot of the stairs. If it wasn't for the water in the atrium, the helicopter in the distance, there would be no sound in the house at all. It comes to her that there is no one here, that she has been admitted only through some electrical fault. That it is not only John who has left, but all of them. The voice of the journalist comes back to her. *Who were you hoping to speak to? Not the Laws, right?*

'Anna Moore,' says a voice behind her, as if her name is a pleasant surprise. Terence stands in the doorway between the halls, hands in jacket pockets. 'They said you'd come back.'

'I didn't hear you,' she says, because it is true, and the bodyguard smiles his sweet, practised apology.

'They said you would, but I didn't believe them. I didn't think you'd dare.'

'They're not here,' she says, not quite steadily. 'Are they?'

'No.'

'Where are they?'

He looks away, taking his hands out of his pockets, as if he expects to see someone. 'Oh,' he says vaguely. 'Here and there. It depends who you're after, really, doesn't it? But it's only me here now.'

'Why?'

'Because that's my job. I'm here to put the house in order. Tie up all the loose ends, you know. Put out the lights.'

'That's not what I meant.'

'You mean why have they gone? I would have thought you might know that. I would have thought that might be obvious, considering. How are you, Anna?'

'Fine.'

'Good,' he says. 'Good. That's something.'

His anger is almost imperceptible. There is nothing in his tone to suggest it. If she didn't know him she would never have noticed. He is between her and the entrance, very small and still, the light behind him. She wonders if he would try to stop her, if she were to leave.

'Do you know where he is?' He shakes his head. 'What about Anneli? Did she take Nathan? When did they leave?'

'That would have been yesterday.'

'Terence,' she says, 'I need to talk to her. I have to find John. It's very important that –'

'Oh, I'm sure it is,' he says, without warmth. 'It's an important job you're doing. Very important, what you've done.'

'I didn't do anything,' she says, but her voice is quieter than she means it to be, meek, almost – as if she is guilty, she thinks, why is that? – and Terence is still talking, as if he hasn't heard her.

'Funny, isn't it, how everyone wants them now. No one much cared about them before. It's the law-suits that did it for her. It's the lawyers who decided her. They've been here every day, calling, asking questions. Raising questions about how they lived their lives. It's hers, you see, all this, but they've been working on that. They say there was decep-tion involved,' he says, staring up the empty sweep of the stairs. 'They say the divorce was improper. But I don't think that's quite right, do you? I don't think Mister Law would do anything improper.'

'You must miss them,' she says, and he looks down, first at her, then at the floor, his expression hidden.

'Miss them,' he repeats. 'Not her. We never got on, if you want to know. No,' he says, 'I won't miss her.'

A silence grows between them. Something has passed, some potential for violence. Though the bodyguard has hardly moved at all, Anna is aware that the anger has gone out of him. She sits down on the lowest step, carefully, the stone cold through the thin material of her skirt. After a while Terence stirs.

'I'll get you a chair.'

'I'm fine.'

'We've got lots,' he says, not moving. And more faintly, 'We've got plenty. You wouldn't believe how many chairs there are.'

She puts her case on her lap, clicks it open. Her computer lies buried in a landslide of papers. She leafs through until she has the one she wants. An A3 reproduction, John Law under an open sky.

'I want you to do something for me.'

'What?'

'Look at this.'

He comes across the hall. As he reaches out she sees that his eyes are wet. 'I remember this one,' he says. 'This is a good one.'

'Do you know where it was taken?'

He shakes his head. 'I always liked it, though.'

'So did I.' He raises his eyes to her. 'Look at the sky.'

'What about it?'

'See the light?'

Slowly, sullenly, he shrugs. 'Now that you mention it. I don't see how it matters. It's something to do with the photography, isn't it? It's not really –'

'It reflects from the clouds. Not from below, though – from above. Even the colours are reflected. Red and green. You see?'

'Well now,' Terence murmurs. He leans his head to one side, squinting. 'Now what is that? Is that a sunset?'

'I don't think so. The colours are wrong.'

'The Northern Lights, then. Is that what you were thinking?'

'Or the Southern. It's supposed to be the same at both poles. At first I thought this might be a picture of Antarctica. I know he owns property there. But it isn't that.'

'No.' He nods. 'I went there a few times with him. Mineral explorations. There are no trees on Antarctica. Not a single tree. It's not something you forget.'

'Is there anywhere else he owns where this could have been taken? Anywhere you went with him?'

'Not as I recall. He never had much time for cities, but most of his property is in the larger commercial centres all the same. Not that I went everywhere. There's places he bought that he never even saw himself. But no, I don't remember anywhere like this.'

She gets to her feet. This close – closer than they have ever been – she finds she is a head taller than him. It seems suddenly ludicrous that she should ever have been frightened, that he should ever have seemed a threat. 'Then there's Anneli.'

'What about her?'

'She's northern European, isn't she? Is she Scandinavian?'

He grunts acknowledgement, as if she is distracting him from the picture at hand. 'Nordic, anyway. Finnish. You thought this might have been at her family home? A summer house? Something like that?'

'Something like that,' she says. But the bodyguard is looking sideways at her, with a kind of satisfaction, and already, her heart sinking back into her, she knows she is wrong. 'Why not?'

'Her parents moved to America before she met Mister Law. She had a lot of work out there at the time. Concerts and so forth. They didn't get on well without her, as I understand it. They didn't get on with Mister Law either. Didn't take to him. Difficult people, I thought. But there's nothing in Finland. I don't think Mister Law ever went to Finland,' he says, as if it is the same thing.

She takes the picture back. 'Where are they, in America?'

'Some island. Somewhere down on the Gulf. Dolphin Island, was it? I don't know. I never went there. I only went with him on business. I don't think you'd see any Northern Lights from down there, or Southern ones.' He clears his throat. 'Well. I'm sorry.'

She doesn't answer. She can feel him waiting for her to say something more. The helicopter is no longer audible, and the water has gone quiet in its pools and troughs, as if all its echoes have cancelled one another out.

'What were you hoping for?' he says finally, a little fierce again. 'Did you think he might be there? Where this was taken?'

'I don't know what I thought.'

'Why would you think that?'

Because he looks so happy, she thinks. It is too foolish to say out loud, and then she is saying it anyway. 'Because he looks happy.'

He takes the corner of the page, turns it upwards. Gazes down.

'He does,' he says finally, and the breath goes out of him, as if he has been winded. 'He does. He looks happier than I ever saw him.'

It is evening before she gets back home. There is nothing there she wants so much as seven hours' sleep. She stands in the back rooms, staring out at the October trees, trying to imagine a continent without them.

She is leaving on lights, dimming them, when her mobile rings. It is downstairs, she is upstairs, and by the time she reaches it, it has vibrated its way across the kitchen table, sideways, like an escaping crab. She catches it as it falls.

A message has been left. The number is not one she knows. She presses the button and Terence

296

clears his throat and says his name, small and tinny with transmission.

'It's Terence. I was just ringing to . . . well, I looked it up for you, the island. It's Dauphin, not Dolphin, my mistake. And I wanted to apologise. It's been hard for me. I wanted to tell you I've got nothing against you. You've got your job to do, I've got mine. Anyway, I don't know where he is, I told you the truth about that. But you asked about her, and I'm telling you. Dauphin Island. Don't forget now.'

She waits for Lawrence on the mansion-block steps. It is almost noon, gloomy and close, and there are few comings and goings. A pair of elevator technicians go in, a woman in a black headscarf goes out, her skirts brushing past Anna, pausing at the canal's edge to hawk into the placid water.

'You're late,' she says when he arrives, and he scowls down at her over armfuls of bread and flowers.

'I'm never late. You're early, in fact, unless my watch is slow. Small thanks I get for buying you breakfast! And since when have you begun smoking? You look *awful*.'

'Alright, don't rub it in.'

'I'm not sure I'd want to. Are you physically contagious?'

She mushes the butt out on the stair beside her. 'Funny. Give me that, I'll carry it.'

'Don't do me any favours.'

'Don't be silly!'

She takes the bread. He keeps the flowers. The elevators are still broken, and they walk up the seven flights in dogged silence. In the kitchen she finds a vase while he fixes them both something to eat. He has bought opium poppies, their crushed-flesh blooms engineered to last for days. She wonders how he could have paid for them. He has never had much in the way of money, and they are no longer something she could afford herself.

She carries them through to the study, arranges them on the window sill. Outside the woman in the headscarf has begun to busk. A violin propped against her chest, her face and hands bent over it, a piece of red cloth spread out at her feet for hard currency.

It is three days since her visit to Erith Reach. Since then she has slept only in the moments it has taken her by surprise. At night her heart has hammered her awake, insistently, striking the hours, as if there is something wrong again; as if one of the Laws has died or been discovered – at nights it seems to her that discovery might be worse – so that the prospect of sleep has finally become exhausting in itself. And so Lawrence is right about her. Apparently she looks no better than she feels. Sometimes it seems as if he is always right.

He comes in with a tray, sets it down on the floor, kneeling on the rug to pour. There are low chairs beside him and she sits and takes the tea he hands her. Only when he offers a plate of French toast does she shake her head. His face falls.

'Not eating?'

'I'm sorry. Maybe later.'

'It's alright, it'll keep. So. Are you sleeping?'

'A little.'

'A little.' Still kneeling he puts the plate back precisely on the wooden tray. 'Not that you ever seemed to need much rest. What can be so bad, though, that it would keep you from your food, I wonder?' He smiles faintly. 'What's eating you?'

'They've asked me to find John.'

'And you don't want to?'

He looks up at her, waiting for an answer. Finally she shakes her head. She doesn't mean it as the reply for which he takes it.

'I'm surprised. I would have thought –'

'No,' she says. 'I do. I want to find him. I need your help.'

He nods. 'You know you just have to ask.'

She puts down her cup, the tea untouched. 'You told me once that you still had contacts,' she says. 'Did you mean it? I'm serious.'

'You're always serious, these days. And I always keep my friends, unless I drink with them.' He levers himself back into a chair, holding his cup level in one hand. 'I have contacts everywhere, if I say so myself.'

'In the IRS?'

'Of course the IRS. They're hardly the FBI. There are certainly colleagues over there from whom I could still ask a favour. If that's what you mean.' He sips his tea, watching her. 'Anna, what is this about?'

'I need to find someone.'

'So find them.' When he brings the cup away he is frowning. 'You have the Revenue at your back. What do you need me for?'

'But I'm not asking the Revenue,' she says. 'I'm asking you.'

For a long time he watches her. His frown fades into something else, an expression almost of amazement. Finally he releases his breath, as if it could leave him lighter.

'I see,' he says. 'You never give up, do you?'

'I never understood,' she says, 'why it was you wanted me to.' And his face twists, as if she has touched on something painful.

'Alright. Alright, I'll see what I can do.'

They drink together. He tells her he has had nothing stronger for a week. She says that she is glad for him, and she is, it is not a small thing. He does not say he is doing it for her. Outside it has begun to rain again. The sound of the violin falters and stops.

He walks down with her to the main door. When he takes her face in his hands his palms are cool, or her face is hot, one or the other. He wishes her good luck. She is down the steps before he calls after her.

'Don't let them decide for you.'

'Who?'

300

'The Revenue, of course.'

She stands in the rain, looking up at him. 'What do I have to decide?'

'Whether you are running or hunting. Whether you are running with the fox, or hunting with the hounds.'

The nearest city is Gulf Shores, the nearest airport Mobile. But the world turns more slowly without Soft Gold. Every airline site she visits has warnings about fuel hikes, price rises and restricted flight schedules. There are no seats available to Mobile for over a month. It is ten days before she finds a suitable alternative, a ticket to New Orleans, a hired car to be there when she arrives.

The flight leaves from the Docklands, rising up through the drizzle, past the grand lit plinths of twentieth-century towers. The moments of take-off are something she has loved since childhood – the clear light above the clouds, lifting the spirits. Now it barely serves to distract her from herself. Her thoughts too far ahead, her hands nervous with anticipation.

The man next to her considers her once, as if to mentally undress her, then settles himself towards the aisle. She keeps her briefcase at her bare-stockinged feet and, once the landing lights go off and she can use her computer again, goes over what she has, reading the same few lines of text again and again until she is sickened.

She sits with her head back, breathing shallowly.

301

The air smells of duty-free perfume and vomit. Finally, to curb her nausea, she stands and walks the lengths of the darkened aisles. The ranked faces contorted with the effort of sleep. The attendants moving smilingly by her, the night rushing past outside.

A house number on Audobon Street, Dauphin Island, Alabama. A telephone and email, neither of which she has used. The abbreviated tax records of a Jami and a Suvi Numminen, aviation worker (male, retired), management consultant (female, retired): the bare bones of two lives. Anneli's family name. For these things she has the Internal Revenue Service to thank, and Lawrence to thank for the IRS. It is an organisation she has dealt with several times in her years at the Revenue, but she knows no one there well enough to call them herself. No one from whom she would ask a favour in confidence. Carl has kept his contacts, no doubt, but it is not Carl who has helped her. It is not Carl she has been prepared to ask.

They land ahead of schedule. The car waits in its appointed lot. She checks for a map and unfolds it onto the seat beside her. Someone has left a cereal bar in the glove compartment, and she tears it open and eats it as she drives, the hunger catching up with her along with the dawn. Now I am really here, she thinks, now I have eaten here. The sky pales and brightens to the colour of rice paper.

She turns onto the interstate, following the coast eastwards. To her right the Gulf of Mexico stretches green and islanded to the horizon. There are signposts to Mobile and Gulf Shores, but no directions to Dauphin. On the map beside her it is a slender shape at the mouth of the Alabama River, horned and tailed, banded green and red and yellow, like an illustration of some exotic oceanic species.

It is several years since she has even seen the sea. As a child she did so all the time, though she has never travelled much. Summer and winter there were holidays in Holland, where her grandparents lived, her father's father and mother at first, then only his mother. Day trips to Zandvoort. Ice in the winter, and in summer, as if in a different country, the smell of heat.

She narrows her eyes, remembering. One year there was a fair and a raffle for some local cause. She and Martha bought two tickets and won a kilo bag of tiger prawns. There is a photograph of them somewhere: two children with the sack held between them, proud as anglers. They ate nothing else for days, sucking the prawns still frozen, like ice cubes. And once they went to an island further north, one of the West Frisians, the ferry ungainly between hidden sandbanks. She recalls the rough grey of the sea and the reticence of the people. Their smiles welcoming but inscrutable. Their conversations gently lapsing into silence in the presence of others. Like a shyness, but ultimately prouder than shyness. Harder.

An island would be a good place to hide, she

thinks. But only for an islander. An island would keep its own secrets to itself.

Louisiana to Mississippi to Alabama. She makes decent time. By eight-thirty she has crossed two state lines. The outskirts of Mobile begin to rise around her, prefabricated industrial structures to the north, ribbon developments along the coast. It is not yet November, and already there are Christmas billboards along the interstate. *Seasonal Greetings from Mobile Quays – The World's Largest Forest Products Terminal!* Santa Claus drawn across the sky by a school of dolphins.

She turns off the interstate too soon, slows uncertainly through towns that are little more than main streets. Ten minutes east of Pascagoula she catches sight of the bridge, an interminable spar of concrete crossing the channel. There is land at its far end, miles off, low and flat as the Gulf itself. Around Dauphin Island the waves are green and blue and brightening.

The traffic around her has dwindled with every fork since the interstate. Now there is almost none. She has crossed half the bridge's length – two miles, she thinks, or more – before a single motorcyclist overtakes her, the biker leaning back into lane as he passes. A school bus heads the other way, all waving hands and mouthing faces. A trawler crawls beneath her, its nets drawn in for the morning.

Now she can make out buildings ahead. The turret of a lighthouse in the clear sea-light. The Martian landmark of a water tower. There are pelicans on the island's northern jetties, rows of them hanging out their wings like dirty washing. As she approaches them the sea breeze catches her, the hired car shuddering in the crosswind.

The water tower looms above her. The streets of Dauphin Island are as empty as the bridge that serves them. At their far ends the sea rises high and foreshortened. Two petrol stations, an oyster bar on wooden stilts (CLOSED TIL APRIL), a car wash, a fish-catch outlet. A broken hurricane window leans against the shop-front of a laundromat. A woman comes out and bangs laundry sacks into the back of a station wagon. In the rear-view Anna watches her make a U-turn, her wheels flinging sand across the blacktop.

None of it is as she imagined. What did she expect? More comfort than this, certainly. A retirement town, a resort house on a stately avenue. Money, she thinks: in John's world she has become used to its presence. Here there is only the memory of wealth. The rawness of its loss, and a dogged, worked edge of persistence. The streets turned in from the sea, as if one night it might try and rise up and wash them all away.

Her map is too broad in scale to carry much detail. The only street named on the island is Bienville Boulevard, which stretches from the horn of the land to its tail, drives and courts extending from its length like vertebrae. She looks out for the appropriate road sign but the main street is obvious before she reaches it, its buildings larger and more permanent than elsewhere. There are cars parked outside the Mobile Union Bank, and figures at the window seats of the Fort Gaines Seafood Diner. She parks and unbelts, yawning gigantically, cat-like, as if she has just woken from a long sleep.

The smell of seaweed and petrol. The breeze lifts at her hair. At the corner of each side street there are signposts, but she can't make out one for Audobon, and the smell of the restaurant is making her hungry again. She crosses the boulevard, tries the door, goes in under the chime of an electric bell.

There are a handful of customers, three men in shirtsleeves, two older women, none hurrying over their breakfasts. The women look up attentively, knives and forks poised. The men only glance. By the *Please wait to be seated* sign there is a stack of news-sheets, and she takes one and reads to be out of their gaze.

The Mullet Wrapper Hot Tips Special.
Including How to Get Your Car Unstuck Out of Sand, Jellyfish Home Remedies & What Is An Undertow?

'Help you?'
She looks up. The waitress is in her fifties, grim at the mouth, kinder at the eyes. A tag on her uniform gives her name and what might be the day's special, though for a moment, the jet lag finally catching up with her, it looks to Anna almost like a surname. *Nancy Catfish Pecan.*

306

'Do you have a menu?'

'Sure. You sit yourself down. Coffee?'

She sits herself. At the next table the frailest of the men glances anxiously at the air around her, as if she has brought in the smell of imminent rain. The menu is long and crudely altered in black marker. She orders coffee and cornbread, pickles and blackened snapper.

'Early for fish. Mike's still doing breakfast. Best else I can do you is popcorn shrimp.'

She closes the menu. 'Breakfast would be fine. Whatever you've got.'

'Wait just a minute.' The waitress walks back to the kitchens. Left alone, the jet lag hits her again. A wave of placelessness. Her head aches, and she lowers it tenderly into the palm of one hand. What would happen, she wonders, if Anneli were to walk in now? Would she be angry, to see Anna in this place where she doesn't belong? Or frightened? Would she throw the cruet sets beside the door? Would she run?

She wonders what she is herself. Not angry, not quite frightened. Her gut feels light with nervousness. Soon she will have to face Anneli, and however she is she will not want to be found. She should be thinking of the right things to say.

Instead she closes her eyes and thinks of nothing. In the background a radio is turned on low. Traffic warnings and tide forecasts, old music and shipping news.

'Okay!' Nancy Catfish Pecan calls from the kitchen doorway. 'He'll do you.'

Anna waves back. A pot of coffee has appeared beside her, though she doesn't remember the waitress bringing it. She drinks while it is still almost too hot to do so, the heat and caffeine flushing her cheeks, bringing her back to herself.

The food is good. Better than good. She eats as if she has not done so for days. When she is done the waitress comes over and smiles as she clears.

'Always a pleasure to see a clean plate. Anything else you want? There's fresh hushpuppies.' She raises her eyebrows, holds up floured hands.

'Just the bill.'

'Sure. You're English, right?'

'Right,' she says, and the waitress smiles again.

'I knew it. Before, we had English folks here. Only the once, though.'

'Can you tell me where I can find Audobon Street?'

Nancy nods eastwards. 'Right off the boulevard, you can't miss it. There's the Dauphin Motel on the corner.' *Dawfinn*, the word sleekly Americanised. She has the dishes cradled in her hands now, though she still stands, shifting from foot to foot. Waiting for something. 'Nothing else down that way but the bird sanctuary. You here for the birdwatching?'

'No.'

'Thought not. I know the type. For the fishing, maybe?'

'The fishing,' she says, as if in confirmation.

'Your gear's in the car, I'll bet. Make sure you

lock your doors, folks take advantage all over. Planning to stay long?'

'Not long.' She reaches for her bag, extracts a moneycard. Nancy takes the payment in her two free fingers. When she leaves it is reluctantly, and when she returns with the receipt she stands again, her large hands at her sides, her eyes kind and flat and searching.

'You know, we don't get many visitors this time of year.'

'Really?'

'Not many visitors at all, these days.' She leans forward confidingly. 'We're a little starved of the company. Excuse my curiosity.'

'No, it's fine.'

'Do you mind if I ask what it is you're here fishing for?'

'I'm not.' She feels herself blush. 'Actually, I'm not here to fish.'

'Fishers of men,' whispers the washed-out figure at the next table, looking only at the radio. Nancy turns on him.

'Bill Raley, you eat up, hear?'

'I was just saying it,' says Bill Raley. 'I meant nothing by it.'

She revolves back to Anna, her warmth returning like sunlight. 'Well. So nice meeting you.'

'Thanks.'

'You have a nice day. There'll be rooms at the Dauphin. Come back soon. Too, we're open late! Anytime, we'll still be here!'

Audobon Street. She stops at the corner by the motel. The advice of the waitress was overly hopeful; like the oyster bar, the Dauphin is closed till Spring. A freight truck heads up the boulevard, dripping ice water, rank with fish and disinfectant. Her mobile is buried in her overnight bag, and when she finally extricates it she finds that it is no longer working. The signal gone or the account cancelled, she can't tell which.

There is an old-fashioned phone-box across the street, the receiver swinging from its cord in the wind. She crosses behind the truck, replaces the handset in its cradle. When she picks it up again there is the purr of a tone.

She knows the Numminen number by heart. There is a smudge of flour on her credit card, the imprint of a finger superimposed on her own golden one. She wipes it clean, inserts the card, dials.

Three rings and she is through. 'Four two nine one,' says a woman's voice, accent overlaid with accent.

'Is Anneli there?'

There is a pause. When the woman speaks again it is less clearly, as if she has moved back a little. 'Who is that?'

'My name is Anna. I'm a friend of Anneli's from England. We're in Gulf Shores for the week and I thought I'd – I just thought I'd call by . . .'

The lie dies on the wind. Another station

wagon goes past, bumper-stickered, bass thumping through its tinted windows. She turns her back, leaning protectively over the receiver, as if to light a cigarette.

'. . . no one,' the woman is saying. 'I am sorry. Perhaps when I speak to her, I should tell her you called. You are Anna –?'

'Moore,' she says. 'Anna Moore. Mrs Numminen, I'm sorry.'

'Oh?'

'I'm not exactly Anneli's friend.'

'No?' Stern, without surprise.

'I'm afraid I haven't been entirely honest with you. I'm with the British Inland Revenue.'

At the far end of the line Mrs Numminen is silent. Anna talks into the vacuum. 'I'm not a lawyer. I have nothing to do with any of that. I don't need anything read or signed. I'm here only on behalf of the Revenue –'

'You are here? On the island?'

'I just need to talk to Anneli.' Awkwardly. 'It's important to the Revenue that I –'

'What can be so important that you would come all the way to Dauphin Island?'

'Her husband.'

A sigh on the line. It reminds her of Terence. *You have a job to do. I have mine.* 'Always him. But my daughter has no husband. She is with us now. And the . . . man you want isn't with her.'

Her head is beginning to ache again. She presses her eyes closed. She should have been prepared for this. A good inspector would always be prepared. She starts to say something, another apology, but the woman is talking again, her voice sure and calm.

'He isn't here. Is there anything else I can do for you?'

'Do you know if he's alive?'

'No.'

'I have to find him.'

'Good luck,' Anneli's mother says, and laughs. For a while there is a careful silence again, as if she is thinking. 'Tell me the truth. Does my daughter know you?'

'Yes, she does.'

'Then wait.'

The line goes dead. From where Anna stands she has a clear view down Audobon Street. The buildings are haphazard, mock-colonial, raised on clapboard or bare pilings, set back behind palms and swamp magnolia. Sand drifts across the asphalt. At the far end there is a flash of white beach. Out to sea there are oil rigs, faint and stilted, distant echoes of the houses that precede them.

'Hello.'

'Anneli.' She turns back into the hood of the booth. The voice is hard and querulous, angry and frightened. Everything she has imagined and more.

'What do you want?'

'I –'

'Wait. Where are you?'

She looks through the distorting curve of the plexiglass. Outside one house an old man works on an upturned dinghy. Under the pilings of the motel a bird hunkers down against the wind, large as a child.

'I'm here.'

'Here? What are you doing *here*?'

'I came to talk to you. I have –'

'How did you find me?'

'The Revenue sent me.'

'To find me?' Her voice rising.

'Anneli –'

'Why can't you just leave me alone?'

Because and because, she thinks. Because something has happened between myself and your husband, who is not your husband, and it isn't finished yet. Because you never quite told me the truth. Because I am still an inspector of the Revenue, and the Revenue gets what the Revenue wants.

'Anneli, listen to me. Alright? No one knows you're here.'

'What? No.'

'The lawyers don't know. The government doesn't. Even the Revenue doesn't know yet. No one knows except me.'

'What does that mean?'

For a long time she doesn't answer. The station wagon returns back the way it came. Slowing to a crawl beside her, accelerating away. As if it has been startled. 'Will you see me?' she says finally, and somewhere in the street on the edge of the Gulf Anneli says, low-voiced, that alright, that she sees, that she will see her.

'Welcome,' Anneli's mother says, and stands back by the open door. The house is cool and dark and aromatic – fresh paint, sea salt, new bread – and there is music playing, though Anna doesn't remember hearing it on the land line. In a corner of the single room a fishing spear and rod are leant, a mask and speargun at their feet. Driftwood is stacked beside the hearth, ready for the evening to close in. It is a home one would never choose to leave. A safe house: a refuge, even. She wishes she could stay herself.

'Suvi.' The woman holds out her hand.

'Anna,' Anna says, and takes it, though there is no need for introductions. She can see the older woman knows it as well as she does herself. She can hear no one else in the rooms beyond, no sound of Anneli or her son or father. She wonders if the woman she has come for is already gone.

The silence is uncomfortable. She searches for something else to say. 'You have a beautiful house.'

'Thank you,' Suvi says, automatically, but as if she has hardly heard. 'My daughter has agreed to speak with you, and you must do what you need to do. But I would like you to know she has not been well. It is not good for her to talk about him. I would like you to be quick.'

'Of course,' she says. 'I will, of course.'

'Please,' Suvi says, and she motions Anna in and through to the garden where Anneli waits.

They sit together on a lawn of Bermuda grass. There are birds in the trees overhead, small and dull with bright, questioning voices. Anneli's mother brings out iced tea and leaves them reluctantly. No one says a word. A helicopter goes muttering over, and Anneli starts and looks up and away.

At first glance she seems well – her face and limbs are tanned, her hair already almost white from the sun. She has put on a little weight, and the new curves are more comfortable on her than her old film-star gauntness. But despite the weight she looks smaller, as if she has retreated into herself. Her eyes are dark, and in her lap her hands won't keep still. She is holding her glass as the helicopter passes, and the iced tea slops over onto her sundress.

'Fuck!'

'Here.' Anna searches through her bag for tissues, but already Anneli is waving her away.

'It's fine! I can do it myself.' From her sleeve she has produced a handkerchief, and as Anna sits back she spits on it and scrubs vigorously at the stain. The activity seems to calm her, her mouth levelling.

'There are always helicopters here. In and out to the oil rigs all the time. My father used to do work out there. I hated them for taking him away.'

'It must be worse now.'

'It is. I always think they're coming for me.'

'No one's coming for you.'

'But they are.' Her eyebrows coolly raised. 'You are.'

'I'm not here for you.'

She has done with the stain. She drops the handkerchief on the lawn beside her and looks up at Anna for the first time. Her gaze is unwavering, as if having begun she is unable to take her eyes away again.

'Have you been here long?'

'Not long, no.'

'And how do you like the island?' Politely, as if she is a hostess, Anna a guest.

'It's very beautiful.'

'Do you really think so? It always feels to me like the bottom of the sea. I never understood why my parents came here. Finland is beautiful. You should be here in hurricane season. In the old days the people used to tie themselves to trees. Otherwise they'd be blown away.'

She stops, distracted, looking across the garden to the rough land beyond. At the end of Audobon Street a weathervane shuttles in the wind. 'I'm sorry you came for nothing. Perhaps I can give you the house,' she says. 'Erith Reach. I can do that, if you like.'

'I'm not here for that,' Anna says gently.

'Oh . . . It must have come as quite a shock to you. All this.'

'Yes, it did.'

'So you know how I feel. It has been a shock to me, more than anyone. There are things I knew. The divorce, obviously. But not much, really.' Her pianist's hands move restlessly, as if to hide something. 'Not very much. You must think I'm very stupid!'

'No.'

'But I am.'

'You told me he was good with secrets, once.'

'Not good enough,' Anneli says. And then, as if only now remembering her name, 'Anna.'

'What?'

'You were kind to me, at the Winter Ball. What did you think of us, the first time you came to Erith Reach?'

She remembers. The children talking, easy in their own confidence, cryptic as John himself. Mister Coldhamsandwiches. There are midges under the trees. Something settles lightly on her neck and she brushes it away.

'Did you think we were strange?'

'I thought you were wonderful,' she says, truthfully, and Anneli smiles.

'Well, at least you believed it.'

They fall into silence. It is not uncomfortable; for a few moments it is almost amicable. From beyond the house there is the sound of a ship's horn, a flat sound echoing across flat land.

She reaches down to her bag, extracts the

photograph. John turning, the light above the trees. When she holds it up Anneli laughs.

'That old thing! Is that what you came all this way to show me?'

'Were you there? When this was taken?'

She laughs again. 'I was drunk, very drunk, but in a nice way. I was having a good time. We were having a really great time.'

'Where were you?'

'Oh, what does it matter? Put it away, will you?'

Reluctantly she does so. 'I just wondered if this was somewhere he might –'

'Please.' Her voice low. Her eyes shining; she shuts them. 'I don't want to look at him. I don't want to hear about him, I don't want to talk about him. Do you understand?'

'Of course.' She searches for something else to say, some means of circling back. 'How is Nathan?'

She regrets the words as soon as they are said. In the other woman's eyes something vicious sparks and almost catches. Her mouth opens onto her teeth. Then the anger has passed. Her voice when she speaks is dull again.

'How dare you.'

'I'm sorry.'

'Don't be. It's not your business to be sorry. None of this was ever *your* business. Except you are here on business, aren't you?'

She doesn't reply. It is not a question to which

318

she is sure she has an answer to give. 'I don't know why I'm here,' she says finally, and when she looks up Anneli is no longer listening. She is staring through her again, as if she is a screen giving onto something else.

'He was a very organised man. Methodical. You must have noticed. I think when we married he hoped I would change. He always seemed to expect that something would rub off on me. Like the Romans in England. Straight roads, you know? But it never did.'

Her voice low and quick. Feverish, Anna thinks. The birds call and call overhead. Beyond the picket fence lie acres of low dunes and sawgrass. Beyond those, the incoming white parallels of the sea.

'You probably think I married him for the money. Everyone does! And in a way I did. He was so clever and handsome and generous. Have you seen pictures of him then? Of course, you even brought one with you. Well, he had more life in him than anyone I had ever met. No one ever said no to him. He said he was going to change the world, and – everyone believed him. And everything he said came true. The money was just something that happened. He was always giving it away. But you can't imagine how exciting it was!

'It was only later that he changed. After Soft Gold there was nothing left to do except – doubt, I suppose. He never enjoyed success. He never told me that, I had to work it out for myself. He kept it from me. Then one morning I looked over at him

319

and . . . I didn't know who he was. It was as if he had become a different person. There were secrets between us. It was the secrets that separated us. We were separated years before we were divorced. Did you love him?'

The question comes out of nowhere, like the wind on the bridge, knocking her sideways. She answers defensively, the first thing that comes into her head. 'You talk about him as if he were dead.'

'Did you?'

'I thought everyone did.'

'Then you were wrong. And that isn't an answer.' She watches Anna, amused and pitying, just as she used to. 'Do you want him? You can have him if you want him.'

She shrugs, abruptly wretched. 'I want to find him.'

'You're just like the rest of them! You ask so many questions, but you can't give any answers. Can you?'

'I don't – I'm not trying to – No one knows I'm here, I told you, not even the Revenue –'

'Don't be ridiculous. What about your co-inspector?'

'My what? I don't have a co-inspector, Anneli. This was my case. I don't know what you –'

'Don't you?' Anneli says, and then stops, staring. 'Oh. I see. You don't, actually, do you?' And she laughs, leisurely and surprised, as if Anna has unexpectedly told a wonderful joke.

There is the sound of the mosquito grille swinging back in the wind. Anneli's mother stands in the kitchen doorway. Her daughter sighs and stands and turns to go.

'I can't help you,' she says. Then, 'You can't keep away, you people, can you? You weren't the only inspector who came for John, you know. Maybe you won't be the only one who comes for me.'

'Anneli, wait –'

'I can't help you,' she calls back again, and then she is gone. Her mother ushering her away into the cool, dark house. Turning back to Anna, impassive, awaiting her departure.

It is a warm winter, one of the mildest in decades. What would have been snow another year falls as rain, so that London becomes a parody of itself. A landscape reproduced in monotone, silver and grey as a lithograph. The drip of water everywhere, from trees onto pavements, from ceilings into buckets, from the braced vaults of the Underground to the tracks below, where over a hundred and sixty years the old leaks have formed stalagmites. It is like being in a city of clocks, Anna thinks. As if every street and corner is counting out the hours.

Every day there is news. Every bulletin contradicts the last. In Macedonia two students of political science confess to writing the Dateline Virus. By the time they have been arrested, their hardware seized, their anarchist leanings reviewed, their claim is already one of many. A bankrupt in South Dakota, a widowed broker in Beijing, a mother of five in Amsterdam, the children confirming everything. *This is just the beginning*, James Seltsam, unemployed, writes to his sister from Anchorage. *We've learned a lot from our mistakes. Just wait till Christmas. Ho! Ho! Ho!*

And still John Law is everywhere. The *Wall Street Journal Online* publishes the emails he sends each week, from London, Paris and Mustique, with faint, unlikely photographs. Two books loaned to a J. K. Law go missing from the Key Street Public Library in Singapore (*The History of Forgery; Delia Smith's Frugal Food*). In Sapporo, a drunken Law visits a downtown hostess bar, sings karaoke, buys champagne, and leaves without paying the bill. The messages from Carl pile up unanswered on Anna's mobile. Insistent, cajoling, ten deep.

It is November before she goes to see him. For three weeks she has avoided him – has been back to the office only once – knowing with less doubt every day what meeting him again will mean.

Nothing is new. She remembers the days in the wake of Soft Gold, when the Revenue briefly seemed a different place. Now it is no longer so. By imperceptible increments it has returned to its archaic routines and forms, as if by force of its recalcitrance the world outside could be un-changed. And perhaps it can, Anna thinks. Perhaps it already has been, as Lawrence has, adjusting to the unthinkable. The floors chiming past her, each one as institutionalised as the last. She only knows for certain that it is not true of herself.

Mister Caunt is in a conference, his secretary says, looking Anna over as if he finds her dubious. Only with the air of one doing her a favour does he let her wait in Carl's empty room.

The air smells of burnt coffee and prefabricated substances. For an hour she sits alone in the only chair, looking out over London. There are no cranes on the skyline; nothing new is being built, while there is no money to do so. The effect is one of stunned peace, as if the city is, for once, at rest.

She waits and remembers the years she has been here. The endless procession of clients, dishonest, angry, terrified. Carl and Janet and Mister Hermanubis, all on one bench in Limeburner Square. Lawrence, teaching her. Twelve years. *That's a life sentence.* She always thought it would be longer. She never thought it would seem so long.

There is a noise in the corridor outside. A subdued murmur of male voices, Carl's crass laughter. From her case she takes her computer and her letter of resignation. She places them together on the empty desk in front of her.

'You must be mad,' her sister says. They meet in an upstairs room in Chinatown, the table too small for the food, which Anna protests is too much, and Martha says is not enough. Dumplings pale and smooth as eggs, clear soup flavoured with abalone. 'What were you thinking of?'

'Funny. That's what Carl said.'

'Not quite so nicely, I should think.'

'Not quite. He said I must be out of my micro-scopical cunting fucktarded mind,' she says, and Martha guffaws and coughs and gropes for water and an empty glass.

'I'm glad I'm not eating with him.'

'You don't have to. And nor do I.'

'But it's not to do with him.'

'Not really. Of course not, no.'

'Then what is it?'

A waiter stops to pour them drinks, Chinese rice wine in china cups. Anna waits until he leaves. As if he'd even care, she thinks. It is quiet, business is slow, and the staff stand by the walls, uneasy with the lack of work. When she looks back her sister is waiting, hunkered forward, staring at her over the half-eaten meal.

'I think you blame yourself.'

'For what?'

'For what happened to Law,' she says, and as she placidly refills her bowl a flush of anger goes through Anna.

'Don't be bloody ridiculous.'

'I don't mean all of it. Calm down. I just think what happened to him, to him and his family, I think you were very close to it. Not that I'm not grateful.'

'You think too much.'

'So tell me, then.' Bowl full and raised to her mouth. Her eyes above it waiting, poised. '*Tell* me.'

'Maybe it's just to do with me,' she says, but her sister doesn't reply. The answer sounds thin in her own ears, disingenuous. She remembers Anneli, amused, pitying. *You ask so many questions, but you can't give any answers. Can you?*

She eats. Fish, rice, fish-and-rice. The early diners come and go. Martha finishes the last of the dumplings and starts equably on the remaining prawns.

'What are you going to do now?'

'I don't know. I'll find something.'

'Of course you will.'

'I was thinking I might catalogue Dad's books for a while. Some of them are quite rare now. Would you mind if I had to sell some?'

'Don't be stupid, of course not. Sounds like a good idea. Healthy.' She leans forward. 'You look after yourself, alright? Otherwise I will. Now, can I pay? It's the least I can do,' she says. 'The least. Don't you think?'

There are no jobs to be had. It is a bad time to be out of work, the worst of times, people say. There is little for those still in employment, let alone for an ex-inspector of the Inland Revenue.

The worst of times. In the days she walks when the rain allows, or sits and listens to music, trying to comprehend it in the quiet ways her father did. She cooks whatever the shops have to offer, enjoying the need for experiment: soybeans, black kale, scabbardfish. She sits and reads her unread books, unpacking boxes of those texts that never interested her before, the ones she can sell, if it comes to that. Engels and Marx, the histories of Israel and gunpowder. The several lives of Albert Einstein. The secret codes of Sparta, the city that turned its back on money.

The nights, too, are her own. At first her friends are insistent, anxious and not to be refused. But their questions are all the same, and she has no answers for them. She spends Christmas with Martha, just the two of them, Eve ringing, full of gin-fuelled cheer, in the company of her luggage man.

It is January before her belongings are forwarded from the Revenue. She signs for the crate – marked *Personal Effects*, as if reports of her life have been greatly exaggerated – and carries it through to the kitchen, hushing Burma to one side. Inside, a note from Goater apologises for 'the tea' and for there not being more to send. There is, in fact, surprisingly little. She wonders how her office looks, and who is there now, in her place.

Three mugs. A slew of books. A sheaf of paper records over which Goater appears to have spilt the apologised-for tea, hastily bundled and still damp. A laser disc in a cracked jewel-case holding those of her files deemed declassifiable. An unopened packet of cigarettes.

She no longer owns a computer to read the disc. She keeps it with some vague idea that it might make a decent coaster. The books she stacks beside the study shelves. The mugs – the ugliest she owns, fit only for the office – she returns to the crate, adding a broken garden chair, to be carried later to the waste transfer station. With the papers and the cigarettes she goes back to the study and sits in the only armchair, unbinding Goater's stained bundle.

She leafs through the pages like a photograph album.

There is more pleasure than she would expect in them. A letter from an eccentric client, an old man then and perhaps dead now. Another – the only one she ever received – sent in thanks. Notes to herself in her imperfect shorthand, indecipherable now even to herself. A card from one of Lawrence's bouquets. *See me soon. I have missed you.*

It is still light outside. There is music playing, an old and much-faded recording, her own for once, not her father's. The broken machine sounds of Tom Waits. A bottle of wine already opened on the desk.

Children are playing at the end of the day
Strangers are singing on our lawn
It's got to be more than flesh and bone
All that you've loved is all that you own –

Nothing has been erased. The papers seem unedited. She would have been more careful, she thinks, if she were forwarding them herself. But then she is not dismissive of paper, as many are, and there is little in these which would be of value to the Revenue. There is little in them that matters even to her. Still she goes on reading them, dutifully, as she would an inheritance.

She is almost through when she comes to the third letter. It is unopened but deeply stained, discoloured as a treasure map. The posting date is a few weeks old, the place of origin blotted out. The writing is not familiar. It is not John's. The stamps are American.

She sits forward to steady herself. Her hands and forearms trembling.

Dear Anna,

How are you? I am – well. It is cold here now, however, they say there is better weather on the way. The island is full of birds which have flown too far or not far enough. Nathan adopts them one after another. He would bring them all home if we let him.

It must be two months since you were here. You said that, if I talked to you, then you would tell no one. Though you didn't really say it, did you? And I didn't believe you anyway. But no one has come, and I am beginning to wonder if I was wrong. So I am writing.

I was unkind to you. I felt, I think, that I was owed a little revenge. Can you understand, I wonder. You seemed to represent all those who blame us for what has happened, all the vultures who come after us. Hopping and flapping. But I remember – you told me you weren't representing anyone. And I said things which you didn't deserve to hear. I am sorry.

Still, I am taking a chance, writing to you. You may have changed your mind. Maybe you will tell them everything after all. But I would like to help you. It's all over with anyway, and you came a long way to see me. It was brave of you to come after me.

The other inspector was an old man. He came three times but I was there only twice. The first time he visited was before I met you, before you came. John told me you were co-inspectors and I believed him. One thing you should know about my husband. I never knew when I could trust him.

They spoke together in private. Never for long. John did so much of his business in private. I don't think I ever heard the man's name (but I am not good with names). I felt that John didn't like him. When I met you I thought you knew. Certainly he seemed to me like a tax inspector.

Now John. I know you want to see him again. I always knew what you were thinking. You are not so good with secrets, Anna. You were always a little obvious.

You showed me a photograph. That was a shock for me, because it was clever of you. I think you will still find him there. He went there for the same reasons I am here. Do you know where his mother lives? I think you do.

It is quite like this place, although closer to home for all of us.

When he asks, tell him we are well.

A.L.

Coll. She had almost forgotten the article, years old and only half believed. She wonders if Carl remembers it too, and if so, how far ahead of her he is already. She has no car, the Revenue having come long ago for that. Nor are there flights, the regular services cancelled, the website says, *for the duration of the immediate situation.* In the end it is the train she takes north, a standby booking on the sleeper and local connecting services. The landscape slipping by outside, her head slipping against the glass every time she tries to rest.

It is evening by three o'clock. The sub-cities beyond London go on for mile after mile and then are suddenly left behind, as if the train has passed over some continental shelf into darkness. She sleeps a little at a time, dreaming that Lawrence is drinking again. Each time she wakes there is the same rise of uplit heath and firs, the same blur of track and cutting, and when she dreams the train comes with her, not letting her go, its rhythms insistent and questioning.

Are you running? Are you hunting? Are you running are you hunting? Are you?

At Glasgow Central a guard wakes her, his breath smelling of cough linctus. She gets out groggily and stands on the cold platform while the sleeper pulls away. The terminus is empty, the shops shut. Frost shines on the macadam. It is an hour until her connection, from a smaller station across town, and there is no one except her so foolish as to wait or walk at this time of night. She is unpacking her winter coat and gloves when the guard comes shyly back, ushering her into his office for directions and linctus-scented tea. The heat of the fire exhausting and gorgeous, her head aching, the smell of him waking her when it is time to go again.

The local train heads out unlit. Glasgow falls behind her, and with it her last hope of rest, whether she likes it or not: the sky is lightening, and she has never been a heavy sleeper. The tenements give way to hills, the hills in turn falling to lochs. Or not falling, she thinks, falling is wrong. It is not as if the land goes down to the water, but as if the water has risen up the flanks of the hillsides, leaving small towns beached at their summits. And the hills are still utterly black, as if something has torn ragged lengths out of the bottom of the sky.

She is thirty-eight, and she has never been so far north. She has never – she tries to contradict herself – she has never seen Scotland. Only one trip to Edinburgh, six hours in a conference room that might as well have been London. She glances around, as if someone might notice her ignorance, but the only other passenger is an old man sunk deep in sleep. It is her job which has always kept her in London, though the work, she thinks, is not to blame. It is not the work which chose her. But it has been a narrow life.

Oban is the end of the line. She makes her way across platforms, down past the seafront to the quays. The ferries loom overhead. A dozen children loiter by the water, in from the islands for schooling, pallid in the early light, sullenly pointing out the Tiree-Coll service when she asks.

The ferry smells of diesel and tar, salt, fried toast and cigarettes. The odours turn her stomach and leave her famished at the same time. She walks through the lounges and halls until she finds the passengers' mess, unsteady with the expectation of motion. The menu offers tea and toast, bacon and mushrooms, farls and poached eggs, and she orders it all and carries it through the fixed tables to a window seat. Only when her plate is wiped clean does she look up to find that the ship is moving. Already she has left the mainland behind. Nothing is visible except the barren humpbacks of islets, the bright sky and the sea.

The Gulf felt closer, she thinks. It is a long way to come with so little to hope for or believe in. From her bag she takes Martha's Eliot, Anneli's letter, the photograph of John, and two pages printed out in a King's Cross Internet café. There are few other passengers to disturb her. A family come in to eat, the four of them all dressed in black, as if for a funeral. She listens to them as she reads.

'Did you remember the cheese and biscuits?'

© Ansel Libera, CNN, 03/10/18, All Rights Reserved. *Mother of the World's Richest Man?* For years it has been the talking point for every hack and rumourmonger with an interest in money and high society (and that makes all of us): where is the family of John Law? Now the cat would appear to be out of the bagpipe. The family – all one of her – is alive and well on the remote Scottish isle of Coll.

'Of course I remembered.'
'Open them, then.'

Throughout his rise and rise, Law has retained an imperious silence on personal issues. What we did know already made good copy. Born in 1984 in a blue-collar sub-city of Glasgow, Law was the only child of a single-parent family, an early school-leaver who spent 18 months in the charge of the Scottish social services.

'They're not for you. Get off! And you, you keep your hands where I can see them.'

Well, we know what happened to the only child. But what about the single parent? Where did she go from such humble beginnings?
Meet Crionna Law, factory worker, sole resident of Cornaig Beag, an isolated homestead on the little-known island of Coll.

Her head aches from the too-small print and the smell of frying food. She puts the papers aside, opens the book. Little by little she reads the fine, cold lines.

It is hard for those who live near a Bank
To doubt the security of their money . . .
They constantly try to escape
From the darkness outside and within
By dreaming of systems so perfect that no one
  will need to be good.
But the man that is will shadow
The man that pretends to be.

She dozes again despite herself, the warmth and motion lulling her into a fitful kind of sleep. Only the shudder of the ferry wakes her. The family has disappeared. Her breakfast is gone too, the formica in front of her wiped down. When she looks out the ferry is already docked, a man in jeans and a red fleece mooring the gangway to bollards. 'Coll,' the ship's tannoy is repeating wearily, as if it has said the same thing too many times before. 'Last call for Coll,' and she jumps up too fast, knocking her knee on the table's edge, crumpling the papers into her bag, running to be gone.

Only the mourners follow her down to the jetty. A battered hearse waits for them, and they get in, still softly arguing, and drive slowly away. There is no harbour, only a single pier at the mouth of a sea loch. The man in the fleece unropes the gangway and stands well back as it is hoisted up, lighting a cigarette. The ferry creaks and groans, the sound of it like some sea creature amplified to colossal volume.

She turns away from the spectacle of departure. Inland the hearse crawls up the one road, past the two outbuildings, the hangar of a factory, its sign broadside, COLL SEA PRODUCT PROCESSING. It is low tide, and the loch is exposed, rocky and treacherous. Goats graze along the water's edge. Otherwise the island is featureless, the wind eroding it down to nothing, the cold so keen and the light so bright they hurt.

She closes her eyes against them. The image of John is with her, but she remembers him only as she last saw him, and she pushes the memory away.

'Can I help you?'

She opens her eyes. The man in the fleece is beside her, hatchet-faced, cigarette cupped in one hand, the other thrust into his pocket. 'Can I help you?' he says again, decorous as a shopkeeper.

'Thanks. I was – wait—' She unzips the bag. The papers flutter madly as she searches through them.

'If you're here for the MacKinnons you'll need to hurry.' He looks her over tentatively. 'You'll want to change, no doubt. If you walk you'll be there –'

'I'm not here for the funeral.'

'No,' he says, as if coming to an agreement.

'I was looking for a place called Cornaig Beag.' As she says it the wind tears at the papers. She catches at the photograph. Anneli's letter wheels out of her grasp, across the kelpy rocks to the open sea. The ferryman watches it go.

'You won't be needing that, I hope.'

She shades her eyes. The letter is still visible, gull-white, riding the waves. 'Probably not,' she says, and it is true, though when she laughs it is unsteadily, her head going light with hilarity.

'The tide's turned, you might be lucky. I'll keep an eye out for it. Where are you –?'

'No,' she says; too quickly, so that he turns back to her. She folds the photograph over in her hands. 'I really don't need it. Thanks anyway.'

'Cornaig Beag,' he says, and looks down thoughtfully at the cigarette in his hand. The wind has whittled it away to ash, and he raises one foot, putting it out on his boot, placing the dead end in his jacket pocket, as carefully as if it were money.

'Is it far?'

He shrugs. 'Not by car. But you'll be on foot?'

'I suppose so.'

'A fair walk, then.'

'Which way –?'

'Go on through Arinagour. Take the right road out of town. Half a mile and right again. Keep going and you'll come to it.'

'Thanks.' She picks up the bag, folds the remaining papers in. She has already started down the jetty when he calls her back.

'You're not the first.'

'Not the first what?'

'Not the first,' he says, 'coming asking for Cornaig Beag.'

She knows it before he finishes, her heart sinking with the understanding, as if it has been pulled under. He puts his head down, walks up beside her. 'Come on. I'll drive you.'

'No, there's no need—' she begins, and then stops herself. She is tired, her leg aches where she knocked it against the mess-room table. He makes a sound in his throat, *ah*, and looks back at the ship as it rounds the headland. She wonders if the questions he asks will be worth the answers he gives.

His name is Michael Gilchrist. His truck is unnaturally clean, as if he spends too much time on it. He talks as he drives, quietly, saying next to nothing. The funeral is the second this year. There hasn't been snow for a week. The ferries call more often now, with the causeway over to Tiree. He sounds, Anna thinks, like a man who talks to himself often, and is not overly concerned by the fact. He reminds her of the waitress on Dauphin Island. The same voice, mild and keen, though less jovial. The eyes cautious and curious. The same islandness.

The landscape outside has changed. Where the east side of Coll was bare, the hillsides little more than rock, here there are tended fields under pocked snow, rising to the west. Sand settled by centuries of grass, the sheep carving the higher dunes into tortuous pyramids.

It reminds her of something too, not a place but a time. The days just after the end of Soft Gold. There is the same sense that money means less, that it has lifted, like weather.

'How long will you be staying?'

'I'm not sure yet. Can I ask you something?'

He cracks a smile. 'You can always ask.'

'How many people are there on the island?'

'Two hundred. More down on Tiree. One priest, no bank, no doctor, and no police.'

'You must know everyone.'

'Some better than others. Ask me another.'

'Do you ever see the Northern Lights?'

'Here?' He glances warily across at her. 'Why?'

'I'm just interested.'

He looks back at the road. Three cows lumber across the single lane. Michael slows, accelerates around them. 'If that's what you're looking for, you've come to the wrong place.'

'Why?'

'*Fir Chlis*,' he says, as if to himself, and then to her, 'The Nimble Men. The Merry Dancers, people used to call them, *Cnoc-na-piobaireached*. If it's them you're after you should've gone further north.'

'Are you telling me . . .' she says, 'hold on. Are you saying you never get them here?'

'No.' He changes up a gear, quiet for a moment, as if his mind is somewhere else. 'No, I didn't say that. This time of year, on a clear night, you might see something. But you'd have to be lucky. You might have a cold wait. It's only once in years we get the real thing. The whole song and dance.'

For a while they drive in silence again. Outside the dunes and marram grass give way to stern outcrops of rock. The few houses they pass are less often whitewashed than those in Arinagour; more ramshackle, easier to miss. The homes of people, Anna thinks, who wish to keep themselves to themselves.

She sits back, his voice running over in her mind. The conversation nags at her, as if she has missed the essence of it. 'So I'm not the first.'

'Not the first,' he nods. 'Not the second either. We had the constable over from Oban, and a week after that two suits from the government. Asking questions. None of them stayed for long.'

'Did they find what they were looking for?'

'I wouldn't have said so.'

'What were they looking for?' she asks, and Michael Gilchrist laughs shortly and pulls off the road. Cuts the engine, sets the brake.

'I'll tell you one thing, they weren't here for the Northern Lights. We're here,' he says, before she can ask, and she turns and looks out at Cornaig Beag.

It is not so much a house as a well-kept accretion of spare parts. Two trailer homes sit up on pilings, boarded together, the wheels planked off, an extension of clapboard and fieldstone adjoining the main structure at an angle. Smoke rises from a red stovepipe. A low-lying privet hedge separates the front yard from the road. Rose stumps, bound in straw, show dark through the hard snow. To one side a hearse is parked, paint peeling from its rusted fixtures, to the other a geodesic greenhouse, the panels fogged, out of place in its modernity. Beyond the house a stand of trees, a slope of land.

'Were you hoping for more?'

'Not really.' She looks back to find him watching her.

'You should've brushed up on your Gaelic. You would've known that *Beag* is small.'

Why would I have expected more, she almost asks; and stops herself. Something clicks inside her, a fractional mental adjustment. *Ask me another.* She almost missed it. She looks back at the house, the hearse beside it, the trees beyond.

'Your funerals don't take long.'

'Oh, they do. That's Ian's old number. He'll be out in the new one for a few hours yet.'

'I thought she lived alone.'

'Not for a while now. Looks like she's in. After you?'

They get out together. There is no gate, the hedge so low and broken that Michael simply steps over it. Anna hangs back as he rings at the doorbell and waits. After a while a light comes on and the door opens.

'Michael. What are you doing here?'

'I've brought you a visitor.'

They both turn to look at her. The woman is a head taller than the ferryman. She wears an apron over sweater and slacks. In one hand she holds the door, in the other a short, dull knife. The light falls clear into her face. 'Who are you?'

'Anna Moore.'

'Who's Anna Moore, when she's at home?'

Kennedy eyes. She looks away, back at the car, the road beyond. All this way, she thinks, to find another person angry, dishonest, terrified.

'What's that?'

'I used to work for the Revenue.'

'What's that to do with me? I pay my taxes.'

'I'm sorry. I'm not here for you.'

'What did you say?'

She looks back. 'I'm not here for you. I've come for John,' she says. Her voice low so it will not break. She says, 'I've come to see your son.'

★　　★　　★

A fire burns behind the stove-glass. The room is all velvet and oak. A mantel clock of ormolu, a driftwood carving of a man singing or calling, arms outstretched. In one corner an easel sits, a canvas cloth hung over it. There is a smell of peat and turpentine, sweet and comforting, and no clue to the scene outside except the motion of the wind as it butts at the thin walls.

Sit, Crionna says, sit, and they do while she works around them, carrying the easel through into the next room, putting a kettle on in the galley kitchen. Michael shifts uneasily, less comfortable, now they are here, than Anna feels herself. The heat has made her drowsy, and when Crionna sets the tea down she has to blink herself awake.

'How are the children, Michael?'

'Fine. We put them on the boat this morning. Off to Oban for the week.'

'You must miss them.'

'Oh well, we do. Laurie misses them.'

'And work?'

'The same.'

'Busy, I should think,' Crionna says, and pours. Two cups of fine china. 'Shouldn't you be getting back?'

'I should.' He stands with reluctant relief, turning to Anna, formal again. 'I hope you'll have a good stay on Coll. Goodbye, then. Goodbye, Crionna.'

He closes the door carefully behind him, as if not to wake someone. In the quiet she listens to the sound of his car turning, the voices of sheep, the tick of the clock on the mantelpiece.

'Milk?' Crionna says, and Anna looks back into the Cryptographer's eyes.

'A little, thanks.'

'So, you've met Michael.'

'He seems nice. He drove me up from the ferry.'

'A man with too much time on his hands.'

'He knows John, doesn't he?'

'Yes, they've been friends for years. You look tired.' She settles back into the empty seat. 'Did you come far?'

'Just from London.'

'London.' She drinks, holding the small cup in both hands. To Anna she looks old, though her movements are those of a younger woman. Clean and sure. 'I went there once. I didn't like it very much.'

'It's where I've always lived.'

'Well, I've tried both. I grew up in Glasgow, where John was born. My grandfather left me land here twenty-seven years ago. I haven't been back since.'

'He is your son, then,' she says, and Crionna lets out her breath, *Tts*.

'I never said he wasn't. You know him, what do you think? I wouldn't deny the fact. What I tell them now is what I've always told them, that it's no one's business but mine and his. They come up here in their shiny government cars and ask me and

343

I say yes and goodbye, and off they go again. Not quite as shiny and not much the wiser.'

'Michael said they were up here recently.'

'Oh, they were. Asking all kinds of people all kinds of questions. Getting no kind of answers at all.' She cracks a smile. 'People here aren't too fond of questions.'

She gets out the photograph. It is seamed now, John's face crumpled in transit. His mother takes it and tuts again. 'I took this. Did you know that?'

'No, I didn't.'

'No, well, you wouldn't. I used to do photography, but the developing took up too much space. These days I paint instead. I don't know how they got hold of this one. I'd complain if I didn't think it was too late.'

'It's a good picture.'

'It's a fair likeness. I've taken better of him.'

'When was this?'

'Years ago. John was just married. They came up together to see me. I liked her. Sharp and pretty. We got on. You could see the Northern Lights that year, and we dressed up and stood out and watched for them. The one night it was clear they were glorious. Oh, we had a fine time.'

'How did you know,' Anna says, 'that I know him?'

'Because he talks about you, of course.'

'What does he say?'

She puts down her cup so carefully it doesn't

make a sound. 'Love, I think you need to ask him that yourself. Don't you? But not now. You've come far enough for one day. Do you think you might like to stay the night?'

The light stays for hours. There is work to be done, gas cylinders and turfs of peat to be carried in from the shed. A telephone pylon has come down beside the house, and Anna helps as best she can, ineffectually, digging into the frozen moine while John's mother, bundled up in thick gloves and a sheepskin coat, mutters over the tangled wires. If she kills herself, Anna thinks, I won't even be able to bury her. I'll have to leave her in the hearse and go and find the one priest. There are clouds building to the north, great promontories and buttresses, but the sky around them is still clear, and from the field below the house she can see white beaches to the west, fringed with surf and blue shoals.

At six Ian comes home, a sallow man, younger than John's mother, with less interest in Anna than the armchairs and the fire. They eat early, Anna finding her appetite despite herself. Collops of beef, bashed swede, whisky from Oban. Crionna and Ian talking as they dine, neither asking Anna many questions nor volunteering any answers. Only afterwards, making up a bed in the spare room, does Crionna mention John again.

'They say it's set the world back a hundred years.'

'What has?'

'The terrible thing my son is supposed to have done. But you wouldn't know it here, would you?' She folds the sheets. Stands back. 'You wouldn't know his money had ever been here at all.'

She wakes late, the sun on her face. Before she opens her eyes she knows the trailer home is empty. From up above come the sounds of gulls and the omnipresent wind. There is a mug of coffee beside the bed, stone-cold, a note lodged under it.

Dear Anna,
     I have to work today. Ian will keep out of your way. Help yourself to what you want, there's bread + cheese etc. There's a parcel in the kitchen you might take with you. Just latch the door when you go.
     Walk back past the house. Go down through the trees. There's a track that goes to a small beach. Go up the cove as far as you can go. There's a caravan. You'll find him somewhere there. My thoughts go with you.
     Crionna

He is sitting on a rock overlooking the sea. Not in a river in Japan, not listening to Schubert in Kristiansund, not eating with the dead. He is not fishing, only looking out over the clear shallows to the west, and when Anna calls out his name he looks up smiling, as if it is her he has been waiting for all along.

'Anna!'

'Hello, John.'

'You never give up, do you?'

'That's what Lawrence said.'

'Lawrence again. Lawrence seems to say a lot of things.'

'Does he?' she says. 'You tell me.'

'Ah,' he smiles, awkward. 'Well, I suppose I could. Why don't you sit down?'

She does, the rock rough and warm through her jeans. He takes her hand in his and looks away again, not letting go.

'Tell me,' she says. 'Tell me what happened with Lawrence,' but he shakes his head.

'Not yet. I missed you.'

'Did you?'

'You know I did. What's in the parcel?'

'I don't know. It's from your mother.'

'Oh, right.'

'What?'

'No. For a minute I thought you might be giving me something.'

She puts the parcel down and stretches her feet towards the sea. 'And what would you want me to give?'

The sun is against the side of his face as he grins. He has aged, she thinks. As if time works differently here. Only in his expression is there still vigour. 'Your pardon.'

'You had that already.'

'Did I really?'

'You always had it. You'll have to choose something else.' But he shakes his head, as if she has asked or given too much.

'How have you been?' she says, and he shrugs so uncomfortably she wishes she hadn't asked. '—I'm sorry.'

'No. You've a right to ask. I've been . . . okay, I suppose. I always expected worse. I've been keeping my head down, keeping out of the way, though they'll find me. One day they will. Maybe they already have.'

Faintly she smiles. 'I left the Revenue, if that's what you mean.'

'Really?'

'Yes, really.'

'Good for you. What do you do instead?'

'I look for you.'

'So you do,' he says, and laughs. 'Do you like it here?'

She looks around at it, his refuge. 'It's beautiful. Yes, I do.'

'I've always been happy on Coll.'

'And now?'

'Now, well. I've friends here, and family. I'm earning a living, of sorts. I've been playing around with the Internet. A kind of lottery. People buy a silver dollar from John Law with a chance to win a thousand. The bank account is in Switzerland, I don't know how long it'll last, still. The odds against them are twenty-four thousand to one.'

'And people do that?' she says, and he grins, wry, for a moment his old self again.

'You'd be amazed.'

A silence draws out between them, not a withdrawal of communication so much as a truce, a tacit acceptance of understandings. As if enough has been said, Anna thinks, though it occurs to her that it hasn't at all. That there is still too much she doesn't know.

'They think you did it,' she says, turning his hand in hers. The shock of its softness. 'The virus. They think you broke your own code.'

'Now, that would be a strange thing to do, wouldn't it?' he says, his voice only a little too smooth. 'Anna, tell me something. Do you think I'm mad?'

'What? No, of course not.'

'Well, that's a bonus.' He squeezes her hand. 'What worries me, though, you see,' he says, 'is that madness might be like beauty,' and when she laughs he peers back at her, as if to see into her mind.

'Alright, now you sound mad.'

For a moment he says nothing, only smiling at her. Then, 'You know how people once saw beauty differently? How in the past the concept was based on different ideals?'

'Yes.'

'I've been wondering if the same is true of madness. This is the age of money. What I was

doing with my life might seem to us to have been
sensible. You say you think I'm sane. How do I
know we're not both wrong?'

'I missed you too,' she says.

'I should bloody hope so,' he says, and leans
to kiss her. His eyes closing a second before
hers, her body tightening against him, her mouth
softening.

'How long do I have you for?'

'As long as you want.'

'You don't know how long I want,' he says.
'Careful what you offer.'

'Alright.' She laughs again, merrily, gladdened.
'How long do you want me for?'

'For good.' He is no longer smiling. 'You could
stay for good.'

She doesn't answer. We could make love, she
thinks. If I kissed him again now he would make
love to me. No one would see us, here. We could
make love and I would never leave him again.

He is stroking her face, her neck, and she keeps
her eyes closed, basking in him. It is what she
hoped for: it is why she is here, surely. Not to know
anything, not in the sense the Revenue would seek
to know it. Just to touch him, to feel the softness
of his hands on her.

It is only the faintest part of her, the inspector,
that insists there are still questions to be answered.
Out of nothing, unasked-for and unwanted,
Anneli's voice comes to her, repeating words
she never said.

One thing you should know about my husband. I never knew when I could trust him.

When she opens her eyes he is watching her, his face so close she can smell the salt on his skin. 'Tell me about Lawrence,' she says, and he comedy-grimaces.

'You know already.'

'But that's what you always say.'

'But I say it because it's always true. What can I tell you that you don't already know?'

'If I already know then you can tell me again,' she says, matter-of-fact. Still, he sighs and sits back up, away from her.

'Alright, let's get it over with. Lawrence had something to offer. Something I thought I needed. It was business, we did business and that was all. I never had much time for *business*. You know that.'

The silence falls again. This time it is less comfortable, and she takes her eyes off him, looks out at the Atlantic. The sun's fierce glitter off the waves.

'Hey.'

'Hey.' Lightly. 'So you tried to stop me,' she adds, and this time he has no smile ready. 'Was that it?'

'I don't know what you're asking –'

'Yes you do,' she chides. As if it is still a game, though she knows it isn't. It isn't something she can smile away, this exchange. She feels a tremor of unease, almost of fear. This isn't what I

351

expected, she thinks, and then; but this isn't what he expected, either. This conversation at the end of the world.

'Tell me.'

'Tell you what, love?'

'Did you use Lawrence to get to me? To make me close the case?'

He closes his eyes. Patiently opens them. 'Alright. Okay. An opportunity was presented to me, and I took it. Listen, Anna –'

'Did he come to you, then?'

'What?'

'Whose idea was it? I know he always wanted money. Did he come to you, or did you go to him?'

'What does it matter?'

'It matters, alright? Did he?'

Only when he laughs – smiling with anger or frustration – does she realise he isn't going to tell her. That he can't. It is beyond him to tell her the whole truth.

'Anna, why do we have to go over this? We're here now, aren't we? Can't we just leave it behind?'

'No, I don't know if we can.'

'What?'

It is the shock in his voice which makes her realise what she has said. She doesn't try to say it again. Her heart is hammering unevenly inside her. Not painfully, quite, but unhealthily, as if the months of cigarettes are about to catch up with her. For a second she wonders if she will faint.

'Anna. Anna.'

'What?'

'Is it Anneli?' he says. She has to laugh.

'No!'

'Nathan, then?'

'No. I don't know.'

'I know you cared about Nathan.' He leans back on the flat of the rock. 'And Muriet, even little Muriet. You're a good person, Anna. Too good for me.'

His voice drifting. *Too early*, she almost expects him to say. *Too late.* For a while neither of them says anything. She is aware of him, watching her, but she doesn't turn to look at him again. She can see gulls, so far out to sea they are barely visible. White shreds of life. She wonders if they still mean rain.

'How is my son?'

'Okay.'

'What does that mean?'

She turns to look back at him. 'She said to tell you they're okay,' she says, and feels a pang of relief when he flinches. After a moment he sits up with a grunt, stiffly, and hunkers forward.

'Anna, why do you think I left them?'

'How many guesses do I have?'

'No, really. Why did I leave?'

'So the lawyers ruin your life, not theirs.' She stops, waiting for his agreement. Instead he stays bent forward, quite still, not answering.

'Why, then?'

'Because Anneli told me to.'

'That's not what she said.'

'But it's the truth.'

'What difference does it make, anyway?' she asks, and he shrugs.

'I thought it might make a difference to us, that's all. I'm divorced, Anna. Anneli stayed with me for Nathan's sake. Now all that's gone, and everyone knows everything. Even Nathan knows. I left because she told me to. I can't go back to them because she won't have me back.'

She looks away from him, taking it in. Remembering Anneli's offer. *You can have him if you want him.* The sun has dimmed behind high formations of cirrus. The air seems colder as she breathes.

'I didn't know that.'

'No.'

'But you can still see Nathan,' she says, and he makes a sound in his throat, *ah*, like an echo of Michael, an expression of amused, forlorn disgust.

'Can I? I wish I could. What hours would they give me, do you think? Would the judge allow us Sundays if I took him to my caravan? If I turned up at a custody hearing they'd laugh in my face at my arrogance and then on the way out, oh by the way, sue me for the skin off my back . . . Anna, I can't see him. Not until he chooses for himself.'

'But the code—' she starts, and he groans.

'The code, the code. The code was just the way it happened to end. It could have just as easily been something else. Maybe the money made more of

354

a difference to Anneli than I realised . . . I don't
know. We weren't fine for a long time before that.
It doesn't matter now, does it? Anna?'

'I don't know,' she says, but she has said it too
many times, and she no longer knows what she is
replying to.

'Anna.'

'Is it true?' and before he can tell her, 'Maybe
you should go back to them anyway.'

'Anna, I've lost them. I've lost more these last
months than most people gain in their whole
lives.' He leans closer. 'Please. I don't want to
lose you too.'

She doesn't reply. *I don't know whether to believe
you*, she would say, if she was going to say anything
at all. And then she almost does.

'I want to believe you.'

He leans down towards her, smiling, shaking his
head, as if he is going to say, *It's alright*. And
then instead he says, 'Of course you do,' and in
a terrible moment she knows that she is right after
all: that she is wrong. She has always been wrong
about him.

It is a long time, a space of minutes, before he
sighs and, standing, looks down at her. 'This isn't
going to work, is it?'

'I'm sorry,' she says, but he just laughs, and not
unkindly.

'It's alright. Really. We'll laugh about this one
day. Will you open the parcel?'

She unwraps it miserably, holding the paper

355

down before it can be blown away. Inside is a tupperware box marked *Spring Stew* in thick green pen, a loaf of bread, a hunk of cheese, a pot of jam. 'She looks after you well.'

'She's a good cook.'

'I know.'

'Will you stay?'

She looks at her watch, not really seeing it, crying a little, then up at him. The sun is behind him, so bright she has to look away.

'I have some time,' she says. 'I think I still have some time.'

It is a long way home to London. Longer, it seems to Anna, than the journey north the day before. And measured in time it is; eighteen hours, as if she is travelling halfway round the world. In her seats and berths and dining cars she sits silently, not reading now, since she has nothing left to read. Only looking out at the land that passes by her into darkness.

The local train is late in, and she misses her connection. At Central Station she looks for the linctus-scented guard, but the shifts have inevitably changed and he has gone, leaving behind two younger men who have little time for her. It is hours before a new seat is found and her ticket changed without penalties, and when she finally leaves Glasgow it is night again. She reaches King's Cross just before four and takes a cab home, watching the tariff rise in hypnotic green numerals.

His voice comes back to her all the way. Not from the island but from an earlier time. Her own answering it. More softly, as if there is less life in her.

I didn't know if I could trust you. I don't know now. Anna.

What?

Can I trust you?

You have to trust, she thinks. Because you need love, you need it even if you hate the one you love. And in love trust is everything.

Now she is almost home. The driver knows the way. Two blocks east, five north. They turn into her road. It has started to rain again. Above the street the winter cherries have come into blossom, white shreds in the lamp-post light.

She pays the driver, leaving him the last of what she has as a tip. It takes a while for her to find her keys in the dusk. She closes the door behind her, leans against it and begins to cry, slowly at first, in great angry sobs, not for herself but for John.

It is almost light, and she is too exhausted for sleep. In the end she manages four hours, her eyes crusted shut with tears, curled in the only armchair, the cat at her feet a miniature. When she wakes the radio is on, the tuner set to timer.

She goes through to the kitchen. She has forgotten to turn the heat back on and the room is cold and unwelcoming. She searches the radio for music with one hand while she checks the cupboards with the other. There is nothing to eat that she can face, and she makes coffee instead. It is just ready, the steam warm and bitter-sweet on her face, when she looks up out of the window and sees him.

He is like the dream. He is standing across the street, on the driveway, under the trees. His hair is wet, pale in the clear nine o'clock light. He is exactly like the dream, and she puts the coffee down carefully, as if she might break it.

Her shoes lie discarded in the hall. She puts them on, belting her dressing gown, and unlocks the door. She is halfway across the road before Lawrence sees her.

'About time. Where were you?'

'Lawrence . . . what are you doing here?'

'Waiting. Hopefully not for much longer. I was just passing through the neighbourhood, unpleasant as it is, and your lights were on. I tried calling, but there's something wrong with your phone.'

'They cancelled it.'

'So they say.' He holds up a bag. 'All for the sake of breakfast.'

'Lawrence—' She pushes the bag out of her way. 'What if I hadn't been here? How long were you going to wait?' And as she says it she thinks, Of course. But he has waited before.

'It doesn't matter now, does it?'

'Alright. What did you get?'

'Breakfast. It's a morning meal, most people try to make it themselves, with varying results. And coffee. Better than yours.'

'Thanks.'

It is a fine day, only the wind chilling the air. The trees move above them. She pulls her dressing gown together, standing watching him until he shifts under her gaze.

'It's my pleasure,' he says. 'What are you looking at?'

'You almost did miss me. I've been away for a couple of days. I only got back last night.'

'Well, good. It's about time you had a holiday. Where did you go?'

'I found him.'

'Found who?'

She doesn't answer. It is only a moment before he understands. 'I thought you would. I always knew you would, of course. You're very good at what you do.'

'Was,' she says. 'Did,' and Lawrence sighs.

'Was, did. What did he say?'

'Not much.' She takes the bag. 'How much did he pay you? To stop me?'

There is a second, less than that, when he says nothing. Then he blinks and lowers his head, as if the light has hurt his eyes. 'Not enough.'

She opens the bag. Two sandwiches, two cardboard cups. At the edge of her vision she is aware of Lawrence, very still, not quite watching her.

'When you left the Revenue,' she says, 'it was me they came to. They asked me to tell them everything about you —'

She stops. His finger is at her lips, her cheek.

'Enough,' he says. 'That's enough, Anna. What are we arguing for?'

'We're not arguing.'

'Of course we are. What else are we doing?'

She reaches up. With one hand she brushes his collar clean. There is something on him there, almost as white as snow.

'What's that?' he asks.

'Blossom,' she says, and takes his hand, and walks him away.

Thanks and Acknowledgements.

Thanks to the Coll Hotel for hospitality, and the Inland Revenue for reluctant answers: also to Stretch and Moners; to Victoria, Sara and all at A. M. Heath, the best agents to be had for love or money; Julian and Angus, Stephen and Rachel, Joanna and Walter, Faber past, present and future; Minim, my number one palindrome; F. Scott Fitzgerald and Alain-Fournier; and any living descendants of John Law.

Acknowledgements to the Estate of T. S. Eliot for the quotations from Choruses III and VI from 'The Rock' in *Collected Poems*, and to the Estate of Ted Hughes for the quotation from *Tales from Ovid*. Acknowledgements also to Rumi, Li Po-Tu Fu, David West's prose translation of Virgil's *Aeneid* (Penguin), Malvina Reynolds for 'The Money Crop' and 'There's a Bottom Below', © Schroder Music 1966 and 1970.